Praise for Robert Magarian

Praise for *You'll Never See Me Again*

"I absolutely loved this book, I couldn't put it down. The details and thought put into this book by Dr. Magarian are absolutely amazing. I felt as if I was in the book myself."

—Brooke, Amazon reviewer

"Loved the book. It kept my attention, kept me guessing and kept me reading. I didn't want to put it down. Highly recommend it."

—Nancy Loyd, Amazon reviewer

Praise for *The Watchman*

"*The Watchman* came to life for me, because it is so well written and instills a sense of caution as you read. I am delighted to have had the pleasure of discovering Robert Magarian and his talent."

—Bea Kunz, reader review

Praise for *72 Hours*

"I was compelled to carry *72 Hours* around with me. It's a blend of trouble both personal and political, with an evil that will stop at nothing and a CDC that may—or may not—have found the only salvation. Here, also, is a family in pain. Suspenseful, timely, and breath-catching."

—Carolyn Wall, author of *Sweeping Up Glass*

Also by Robert Magarian

Fiction

The Watchman

72 Hours

You'll Never See Me Again, A Crime to Remember

Essays

Follow Your Dream

A Journey into Faith

THE
TONGUE
COLLECTOR

—◆—

ROBERT MAGARIAN

SCOTT WALDRUP

Light has come into the world, but men loved
darkness instead of light because their deeds were evil.

John 3:19

Dedication

In loving memory of our son,
Robert (Bob) Dwight Magarian,
who left us much too early
(July 6, 1962 – August 7, 2017).

Chapter 1

He slips in like a cat burglar.

Not there to steal.

No one is at the nurses' station. They're at the hall closet, pulling evening meds for their residents. Dressed in dark clothes, black wool cap pulled down over his ears, sun glasses, this tall, muscular man, looking like the Unabomber, enters this single-story building as if he's been there before, not concerned about signing in at the desk. He never plays by the rules.

With the stealth of a black cat, he moves through the soft-pink painted hallway to his right. The smell of urine and Pine Sol is prominent. Laughter from TVs and snoring from the tenants travel into the hall from the rooms he passes.

Slips into room 127.

Closes the door and shoves a chair up under the door handle.

Hannah Clay, his mother's church friend, in her nineties, dying from breast cancer, is sedated and unconscious in bed. He hates the woman. Like his mother, she verbally abused him. He hasn't forgotten the other visits to deliver Hannah's clothes washed by his mother. She slapped his face and spit on him because he didn't bring her any sweets. Her hateful actions engendered such fury in him that he couldn't get her out of his mind. She had to be eliminated; otherwise, no peace of mind.

Deep into the room, the intruder stands next to Hannah's bed, eyeing the cadaverous body covered in a white sheet. He places a pillow over her face. His large gloved hands press hard on her face.

She squirms violently.

Claws at his hands, but he's much too strong.

Seconds later she is motionless. An immense thrill comes over the intruder as he removes the pillow and stares down at the lifeless body. He feels no guilt, no emotional attachment to this being.

This is no different than killing those useless dogs and cats, he thinks.

She shouldn't have spit on him or cursed him. He's done her a favor, keeping her from suffering. Lifts her out of bed, carries her inside the bathroom, sets her on the floor. Goes out. Pulls the call light cord above her head board, ties one end around her neck and the other end around the inside door knob behind her, leans her forward on her knees to mimic suicide. Forensics has taught him that the elderly often commit suicide in this manner.

He edges around the bathroom door, not to disturb the position of the body. Walks to the door leading to the hallway, removes the chair and peers into the hall. He slips out and hurries toward the exit passing the busy nurses' station without being noticed. Outside, he treads like a black cougar between the bushes, slips into his black SUV parked a block away.

And speeds away.

Chapter 2

Three o'clock the next afternoon, a Saturday in late November, Jack Carter heads west from Atlanta on Interstate 20. Several miles from his turn-off, the highway divides around a median filled with a beautiful grove of evergreens. He turns off on Water Valley road and maneuvers the white Caddy through two miles of winding gravel road and over a small wooden bridge before arriving at his cabin. Carter drives up the gravel driveway to the cabin that sits on top of an incline, swings the car to his left, stopping in front of the steps. Flips the trunk from inside, hops out, reaches in for a suitcase, two bags of groceries, enough food for the weekend—sandwiches, chips, trail mix, salmon, canned smoked fish, two six-packs, and a bottle of 12-year-old Glenlivet scotch, his favorite— sets them on the porch. Returns to the car, and removes a small box of fireworks, an AR-15, and ammo—much of which he keeps with his arsenal in his storage unit back in Atlanta. Slams the trunk shut. The fancy fishing gear his dad collected over the years is stored in a special cabinet his dad built in the utility room in the back of the cabin. After settling in, Jack opens the can of smoked fish and pours himself a three-finger glass of scotch. He finishes off the fish and throws the can into the trash can under the kitchen sink, pours himself another three-finger scotch and heads out on the porch. The scotch is making its way to his head now as he stares into the twilight toward the lake some hundred yards down a slope through a heavy wooded area. The air is cool and fresh. The smell of evergreen is prominent. It's quiet except for the wind murmuring through the trees. The log cabin with fifty acres he inherited from his dad is Carter's prize and joy. The old man renovated the place before he divorced Jack's mother. She wasn't an outdoors person. It thrilled Carter that she never wanted anything to do with the cabin. She was very critical of everything his dad did.

Most of the other cabins in the area rent out from April to the end of September. He has never met the owners. This being off-season, very few cabins in the area are occupied. No lights, which means he's probably the only one in the area, and that's the way he likes it.

Carter had to get away from the City after what he did to the old bitch, Hannah Clay. He inhales the cold air. Killing her thrilled him beyond measure, and he had never realized how much joy there is killing a human. Jack inhales another deep breath and takes a drink of scotch. Much different feeling than killing animals. He looks at his hands. The power in them and how much control he had over his victim pleases him. *The old bitch was going to die anyway*, he rationalizes, finishing off his scotch. He turns and goes back into the cabin. Thirty minutes later, Carter returns with a small box, collapsible fishing chair, and a large flashlight, heads down the path that he and his father made through the years to and from the lake.

Bull frogs hibernate in winter in northern U.S. but in southern U.S. they are active year around. They favor living at the edge of the water in swamps, lakes, and ponds. Jack has seen them travel on land during rainstorms looking for a new habitat. He doesn't like them because they carry viruses, bacteria, and parasites, and he gets a thrill blowing them into smithereens with fireworks he made himself. He walks the edge of the lake with his flashlight whenever he's here looking for the critters. He now spots three bull frogs, grabs them one at a time and pitches them over near his chair. Once he settles them on a large boulder, he reaches in the box for some little bombs he had prepared, places them under the critters. He lights the fuses and watches with great delight as pieces of the animals' flesh fly into space. He yells and whirls in a circle. The thrill he receives is like riding a roller-coaster.

The next morning around eleven, Jack comes out dressed in a fly-fishing vest, carrying a tackle box hooked to a cooler filled with sandwiches and beer, fishing poles, and a portable chair. Once at the shore, he sets the cooler and poles next to the boulder in a small open area, which marks his favorite spot. He flips open the fishing chair, pulls out lures from his jacket and sits in the chair to ready his poles.

Suddenly, he hears a cry for help. He looks up, A teenager about twenty yards up stream is sliding down the muddy bank, slams into the water, flailing his arms to keep his head above the water, and is screaming as he moves in the current toward Jack. A strange vision comes over him as he watches the boy struggling in the water. Carter sees water as life's challenges and the boy as one who is fighting through them, or he'll be taken down into the depths of defeat.

"Help, help," he screams as he comes closer. "I can't swim."

Jack flips off his vest and shoes and dives into twenty feet of ice-cold water. His sportsman body is in good shape and his arms are strong. Jack is a very good swimmer and gets to the boy before he travels too far down stream. He grabs the teenager around the neck and tells the kid not to fight him, that he'd get him to the shore safely.

"Try to float your body, son," Jack says.

When they get to the shore, he drags the boy up on the bank and collapses by his side. After getting his breath, he says, "Are you okay?"

"Yes. Thank you, sir."

"What's your name?"

"Jimmy, sir," he says as he tries to get up.

"Take it easy for a while. Are you by yourself?"

"No, my dad and grandpa are up the way. I decided to move down stream since the fish weren't biting.

"Okay. Come over and sit in this chair. There's a towel in the side pocket on the right side. Dry yourself off."

Jack wonders why a young guy around these parts never learned to swim. "How come you can't swim. You must be 15 or 16."

"Sixteen, sir. I'm afraid of the water." He turned away. "I'm not much of a fisherman, either."

"You're pretty tall. I imagine basketball's your thing."

"Love it, sir."

"Any good?"

"Varsity. Best 3-pointer on the team."

"Stay with it, Jimmy. Always do your best." He thinks about the encouragement he got from his dad.

"Thanks—"

"—Jimmy, where are you," a call comes from the area where the boy fell into the water.

"Over here, Dad." He hands the towel back to Jack. "Guess I better get going, mister. Thanks for saving me." He stretches out his hand to shake Carter's.

Jimmy rushes over to his dad, who doesn't appear too happy.

Carter looks on.

Jimmy's talking a mile a minute. Probably telling dad what had happened. That this man saved his life.

The brawny man, around six foot with a ruddy complexion, dressed in overalls, comes over to Carter, holds out his hand.

"Appreciate what you did for my boy, man."

"You have a nice boy there."

"Name's Kyle. My boy, Jimmy, well, he's not much of a fisherman, but he wanted to come with his grandpa. Doesn't see him much."

Jack looks around but doesn't see anyone fitting that description.

"Oh, he's up the way. Once he's put his poles in, only a tornado or earthquake can drag him away from his spot. Afraid someone will catch all his fish if he leaves."

They laugh.

"You have a cabin around here?" Jack asks.

"Naw, man. Can't afford 'em. How about you?"

Jack points up the slope behind him. "Been in the family for years."

"Well, we'd better get going," he says to Jimmy. "Grandpa will wonder what happened to us."

He watches as they disappear in the woods. Gathers his things and walks along the path up to the cabin.

Chapter 3

Noah McGraw, sitting on the porch of his home at the Circle M ranch this sunny Friday morning in December, several days before Christmas 2011, drinking coffee as he watches Holly Roark ride Majestic Lady and her son, Dusty, on TR (Texas Rodeo). He has enjoyed having them on his ranch since he and Holly returned from Mississippi last month. The wounds he received on the Ole Miss campus during his shootout with Max Kingston, the perpetrator in the death of Eva Bingham Hamilton, have healed. The doc has released him to return to work after the New Year. McGraw hasn't been totally at ease since his return from the south. The battle with the perp could have ended differently, with Noah as the victim instead of Kingston. Thoughts about one's mortality are not unusual for those in law enforcement. Protocol has compelled him to see the psych doc to integrate his experience as a new normal, knowing things will be different.

She released him for duty.

All that is left now is for him to go to the firing range to demonstrate that he can handle himself to satisfy HR (Human Resources).

What's been bothering him more lately than his wounds is an old case, the Manchester Case. With so much time on his hands, old dreams have returned. In every detective's life, there's a landmark case that follows him around. McGraw is no different. Manchester, a maniac, who had a pretty little wife and three small beautiful children, killed them all. The scene was bloody and horrific. The details stuck in Noah's mind for weeks; especially, the children, with half their heads blown away. He has told no one about these haunting images that lingered after the case was closed, except for his friend Zee, his former partner, retired. Noah still sees every detail as if it happened yesterday. He knows better than to dwell on the case, but no matter how hard he tries to shut out the images, they keep popping up in his head. It happens mostly when he's idle. But what troubles him the most is knowing that there are still many Manchesters out there filled with evil.

He finishes his coffee, reaches for his Stetson on the small table next to him, rises and heads to the barn. When troubled, Noah talks to his horses, usually in the morning before heading off to work. Sometimes he rides his dad's motorcycle around the grounds to drive out the tension. Two things he likes the most: roaming the property in early morning hours drinking his coffee, and talking to Majestic Lady and TR. There are times he lets loose with his thoughts to his best friend, and ranch hand, Whitey Berry, but his most powerful thinking takes place at the fence outside the barn. He moves to the fence, pushes back his hat, slips a boot between two planks, leans his arms on the top log, interlocking his fingers, and gazes into the grove 50 yards in front of him. Feeling relaxed now, he inhales the moist air. Noah sees things he never tells anyone. A sixth sense came to him when he was working with horses in Texas near the Four Sixes Ranch east of Lubbock where Noah was raised. This particular day, an untamed black stallion was driven into a 40-foot-round pen, stomping and kicking and racing around in circles. McGraw got the urge to grab the rope dangling from this wild creature as he raced by. Once the creature stopped and gazed at him, Noah slipped off the fence and moved slowly and spoke softly to him, remembering what an old ranch hand taught him: 'a horse can see deep into your soul and sense your fear.' Holding the rope as tightly as he could, McGraw was witnessing the old guy's saying as being true as he looked into the eyes of this beautiful creature. The horse sensed something in Noah McGraw, maybe his kindness and the warmth he felt for him. McGraw's mentor, the ranch owner, watched and listened over the course of thirty minutes as the horse changed from being wild to becoming calm. McGraw saddled the stallion and rode him around the pen. The ranch owner told McGraw he had the gift—a sixth sense—that only a few have.

McGraw inhales a second time as he refocuses his attention in the grove. A rock's throw away, a mist begins to form, becoming thicker and thicker, swirling and swirling. A huge mass explodes out of the fog.

On a black horse is this creature dressed in black, eyes blazing red, galloping towards Noah, who recognizes that he's the horse, struggling to free himself of the rider. The horse comes to a sudden stop, neighs as it rises up on its hind legs ten yards from the fence. Suddenly, a transparent figure dressed in a white garment, infused with a bright Light, appears above the horse. Satan vanishes. The horse becomes calm. Noah hears in his mind words from the angelic figure saying: "Do not remember former things or consider the things of old. I'm about to do a new thing, now it springs forth, do you not perceive it?"

Noah knows these are God's words from the old testament. They mean he's no longer bound to the Manchester case.

He is awakened from his reverie when Prince and Tucker, his German Shepherds, jump on him. He squats down, rubs their heads and backs. The playful canines run in circles, wagging their tails, barking.

Anna Marie calls out as she approaches. "Kinda thought you'd be here. You okay?"

"I'm fine now, ma. What's up?"

"A man said he was with HR. That you should report to the firing range Monday morning at eight."

"Got it."

Holly and Dusty, still on their horses, race by waving, having the time of their lives.

"Son, we gotta talk."

"I know, ma. I've been expecting it."

"Let's have it now. I've made your favorite coffee."

Heading back, they step up on the porch. Noah goes to his favorite chair. Anna Marie walks into the kitchen.

Anna Marie taught her son to cook at a young age. She said learning recipes would warm his heart. He became pretty good in the kitchen. She also instilled respect for God in him, reading Scripture to him in the evening. Proverbs became his favorite book.

She returns with a large mug of latte and her glass of lemonade, sets them on the table between them. She chooses her rocker with the flowery covered cushions, sits, and drinks some of her lemonade, staring at Noah.

"Noah, you know Holly and Dusty will be returning home in a few days, and I see trouble acomin'."

"Trouble, ma?" he says, as he picks up his coffee mug and takes a couple of drinks.

She nods as she rocks herself holding the glass of lemonade. "You're frowning, but you know what I mean. You and she...well, you've become close. Very close. And Dusty, he's like a grandson to me. I'm concerned about him. I see him watching you two, and I'm afraid he's getting the wrong impression, son."

She pauses, waiting for his answer.

He smiles to himself. She pausing to make sure I'm listening.

"Listen to me," she says. "Dusty told me you and his mom really like each other, and I know where he was going with that."

"We do like each other," he says. "That's become obvious."

"Enough so that you'll become Dusty's dad?"

Noah doesn't say a word. Instead he drinks his coffee and stares out at the barn. Seconds later, he says, "It could happen, but Holly and I haven't talked about it. Not yet."

She shakes her head. "And then I'll have two loved-ones to worry about out on the streets."

"Ah, ma. You worry too much."

"Yeah. Look what happened to you in Oxford. It could have been worse."

"But it wasn't. Holly and I have each other's back. What happened down there was a slipup. Won't happen again."

"Slipup? That's what I'm talking about. That's all it takes is one slipup."

"Nothing to worry about."

"What about Dusty?" she says. "He adores you."

"I need to think on that."

"You need to have that talk with Holly, son."

He looks away. "I will. I will."

Holly's always on my mind.

She's outgoing, easy to talk to, vivacious, and those big brown eyes of hers can get to you. Her mother and father still live in Cleveland. Holly has no siblings, comes from a family of cops, beginning with her paternal grandfather, a homicide detective who took a bullet and died when Holly was 15. His death crushed her and took some time for her to get over. He lived with them. She carries a picture of him in her wallet, and has a larger one in her bedroom. When she gets miserable, she looks at his picture. Her father is a detective, and her uncle is a supervisor in the Patrol Division. She wanted to be like grandpa. She told McGraw when she finished high school (with honors), she went to college, earned a bachelor's degree in law enforcement, entered the police academy, and worked as a police officer at the CPD. She's always been a reader and early in her career became very perceptive in analyzing things. She developed certain skills—multi-tasking, empathy, leadership and communication skills, serving several years in Patrol and in Burglary, but became frustrated with the lack of opportunities in the Cincinnati PD. At a conference, her father happened to mention to his detective friend in Atlanta about his daughter's unhappiness in CPD. His friend told him there were many opportunities for advancement and specialization at the Atlanta PD, and that she should apply and he would do what he could to help. Holly was accepted into the Police Academy in Atlanta and moved up in Patrol. She took the detective exam and was assigned to Burglary, and later moved into Homicide to join McGraw's team.

Chapter 4

His lair is off limits.

The only ones allowed in it were he and his father before he was killed. His mother was not allowed within 50 yards of the place after his father kicked her out the time she came to berate their son for not doing his chores. Jack Carter's hideaway changed into his living quarters as he grew older. He added three rooms, no windows. He helped his father build the structure to appear as an extension off the two-car garage. The entrance is from the rear. What would be the front has trees and bushes to hide the place. There is a small bedroom; small room with a shower and toilet; a combination living room/kitchen area that has a couch; kitchen counter where he keeps his coffee pot, a fridge, a wooden book case with forensic books that slides to one side, and a mahogany desk he got from a garage sale, on which sits his laptop. Behind the bookcase is a false door about four feet by three feet, behind which is enough space for him to kneel into. The space is used as his trophy room, where he keeps small cats and dogs he killed and skinned, preserved in jars of formalin.

Pictures of bodies of women victims around his mother's age, cut out of forensic and detective magazines, are posted on the wall next to famous serial killers. and also, on a stand by his laptop. He's intrigued with their methods used to kill their prey. It gives him an erotic potency.

———•••———

The next afternoon, Laura Evans, Jack's mother, is on her cell phone talking with the church secretary. She learns Hannah Clay has committed suicide. Relaying the message from the nurse in the retirement home, the church secretary tells Laura that Hannah was depressed this Christmas season more than usual. She complained that she had nowhere to go for the Holidays and no one came to her with presents. As she turns off the phone, Laura, standing by the kitchen window, sees Jack drive pass in his white Caddy, heading to the back. He had promised to take Hannah some treats she had made for her. She hurries out the back door and sneaks up behind him as he bails out of his car and hurries to the back of his hideaway. Laura pushes her way in behind him, shocking Jack. She screams at him. "You imbecile. Did you kill Hannah? Have you now gone from killing animals to killing humans? You're a sick bastard!"

Jack flies into a violent rage. "I'm sick and tired of your tongue lashing!" he shouts. "Get the hell out of here. You know better than to come in here."

She knows he can see the shock on her face as she glances at the dead women in photos next to his laptop. "I knew you were crazy the day you were born," she shouts. He lunges at her. She grabs a heavy paperweight off his desk and bashes him on the side of his head. He's dazed but doesn't lose consciousness. He socks her. She goes down. He jumps on her, strangles her until life gushes out of her. He's surprised again at the strength in his hands. He jumps up. Hovers over her limp body. Feels nothing—no guilt, no sorrow, no sympathy for the woman that brought him into this world. The emptiness in him is the same he felt for Hannah Clay. He takes a picture of her and places it in his photo album. Too bad he didn't have one of Hannah. Jack slides the bookcase to one side to open the door behind it, places the album on the top shelf. The lower shelves are occupied with jars of dead animals. Jack closes the door and resets the bookcase.

He goes to his mother's body, which is still on the floor. Stares at her.

"For what you've done to me, I'll fix it so no one will ever recognize you. It'll be like you never existed."

Chapter 5

Under the moonlight, Jack Carter, dressed in black sweats, a miner's helmet, face painted dark like a sniper, pulls the black Tahoe through the arched entrance of the Pinelawn Cemetery where his father is buried, drives on the blacktop around an island of headstones with his headlights off. He spots the canopy covering the open grave, pulls the SUV off the road to the side. He jumps out. Opens the back, turns on the helmet lamp, removes the tarp that's over his mother's body and lifts her out of the back, dodges several headstones on his way to the open grave that's awaiting the body of Congressman Sunday to be interred the next day, according to the Atlanta Journal-Constitution. Carter drops her at the edge, adjusts the helmet light so it is directed downward and not up in the night sky, then rushes back to the Tahoe, removes the pick and shovel from the back. At the edge of the grave, he drops in the pick and shovel, jumps in and grabs the pick. Carter curses his mother with every thrust of the pick as he imagines her flapping tongue lashing out at him. Minutes later, he grabs the shovel. "Bitch," he shouts with every shovel full of dirt he throws out. For years, he's taken her abuse. Soon, he'll be free of her forever. The cops will never find her once the grave diggers lower the casket of Sunday on top of her.

Such a brilliant plan. The cops aren't smart enough to match wits with me.

He climbs out, rolls her body over until it falls into the grave, jumps in, arranges the body so her face is looking up at the dark canopy, then begins scraping the pile of dirt at the edge of the opening into the grave until it covers her whole body and smooths the top layer over her. He buries the tools next to her body, hops out and looks down into the hole and says, "Good riddance." He rushes to the SUV and heads toward the exit. Headlights from an incoming vehicle flash in his direction as he approaches the exit. Carter stops, pulls his wool cap down to hide most of his face, turns on his brights as he maneuvers closer to the car coming deeper into the cemetery. When they pass each other, he looks straight ahead as if he hadn't seen the guy entering.

Back at home, he pulls the vehicle into the garage next to his hideaway, examines the back of the SUV to make sure he hasn't left any incriminating evidence. He'll check the vehicle in the daylight to make sure it is clean. He enters his lair, washes up and hits the sack.

Around four in the morning, Jack bolts up in bed. He heard a voice. Was that his mother's? Couldn't be, just buried her a few hours ago, He lays back down, breathing hard, closes his eyes.

You got a thrill killing me, didn't you, Jack? Admit it. You got a high and were excited just like when you were ten, killing those animals.

He grabs his head at the temples and screams. "Yes, yes. I did! I loved the feeling I got killing you for what you did to dad and me. I should have killed you long ago!"

Chapter 6

At the breakfast table the next morning, sipping black coffee, Jack Carter is feeling dizzy, his headaches becoming worse.

Maybe I have a concussion with brain swelling.

That bitch of a mother slammed a paperweight into his temple. The headaches are affecting his eyesight and he doesn't think he can drive. He could call Megan Turner, one of his forensic criminalists, to take him to the doctor.

Carter enjoys using people. Megan's easy to manipulate. He's an expert at playing to women's emotions, using his charisma and good looks— narrow face, black hair, dark eyes and muscular built. As Megan's supervisor, he's been playing her to see how much material things he can get from her. He has no sexual feelings for her; he's incapable of having intimate relationships. They have been dating but haven't been intimate. Megan is a high empathetic person, has a good heart and loves to help people. She took care of her sickly parents until they died. Jack is attracted to such women, those who yield to his demands.

Megan is attracted to his extroverted ways. She has been pressuring him about living together, but he likes being alone. Lately, however, he's been thinking she'd be easier to control if they did live together. Her family left her lots of money and he's been enjoying nice clothes and jewelry from her.

Megan is driving Jack home from the doctor's office in her silver Nissan. Jack has a mild concussion and has to take the meds prescribed, rest for a week, no alcohol, and no heavy lifting. Megan is eager to stay with him, since Jack told her his mother is in Charlotte taking care of a sick cousin. He assures her he'll be okay. She drops him off at his mother's home. He waits until Megan pulls away, then goes out the back door to his shed apartment.

Chapter 7

Noah McGraw pulls his sky-blue RAM 3500 pickup into a parking spot in front of McAteer's Coffee Shop around eight this cold, cloudy morning, several days after Christmas. He reaches over and shuts off his favorite classic country music station, slides out and adjusts his white Stetson, and walks to the entrance, dressed in a starched white shirt, jeans, jean jacket, and his seven-hundred-dollar Lucchese boots with exotic square toes. He opens the door to the coffee shop and waits until a couple of women dressed in business suits enter. They eye the cowboy and smile. Noah tips his hat and follows them in. The warm air from the kitchen behind the counter blasts him as he enters. The smell of coffee and cinnamon bagels permeates the place. He waves to his former Italian partner, Zamperini, known as Zee to his friends, sitting in back at their favorite booth drinking coffee in a McAteer's cup. Noah moves to the end of the counter next to the register. Shane, the owner with his wife Ruth, is at the far end talking to a cop. This is a favorite place for the guys, since Shane was one of them. Ruth, a pretty blonde ten years younger than her husband, is in her white uniform, serving coffee to a couple of uniforms at the counter nearest to Noah. She glances at him, smiles and raises the glass coffee pot in the air to acknowledge him. He tips his hat. Shane, like Zee, is much older than he. Noah partnered up with Zee, but Shane partnered with another officer. Both were good cops, too.

Several uniforms and a couple detectives are seated on the stools around the curved counter. They nod, a couple even wave, not one says what he's expecting. He finds this strange. Shane wipes his hands on his white apron, nods as he ambles over to the register to take McGraw's order.

"Shane," McGraw says as he nods.

"Noah. Good to seeya. Heard you ran into some bad luck in Mississippi. You okay?"

"Much better. Thanks."

"Good to hear. What can I get you, your usual? I'll throw in one of our bagels, on the house."

"Thanks, just the skinny latte."

"I'll wrap a cinnamon for your mom. They're her favorite."

"She'll appreciate it."

McGraw takes the bagel and cup to the condiments stand against the large window facing the street, adds cinnamon and vanilla to his coffee and moves down the aisle between the row of black-top tables, heading to the back. The place is packed. Tables are occupied with neatly dressed white- collar workers, many of whom aren't talking but texting or reading things on their cell phones, while others are typing on their laptops.

Give it a rest, McGraw thinks as he passes them.

Noah hasn't seen his old partner since he got back from Ole Miss, but did talk to him on the phone. Zee is munching on a cheese omelet, and looks like he's really enjoying it.

"Good to seeya, Zee."

The Italian, who resembles Tony Soprano (James Gandolfini), looks up and frowns. "Where in the hell is that sling you're supposed to be wearing?"

"Don't need it."

"Bullshit!"

"The doc released me. You my babysitter now?"

"Damn right. Hop in cowboy. Let's talk."

That's about as good a 'hello, how are you' as Noah is going to get from the old Dago.

McGraw slides in the booth opposite Zee, places his coffee and bagel on the table in front of him, removes his Stetson and sets it next to him on the red leather seat, reaches for his coffee, removes the cover.

"What's up with the guys at the counter?" McGraw asks as he takes several quaffs of his coffee. "Hmm, that's good."

Zee frowns.

"They nodded when I came in but didn't do that name calling thing."

The cops usually greeted him in a playful manner saying, "Howya doing, cowboy?" or "There's the Marlboro Man," or "There's the D that talks to his vic's." Then everyone would burst out laughing. Zee had told him The Marlboro Man stuck to him because he's cool, calm, and has his act together just like that cowboy on the horse who used to appear on the billboard signs around town advertising Marlboro cigarettes before smoking became bad for you. The homicide detectives at the Atlanta PD would swear that cowboy McGraw has some special talent for solving crimes. They believe the dead speak to him, the way he goes about processing a homicide scene.

"They're just concerned." Zee says. "They know you went down in Mississippi. We stick together when one of ours is hit."

Noah shrugs. "It's just that I thought it wouldn't have made any difference to the guys."

"Naw, man. They're on your side."

Zee's stomach growls as he takes a drink of his coffee and stares at McGraw over the rim of the cup. "Excuse me a minute, partner, I gotta go to the John." He slides out the booth and heads to the restroom area, leaving a plate of half-eaten ham and cheese omelet with pieces of biscuits.

McGraw thinks about his decision to go into the Marines before college, where he served four years in the military police, then to Harvard, graduating with a degree in psychology, and then on to the University of Maryland, earning a Master's in Criminology and Law Enforcement. His years as an investigating officer for the Maryland Highway Patrol were beneficial in developing his investigative skills. He applied for an opening in the Atlanta PD when he learned of the opportunities there. When he was promoted to lieutenant in the Homicide Division, the department allowed him to go back to wearing starched white shirts, jeans, boots and his white Stetson. The other officers at the APD began calling him The Marlboro Man in jest. And it stuck.

McGraw reaches for his coffee. Finishes it. "Gotta get another," he says to Zee who has returned to the booth from the restroom. "Be right back."

At the counter, McGraw walks around talking to the officers, which is a first for him, thanking them for caring. Minutes later, he returns with another latte.

"Better be careful, cowboy, that coffee can stunt your growth."

McGraw smiles. Takes a drink from his cup.

"Okay. Let's have it," Zee says.

"What?"

"The details. Couldn't get them out of you over the phone."

"Oh, the Oxford thing."

"Hell, yes, the Oxford thing."

"Nothing much. We had Kingston cornered in a parking lot behind a fraternity house late in the fourth quarter of the football game. I returned fire while Holly made her way around the cars to get a bead on him. In the process, he put a couple in me, but she took him out."

McGraw takes another drink of his coffee. "That's it. I'm healed."

"Holly's okay, too, right?"

He nods. "She's been taking care of me ever since I went into the Oxford hospital."

"Good. You're lucky on two accounts, my friend. One, you're alive, and two, you have that beautiful partner."

Noah nods again and sips his coffee while watching his old partner eating, who is staring back between bites.

Neither one speaks while Zee finishes his omelet and drinks the last of his coffee. He pushes his plate to one side and says, "Okay, what's bothering you?"

"Nothing."

"Bullshit! I know you better than you know yourself. Remember me?"

McGraw's isn't surprised that Zee can read him. He's reluctant to bring up the Manchester case.

"I've told you everything."

"C'mon, man. How many years were we together? You can't bullshit your old partner. You're all smiles but behind it, I see sadness."

"I knew I couldn't hide anything from you. That's why I didn't want to come." He shifts in his seat and looks away for a few seconds. "I'm having those…dreams again," he says, gazing into Zee's eyes.

Zee scowls.

"They've returned." He raises a hand. "But they're appearing less and less."

"Too much time on your hands. It's good they're fading away. Means you're getting control of your emotions." He frowns as he waits until a young woman dressed in a business suit passes their table. "Man, have you forgotten how I taught you how to detach yourself from a crime scene? It's as much a necessary tool as forensics."

"That you did," he says. "You reminded me often that: 'crime scenes must be viewed at an emotional distance.'"

"It helped us survive," Zee says. "Without the right attitude, this work can make you callus. It can change you."

"I'm with you on that, Zee. I'm handling it."

"Have you seen the shrink yet?"

"Yep. Capt. set it up. I've been cleared. She said I'm good as new."

The psych doc had to determine if McGraw was having any recurrent dreams about being shot. To excel in his field, McGraw had developed certain traits—a sharp mind, bull-dogged determination, and an impatient nature. These traits were necessary to match the emotional distance that was necessary to do his job.

"Been to the firing range?"

"Done that, too. And the medical doc says my wounds are healed and he released me."

HR (human resources) wants to know if McGraw is able to lift objects, not impaired in his thinking, or impaired in firing his weapon. He has to be as good as before getting shot.

"You're a survivor, partner. I did a good job in molding you."

McGraw laughs. "Thanks."

"Now, tell me how that movie star partner of yours is doing. Who did you say she reminds you of? Oh, yeah, Sandra Bullock."

Zee winks at McGraw. "And you're George Strait? Right?"

He laughs again.

"That's the spirit, Noah. Laughing's good for the soul."

McGraw finishes his coffee. "Holly and Dusty have been with me at the ranch since she and I got back." He takes another sip of his coffee. "She and I…well…we're becoming very close."

"I approve," Zee says. "What the hell took you so long? I was beginning to think you were losing your eyesight."

McGraw looks away. "I'm concerned, though," McGraw says, "about working together—"

"I know what you are thinking," Zee says, interrupting. "But partners look out for each other just like you and I did, and she did for you in Oxford."

"Yeah, but if it were the other way around, and she went down for good, I don't think I could handle it."

"I know you both and if fear becomes too much, you both'll work it out. Give it a try."

Chapter 8

Capt. Norman Dipple, Chief of Detectives, sits at his cluttered desk in a spacious office in the Homicide Division with his tie loosened, shirt sleeves rolled up to his elbows, suit coat hanging on the hall tree behind him, looking into a mirror. The ex-hockey player from Minnesota, in his late forties, over six foot, has a muscular built, high forehead, dark hair, and thick eyebrows. Friends tell him he has the smile and face of the actor Ernest Borgnine. Reminding himself of that while shaving in the morning makes him proud.

But something is disturbing him. He heard through the grapevine some weeks ago that a detective said he has bulldog jowls. He'd put his money on McGraw. As a result, Dipple has been on a diet and now, rubbing his face as it appears in the mirror, believes his jowls have shrunk some. When he first heard it, he had to admit that the first thing his detectives noticed when they approached him was his jaws, not his eyes or ears or nose. That's changing. In a way, it is good that he can't see his face—of course, not unless he looks into a mirror—he doesn't want to be reminded of his jowls every minute of the day.

He inhales a deep breath, reaches over to the intercom, pushes the button.

"Yes, Capt."

"Bonnie, bring me the medical file on Noah McGraw. All reports should be back from HR."

"Yes, sir," Officer Barber says.

Dipple leans back in his chair and thinks about the guilt he's been working through resulting from recommending his financial advisor, Max Kingston, to the squad. Max hoodwinked the Capt. into thinking a financial advisor could help them. But that's not how it played out. Max turned killer. He targeted McGraw in a shootout on the Ole Miss campus. But now Capt. is trying to leave it all in the past. The Bureau Counselor has helped him do that.

The bulldog sighs and turns his attention back to his squad of detectives. The name fits him. He likes the tough guy role. That way he can't get too close to his officers. But he understands the chemistry and the camaraderie cementing his detectives together through the skills and leadership of his outstanding investigator, McGraw. Kramer and Gomez have been asking when McGraw and Roark are coming back. This team has made Dipple look good in the eyes of the Police Chief and the Mayor. He thrives on his detectives' kudos. Dipple's favorable relationship with the Mayor is through their wives being first cousins.

The door opens and Officer Barber enters with a half-inch-thick file.

"Here's the file on Lieutenant Noah McGraw, sir," she says. Barber is always proper when addressing the detectives. Never uses just their last names. "I hadn't filed it yet with all of his other stuff."

"Good."

Officer Barber stands in front of his desk waiting for instructions.

Dipple opens the folder. Minutes later, a smile comes across his face. Dr. Joe Kirkpatrick has given McGraw a clean bill of health and released him to return to work. Attached to her evaluation of Noah McGraw, Dr. Sherri Frey, the Department Psychiatrist, reports that McGraw is able to perform his duties as well as before. *He's the same old McGraw*, Dipple thinks. Included is another report asserting that McGraw has been to the firing range and has qualified, better than before.

"Great." He looks up. "Have Ed Kramer and Juan Gomez come to my office."

"Yes, sir," she says, turning and rushing out the door.

Feeling more relaxed, Dipple returns to reading the file. The psych evaluation on McGraw describes the psychological issues that McGraw has faced.

Officer Barber returns. "Sir, Detective Kramer is in the squad waiting for Detective Gomez who's on his way from the hospital. Sick kid."

Dipple nods. "His boy struggles with chronic asthma. The attacks can be severe. Tell them to report to me as soon as Gomez gets back."

"Will do, sir." She hurries from the office.

Next, the Chief's eyes navigate back to the psych evaluation on McGraw. Dipple's curiosity is getting the better of him and he yields to his eagerness to read it. Minutes later, he looks out the window at the busy street in the distance.

I know those feelings McGraw was having, he thinks.

Dipple runs his fingers over the report as if to drive out McGraw's demons. The doc states that McGraw's clash with Max Kingston triggered the lieutenant to reflect on his mortality, which is reasonable and expected. McGraw expressed concern for his partner, Holly Roark. In addition, the confrontation in Mississippi had conjured up nightmares of an old multiple homicide case McGraw had worked. She states with assurance that they have worked though these issues and McGraw is capable of performing his duties.

Finding himself in a situation where he must act with deadly force, the Lieutenant will be able to fire his weapon to protect himself and his partner, and the public.

It'll be great having him back, Dipple thinks.

He closes the file. There's no better detective than McGraw, he grudgingly admits to himself, but he still likes to come down hard on him. McGraw was one of the few officers he ever had who came up through the ranks in record time. After the academy, he demonstrated street smarts working patrol and an ability to read people and to get them to talk. These exceptional skills propelled McGraw into the Investigation Bureau, Narcotics Division, where he was promoted through the ranks. His ability to multi-task and to lead an investigation opened the door to the Capt.'s Homicide Division.

McGraw has asked again for a black Silverado SSV police vehicle before his return to duty. Dipple had a hell of a time getting it approved. He would do anything for his best detective, but he'd never tell McGraw that. The surprise is waiting for him in the mechanics garage. They are preparing it for police work.

A knock on the door brings the Capt. out of his reverie.

Detectives Kramer and Gomez step into the office without saying a word. They could be the odd couple. Kramer is over six feet and medium-built, while Gomez is five-foot-five and a little plump. Kramer is the somber one, while Gomez is always smiling and playful. Both are good cops.

"Ed and Juan," the Capt. says. "You'll be glad to know that McGraw and Roark will be returning to work next Monday."

They glance at each other. Gomez allows himself a smile.

"The place has been dead without them, Capt.," Gomez says.

Dipple nods. "It has, but for now, we have a suspected suicide. The subject's name is Hannah Clay, a ninety-year-old living in the Reagan Retirement Home. There is evidence of depression, loneliness, and isolation according to the nursing staff. Christmas and New Year's Day are big days for suicides. Some poor souls see this as a time to end their lives."

Kramer and Gomez leave the Chief's office and return to the squad room. The mornings haven't been the flurry of activity like most days when McGraw and Roark are in the room.

"When did the Capt. say the lieutenant and sergeant are coming back?" Kramer asks.

"Next Monday," Gomez says. He shakes his head. "And, brother, it won't be too soon. This place's been a morgue without them."

Outside, Gomez slides behind the wheel of a black detective unit while Kramer takes the passenger seat. As they pull out of the parking lot, Gomez says, "Have you noticed the change in the Capt. since McGraw's shooting?"

Kramer nods. "Yeah. It really hit him. He misses the lieutenant as much as we do. McGraw and Roark make a great team. They enhance the Capt.'s status, and he knows it."

"And ours, too, man," Gomez says.

"Without a doubt," Kramer says.

At the Reagan Retirement home, Gomez pulls up behind a patrol car.

"Howya doin,' detectives," a patrol officer says to the two men dressed in suits, white shirts, and ties. They nod.

"Has the M.E. been called?" Gomez asks.

"Her assistant is inside, sir."

Gomez likes it when patrol calls him 'sir'.

When they enter, they find a uniform officer interviewing two nurses at their station in the center of the room.

The detectives turn down the hall and greet the officer standing outside the entrance to room 127.

"Howya doing?" Gomez says.

The officer nods. "Okay, detective."

They enter, slip into gloves, and move around the room. Only a few magazines and a bible are on top of the dresser. Candy bars and crackers are in the drawer. Nothing under the bed.

Kramer finds an opened letter from Hannah Clay's attorney. He reads through it, then turns to Gomez.

"Looks like our subject has no living relatives. The attorney is the executor of her will. She wants to be cremated and is giving most of her money to her church. Have you seen a suicide note?"

"No note of any kind," Gomez says.

The assistant medical examiner, Larry, is in the bathroom on his knees examining the subject's head and neck. The decedent is kneeling and leaning forward with a wire around her neck. He looks up. "Well, there's Mutt and Jeff," he says, jokingly.

"What's up, doc?" Gomez says, smiling.

The examiner looks up and frowns. "Not funny. Gomez. That's from an old cartoon."

"C'mon, you know you like it. Makes you feel important."

"Yeah. Doing what I do. Really important, working in people's shit."

"Determined anything, Larry?" Kramer asks, seeming a little impatient.

"Apparent suicide. Appears she pulled the call cord out from above her bed, the one she used to call the nurses, and strangled herself with it. It's common in the elderly. We'll do x-rays."

Kramer nods.

"The place looks clean," Larry says. "You can look at the body if you wish."

"We'll wait for your report since she hasn't been shot or stabbed. No gun, shells, or weapon to look for," Kramer says.

"Can we take her?"

"Sure thing," Kramer says.

Larry leaves the room, and several minutes later returns with a gray-haired guy pushing a gurney with a black bag on it. "Call me when you get back, we may have something for you. Should be quick," Larry says. "Dr. Philips won't do an autopsy."

"Thanks," Gomez says as they knuckle punch.

The detectives head to the nurses' station to interview them. A few residents have taken their lives during the Holidays, especially when they have a sickness like cancer. In Hannah's case, there's evidence of depression and desperation.

The poor thing had no one and was lonely, Gomez thinks. *No reason to write a suicide note. This is a closed case for now.*

Kramer and Gomez ask for Hannah's med list, thank the nurses and move out behind the stretcher with the black body bag being wheeled down the sidewalk and loaded into the back of the coroner's white van. They head back to the precinct.

Kramer reports to the Capt. that the assistant M.E. at the site found no bruises—no defense marks—and took the body in for x-ray. He believes Hannah Clay committed suicide by kneeling on the floor in the bathroom, tying one end of a cord around her neck, and the other end to the bathroom door handle, and then leaning forward. Her attorney is the executor and he's waiting on her body to be released so he can proceed. Calling down to the M.E., they learn Hannah Clay had no finger marks around the neck or broken hyoid bone from strangulation. Knees showed lividity. Nothing suspicious. There will be no autopsy.

Chapter 9

Walking to his Caddy from his favorite coffee bar, *The Kitchen Door,* Jack Carter carries a sack containing a slice of chocolate cake and two coffees. He depresses the remote to unlock the car and slips in with the goodies. When he arrives at Megan's apartment in west Atlanta, he uses his key she gave him to open her door. She's on the couch watching a movie on the TV, crying at the commercial that is telling the story of children with cancer in a research hospital. Carter watches from the table in the kitchen while placing a slice of cake on a plate. One little girl is bald-headed, another has a mask over her mouth, and the little boy has an arm amputated at the elbow. He turns away so Megan won't hear the laughter that is rising up in him. He envisions the little boy rotating his stub in the air, which Carter finds amusing. Megan would think he's sick in the head if she knew. He can't help from laughing at those who are hurting or have special needs.

He carries the plate of cake and two cups of coffee from the kitchen. She's told him several times how much of a gentleman he is. He takes pride in acting as the good Samaritan. Carter places the plate and coffees on the round table in front of her. He's about to play to Megan's feelings when the movie goes off. Megan turns to him. Asks about his family and wants to know everything about them. Carter has been waiting for the right moment. And it's now.

"You want to hear about my family?" he says taking a couple of swallows of his coffee. "Are you sure? It's not a pretty picture."

"Oh, yes. Please."

"We'll, okay."

She takes a drink of her coffee, cuts off a small piece of cake with her fork, then turns to face him. "The cake is delicious. Thanks for being so thoughtful."

He only smiles. Then, taking his time since she's so interested, he begins by telling her that his mother screamed and berated him ever since he could remember. He'd hide under his bed. Sometimes he'd wet the bed and she'd get so angry she'd lock him in the basement.

"You poor thing," she says, squeezing his hand.

When Carter didn't make it into the police academy, his mother called him all kind of names and told him he'd never amount to anything. To prove her wrong, he enrolled in college with a major in forensic science, which always thrilled him, especially since his dad told him not to be a cop when he was 10. He should choose something where he wouldn't be gone from home so much. Carter graduated at the head of his class. went on to earn a master's degree. His mother never congratulated him.

"Oh, you poor thing," Megan says as she wipes away the tears.

Carter is pleased. He wants her motherly instincts to kick into action so he can manipulate her. He senses her love for him even though he has none for her.

"Finish your cake," he says. "Maybe I shouldn't have told you so much."

"No, no. I want to hear it all." She eats a few more bites and washes it down with several swallows of her coffee. "Please go on."

Carter tells her about his dad, Nick Carter, a former APD cop being killed in the line of duty in a shootout when Jack was nearly eleven. His parents had divorced when he was much younger. Laura, his mother, couldn't take her husband being gone so much; she started drinking and began treating his dad badly. Nick left and they divorced. But he and his dad continued seeing each other until he lost his life.

"Oh, I'm so sorry," Megan says.

He puts his arm around her and explains how his mom took back her maiden name, *Evans*. Jack's parents fought for as long as he can remember. He has no brothers or sisters. His mother told him she never wanted him, even thought about having an abortion. She verbally abused him. Her mantra was "You're a loser." There were times when he wasn't in school she'd chained him in the basement like an animal so she could go shopping or to have lunch and drinks with her lady friend, Sally Crane.

"They both are selfish divorcees in their early sixties who love to drink and gossip."

Now tears are streaming down Megan's checks.

"I called them peas in a pod. I never liked Sally. Everyone thinks my mother is a nice person. She's a devil, and great at deceiving people."

Megan lays her head on Jack's shoulder.

"I think I've said enough. Do you want more coffee?"

"Yes, please."

Jack rises, goes to the Keurig in the kitchen and puts in a Hazelnut K-cup, Megan's favorite. He doesn't want to tell her how he remembers the last time his mother locked him in the basement as if it were yesterday. She chained him without food and water for an entire day to get even with him for killing her precious cat. After his father was killed, Jack began setting fires, dismembering animals, hiding from his mother in his special hiding place behind the house.

Megan doesn't need to know this, he thinks, as he waits for the coffee cup to fill.

Carter moves to the couch with a fresh cup. After finishing half of her coffee, she hugs him, slips into heavy kissing, Megan reaches between his legs, rubs him and then unzips his pants, reaches in and works him until he's hard. She grabs his hand, pulls him up from the couch and escorts him into her bedroom. While he doesn't enjoy the sex part as much as she, he acts like he does. No feelings for her. Megan is playing into his hands.

After they finish rolling between the sheets, he leaves and returns to his lair before midnight and hits the sack. During the early morning hours, he bolts up in bed awakened again by this recurring nightmare involving his mother—her fluttering tongue screaming at him to kill.

If I get caught, she'd have her revenge.

Chapter 10

The City Crime lab is located in the west side of the police headquarters annex building occupying the entire first floor above the City morgue. Jack Carter, Crime Lab Director, has an elevated office at one end of the spacious lab where he can look out over his scientists as they work in their respective sections. Some of his specialists perform their duties in lab analyses after returning from the crime scenes.

The lab seeks answers for the detectives and Carter's cooperative attitude has won him high praise from the Police Chief. Even though the detectives are demanding, Carter never shows any displeasure. His charisma works in his favor. They like him. Little do the detectives know that he has disdain for them. His arrogance permits him to believe that he's smarter than they are.

Carter is in a perfect position to review evidence as it is brought into his lab—latent prints, implements of assault, suicide cocktails, clothes, hair, fingernails, fiber, blood, bullets, powder, DNA, altered checks, receipts, and notes—before distributing it. He would never tamper with evidence unless he needs to avoid detection.

Carter is proud of his lab. It is one of the best in the country, being relatively new. He has one thing going for him, he knows how to negotiate for what is needed in his lab for his scientists to do their job. Different scientific methods are used to examine evidence. Each scientist works in his area of expertise, such as chemistry, biology, blood spatter, ballistics, and document examinations. Most will work in a variety of different scenarios and will do many things. They are very much involved in a satisfying hands-on profession, observing results of their work. Every case is different and involves specialized expertise, requiring that the specialists work closely together, meeting evidence requirements of the law.

The lab contains fume (exhaust) hoods, and particulate control hoods that have special filters to control particulate matter; long tables needed for examining various bits of evidence that come in from the different crime scenes. Optic microscopes, and for deeper analyses, a scanning electron microscope are available, as are computers with high-definition monitors and a latent fingerprint imaging chamber, AFIS (Automatic Fingerprint Identification System), variety of lasers, and ballistic catch barrels.

A special room houses spectroscopy and chromatography instruments. Forensic scientists prefer using nondestructive methods first, such as, Thin layer chromatography, HPLC (High Performance Liquid Chromatography), and Fourier Transform Infrared spectroscopy to preserve evidence. Destructive methods include: Atomic Absorption Spectroscopy and GC-MS (Gas Chromatography-Mass Spectroscopy). Which method is used is determined by the one that would produce the best results.

Quality assurance and quality control of their results and their instruments are of utmost importance to his scientists. To ensure accuracy, their instruments are calibrated and certified for accuracy, and are able to detect and measure various quantities of different substances.

A special unit performs all DNA analyses.

Carter's scientists have no clue about his dark side. At night in his lair, he surfs the Internet on his laptop for females around his mother's age and older, and blocks out time at work to continue his Internet search during the day using his laptop. He takes great care not to use his lab computers, which are reviewed. After killing Hannah Clay and his mother, Carter is no longer inhibited. The urge is becoming stronger and stronger when he sees these women on the dating sites. He first wondered how it would feel to kill a human being when he was a teenager killing animals. He's fascinated with his double life—a normal one and the one that gives him erotic excitement in taking a life. His hero is Ted Bundy, who led a well-documented double life. He was a serial killer, rapist, kidnaper, burglar, and necrophile who assaulted and murdered numerous young women and girls during the '70s. He committed thirty homicides in seven states in four years from 1974-1978. He was handsome and charismatic, traits he exploited to win his victims' trust. Bundy called himself, "the most cold-hearted son of a bitch you'll ever meet."

Chapter 11

After a hard day, Jack Carter ambles out of the lab into the late afternoon cold to the parking lot and slips into his white Caddy, slides in a CD, listens to *It's all in the Game*. On the way home, he stops for a cheeseburger and a drink. When he arrives at the homestead, he finds his mother's drinking buddy, Sally Crane, parked in front of the house in her red SUV. He pulls into the driveway and sits for a few minutes wondering what he's going to tell her, before stepping out.

The bitch is a damn pest.

Sally is standing on the porch looking his way, waving. He steps out of the car, leaving his sandwich and drink on the passenger seat, and strolls from behind his car over to the porch.

"Hi, dear," Sally says with open arms, coat unbuttoned. That's her signal for a hug even though she has a cigarette between her fingers, covered in red lipstick at the end. They embrace. "I stopped by to see Laura. She hasn't been answering my calls. Is she okay?" she says, taking a puff on her cig, blowing smoke in his face. "She's not sick, is she?"

Sally and his mother go out at least once a week, like clockwork, for lunch and drinks. She likes Jack and thinks he's very sweet and hugs him whenever she sees him. He smells liquor and tobacco on her breath. He despises her, but lays on the charm; his good looks—short black hair with a little gray in it, thick eyebrows and dark eyes. Sally tells him how handsome he is, and squeezes his cheeks instead of a hug.

"You're sexy and if I was younger."

The slut, with breasts about to pop out of a low-cut blouse, has heavy rouge and red painted lips, doesn't say what she would do, but he could guess what she'd want.

"Mom went to Charlotte to take care of a sick cousin but she'll be back in a week or so. I'm sorry I didn't return your calls. Mom told me to call you but it's been a rat race at the lab the last week and when I get home, I just grab a bite and hit the sack."

Sally believes him. "That's okay, honey," she says as she heads to her car. "When you talk to her, tell her to call me."

"Will do, Ms. Crane."

"Oh, honey, call me Sally," she says as she takes a draw on her cig and drops the butt by the curb, opens the door and slips in behind the wheel of her SUV.

Jack waits until she pulls away, then moves to the curb and picks up the red lipstick-stained cigarette butt, still burning.

If you bother me again, you'll end up like the others.

Don't even think about it, he hears a voice say in his head.

It's her again?

Chapter 12

Nick Carter began taking his son Jack on fishing trips to the cabin, which he bought when Jack was just three. Jack enjoyed being with his dad during those years they had together. Sergeant Nick Carter told him once while fishing on the lake that their time together meant the world to him, and someday this cabin would be his. Jack knew that besides their fun together, his dad was glad to get away from his mom, the abusive alcoholic.

This cloudy Friday afternoon, Jack and Megan are sailing along in his white Seville, heading toward Sweetwater Creek area. It takes a little over an hour drive to his cabin once out of Atlanta. Megan is dressed in jeans and low-cut blue blouse tied at the waist, with plenty of cleavage even though she's wearing an open jacket. Jack has on fishing clothes and his favorite beige fishing hat with little lure trinkets pinned around the rim.

"Watch out!" Megan shouts, shooting forward in her seat. "That dog over there," she says, pointing, "he's about to dart into traffic."

An oncoming car on I-20, hits the dog. It flips under the fender and is thrown to the side of the road, yelping. The driver continues on at top speed without stopping.

Megan screams for Jack to stop, but he speeds up and doesn't look back.

"Didn't you hear me! Stop! The poor thing is in great pain."

"Let someone else stop and take care of the mutt," he says. "We're going in the opposite direction and need to get to the cabin. I want to be on the lake while there's daylight.

"Don't you have any feelings for that poor thing?" she says, looking out the back window. "You should have stopped? No one's stopping."

She's in tears.

"We couldn't have done anything. The mutt is probably dead by now." He looks over at her. *Poor, Megan. Her empathy always gets in the way of her reasoning. She should be pitying me for what I went through in my life and not that dumb animal.*

They both remain quiet during the last stretch of their drive to the cabin. Jack makes a right turn off the divided highway onto Water Valley Road and travels the dirt road, thick with climbing Magnolias that provide inviting shade, drives past several cabins along the way, trying to avoid the ruts in the winding road. After meandering for a couple of miles, they finally turn onto the road to the cabin, cross a wooden bridge that he and his dad had made repairs on several times. Up ahead is his three-bedroom cabin with dozens of Dogwoods and Southern Magnolias on the property of one acre. Good thing it hasn't rained in a while. He drives up to the pine wood cabin with its large windows, twenty yards up an incline, and pulls up in front. The panoramic view out over the lake with beautiful White and Southern Red Oaks close to its banks across the way is breathtaking. Jack and Megan hop out of the Caddy, He opens the back door on the driver's side, grabs his luggage and a box of groceries off the back seat. Megan opens the door on her side and removes her overnight bag and more groceries. They carry the items to the front porch. Jack returns to the Caddy, opens the trunk and removes a rifle and fishing gear, then hikes back up to the wooden steps and sets them on the porch.

"This view of the lake from here is so picturesque," she says. "Love those trees how they appear to protect the water."

"You'll love it here. The cabin is well-stocked and we have all we need," he says as he opens the door. They carry their belongings in and begin putting the groceries away. Jack takes her hand and pulls her out into the Lanai in the back. The porch is surrounded with brick about three feet high, a white ceiling trimmed in brown, with fans. White lights are strung along the sides at the top. An electric fire pit for heat separates a table with chairs for dining and an area with lounging furniture. An ornate built-in grill is to one side. Beyond the brick wall is a steep drop-off.

"Did you and your dad build all this?" she asks, looking around.

"The cabin was an old hut on a large sewer line that went to the lake, but that all changed when Dad bought the property and we enlarged the old building. It took us a few years, but we laid every brick, hammered each piece of wood, installed the electric wiring and fans. I was small, but I handed things to dad. I was able to shove and pull stuff." He laughed. "My dad was really good to me. Being under ten when we started, you can't do too much. But he acted like I was a big help. As the old commercial used to say, "And, I helped."

Megan smiled. "That's cute." She looks out over the property. "What do you keep in that garage? Do you have a jeep?"

"No. I keep my ATV in there."

"What's an ATV?"

"It's a utility vehicle. The acronym ATV stands for All-Terrain Vehicle, which means you can drive that baby anywhere. Maybe I'll give you a ride in it later."

"Oh, I don't know. It sounds like a rough ride."

He turns to leave and stops. "You'll need cushions for out here. They're stored in the large closet in the hall," he says, "I'm going to go to the lake to do some fishing before dinner. I'll grill the steaks and we can eat under the lights." He starts to go back into the cabin but stops, turns and says, "There's beer and wine in the fridge."

"I think I'll bring a glass of wine out and enjoy the peace and quiet. I can even hear the critters singing."

"Sounds great."

Jack grabs a couple cans of Bud Lights from the fridge. Out the door, he picks up the portable chair, fishing rod, and tackle box off the porch and heads down to his favorite fishing spot. He arranges the chair close to the edge, opens his dad's tackle box with all his lures. He taught Jack about the six best bass lures ever made, guaranteed to catch bass: plastic worms; spinnerbaits; jigs; crankbaits; buzzbaits; and jerkbaits. His dad liked the jigs but Jack preferred plastic worms. Today, in honor of his dad, he's gonna attach a personalized fishing lure with skirted jig, the best. After thirty minutes of casting with no luck, he sets the rod and opens a can of Bud and sits. He takes a couple of swallows and sighs.

Looking out into the water he sees a vision of his dad casting into the waters, the strong, healthy cop who loved the outdoors. How Jack misses him. The only person in the world who ever hinted at loving him through his smiles and touches. Never said the words, but Jack knew his dad loved him. Nick Carter never knew his son used to sneak down to the pier at night, catching bullfrogs to blow them up. The urge to kill was strong at times. He stuffed fireworks into the mouths of several frogs and watched as the explosion blew them to smithereens. Even now he feels the thrill of that moment. He told his dad that he found the frog pieces on the bank and they were used as fish bait.

A call from Megan stirs him from his reverie.

"Jack, are you about done? I'm getting hungry and it's beginning to get dark."

"Up in a minute," he says.

Jack gathers his things and heads up to the cabin. Once inside, he notices two steaks and a salad on the counter, goes to the grill and removes the cover.

Out in the Lanai, Megan has decorated the table with colorful placemats, candles, water and wine glasses. The little white lights around the ceiling are on. It looks like a celebration. He starts the fire and goes for the steaks.

"This looks like a celebration," he says. "What's the occasion?"

"Oh, just felt in the mood to have a relaxing dinner and a little talk."

A little talk. He doesn't know if he likes that. Certainly, she isn't thinking about him proposing marriage?

"You like your steaks with just a little red, correct?" he asks.

She nods. "You remembered."

When the steaks are near ready, Megan fills the water and wine glasses. Then she lights the candles.

Jack carries the steaks to the table and they sit. She takes a bite of her steak and smiles. "Just the way I like it."

After the meal, they fill their glasses with wine and Megan asks that they sit on the couch a few feet from the table. They sit together in silence for a few minutes savoring their drinks. Jack is wondering what's going through her mind this very moment. Did she discover something of his? Maybe the dating site he visits? That's crazy. There's no way.

"Why didn't you stop for that dog this afternoon, Jack? Don't you like animals?"

This really takes him by surprise. "It's not that," he says. "It's just…it was dead and we couldn't do anything."

"But we could have checked to make sure. Maybe it only had a broken leg."

He took another swig of his wine. "I guess I wasn't thinking. I'm sorry."

She frowns. "What do I really know about you, Jack? Oh, sure, you've told me about your family and how you were abused by your mother, but you never talk about what you are thinking or what ideas you have, you never express your feelings towards me…never talk about your interactions with anyone or about other family members. You must have grandparents, aunts and uncles. Your mind always seems preoccupied."

He sets his wine glass on the glass-top coffee table.

"I'm a loner. You knew that ever since we started our relationship. I never talk about family because I didn't know them. You know from this place, the only person I was ever close to was my dad. The abuse I took from mother made me shy and withdrawn. In my younger years I was afraid of everyone and began not trusting anyone. When I got older, I realized I had to make my way in the world like my dad. He influenced me at an early age not to be a cop, so I chose forensics. As a cop, his time away from the family broke us up. You know the story.

"I know women think they can change men. That can never happen. While no excuse, I'm the way I am because of my mother. I've worked hard to change, to make something of myself, but can't seem to be any better than the person I am."

Megan sets her glass on the table and scoots over to him and they embrace for several seconds. She whispers in his ear, "I'm sorry. I understand."

He grabs her hand and leads her inside. "I want to show you something."

He takes her to a door in the kitchen, opens it, flips on the lights as they descend the stairs, ending up in a decorated basement that fits the definition of a man's cave, filled with leather couches, a TV screen that covers the entire wall, table lamps, and several pieces of exercise equipment. He goes to one of the several table lamps and turns it on.

"Wow. Nice. I didn't know this place had a basement."

"You'd never know it from outside," he says. "We think this could have been the storage area for a drug house. It had an escape route that was made to look like an old sewer line running about one-hundred yards out from here. There was no need for a sewer pipeline, that's when my dad determined it had to be an escape route."

He pauses, wondering if she's going to ask him where it is exactly.

"The hole was large enough for a person to run through. We walled off all sides of this room and then poured the concrete floor."

"The brown rug and walnut paneling look very nice." She looked up. "And the varnished overhead beams are very attractive. This place gives me a warm an inviting feeling."

"I love working out down here and watching some of my sports."

"I'm impressed. You mean you and your dad did all of this?" she says, extending her arms out and rotating her body.

He smiles. "It took a lot of work." He pauses. "I… I have to confess. We did have help."

"Oh?"

"Yes. Many of my dad's police buddies had the skills we needed. That's how we remodeled the whole place."

"So, you helped, but not as much a superman as you liked for me to believe?" she says, smiling.

He shrugs. "It sounded good. I guess I was trying to impress you."

They laugh.

Chapter 13

It's a sad day.

Dusty is gathering his things in the bedroom while his mother, Holly Roark, finishes packing her suitcase.

"Are you about done, Dusty?" she asks.

He is slow to answer. He slips something into his pocket.

"Did you hear me, son?"

He snaps back. "Yes, I did! I'm done."

"Young man, I don't like your attitude!"

He pulls his suitcase from the bed to the floor. "I'm sorry, mom, but...do we hafta go?"

"We have our own home. You knew when we came here, it was only temporary until McGraw got better."

"I know, but I like it here. There's no fun at home."

"Mattie and Lloyd miss you. They've been asking about you."

"I know, but—"

Anna Marie steps into the room. "Well, it seems you both are ready. Noah is waiting on the porch." She moves to Holly with her arms out. "I will miss having you both with us," she says. They embrace.

"I'm sorry," Holly says, wiping away tears from her eyes. "I told myself I wouldn't do this."

"Oh, dear, don't be sad. You can come anytime. I know Noah would want it."

"Thank you," she says.

Dusty is sitting on his suitcase with his back to the ladies, looking at the floor.

"Let's go, son," Holly says. She follows Anna Marie out of the room and down the stairs to the front door. Dusty drags his suitcase across the floor and down the flight of steps, hitting each step with a bang.

While waiting for Dusty, Holly can see Noah through the glass door, standing at the edge of the porch, dressed in his cowboy hat and jeans. All he needed was a guitar and he'd be George Strait's twin, about to sing a love song to her. She shakes it off as a schoolgirl fantasy. Like Dusty, she doesn't want to go, but knows they must.

Anna Marie opens the door.

"They're ready, Noah.

He turns to face them, reaches for the suitcases. "Let me take those."

They walk at a snail's pace down the flagstone sidewalk, as in a funeral procession, ending at his blue pickup.

Noah throws the suitcases in the bed of the truck and walks around to opens the passenger door for Holly to slide in. Dusty has vanished.

"Where did that boy go?" Holly asks. "He doesn't want to leave."

"I know. Back in a minute." Noah moves round the front of the truck to face his mother, who looks puzzled.

"I'll be right back, ma."

Noah heads to the barn. Whitey Berry, the handyman, says, "You'll find him inside with TR."

Noah moves through the open doors, hears Dusty's voice but doesn't see him. As Noah moves in deeper into the barn, Dusty is talking to Texas Rodeo. He's on the opposite side of the horse and isn't aware that Noah is a few feet away.

"You know I'm going to miss you," he says sobbing. "I don't know if I'll ever be back. They say we can come on weekends, but my mom is always busy at work." He wipes his eyes on his shirt sleeve. "Being a cop, she's gone a lot." He sighs. "I miss not having a father around." He looks into TR's eyes. "You're the only friend that I can talk to, even though you don't talk back." Dusty laughs. "Do you understand me?" The horse neighs. "Okay, okay," he says as he strokes him. "I know my mother loves McGraw. I wish he was my dad. We're really great pals. I want them to get married so bad."

McGraw moves backwards out of the barn, so not to be heard, and acts like he has just entered, calls out his name. "Dusty, are you in here?"

"I'm over here," he says, stepping around the horse. "I had to say goodbye to my friend."

"You can come and ride him, anytime," Noah says as he enters the stall.

"Thanks," Dusty says as if he doesn't believe it.

McGraw rubs TR. "Dusty will be back." He turns to the boy. "Your mom is waiting in the truck."

Dusty walks out of the stall without saying a word, but looks back at the horse as they head towards the door. On the way to the pickup, Noah tells Dusty that just because he's going back home doesn't mean he won't be coming back to the Circle M again.

"It won't be the same," the ten-year-old says.

"You can stay the summers and holidays. How does that sound?"

"Okay," he says in a tone that's doesn't sound convincing.

McGraw puts his arm around him as they walk to the truck. Anna Marie, standing at the passenger side talking to Holly through the open door, turns as they approach and hugs Dusty. He hops in next to his mother.

"Come and visit us anytime," she says.

"I will, Mrs. McGraw," Dusty says.

Noah slips in behind the wheel next to Holly without removing his Stetson. His mother waves as they back away. No one says a word as they head to the Roark home.

⎯⎯⎯◄►⎯⎯⎯

Holly glances over at Noah. He's concentrating on the road and Dusty is staring out the passenger window. She's sandwiched between two sad people. What about her relationship with Noah?

Does it have to change once we're working together again? she wonders. They've gotten much closer the last few weeks without any interruptions, no cases to solve, and no reports to write. Their minds were clear to concentrate on relaxing and enjoying each other. They talked about their future together without mentioning marriage. Could they have a happy marriage working as partners, gone from home at all hours? She's only known one couple in another precinct, but they eventually divorced. She doesn't want to think about that for her and Noah. But there's also the dangers they face as cops. When he was hit in Mississippi, she felt a piece of her was gone until she learned he was going to be okay. She couldn't take it if he went down again. She has to think this through. If they were to marry, would the Capt. transfer her to Vice or Burglary? She didn't want either.

McGraw pulls into her driveway. Mattie and Lloyd Martin, the neighbors who care for Dusty, rush out of their home to greet them.

"Oh, we've missed you," Mattie says, hugging Dusty, who collapses in her arms like a ragdoll, not saying a word. She looks at Holly, frowning.

Holly whispers, *"He's sad."*

Mattie winks, indicating she understands.

"We'll stop over later," Lloyd says, as they head back into their yard.

McGraw steps out of the truck, reaches in the back for the suitcases. Dusty rushes to him.

"McGraw?" he says, reaching into his pocket. "I've got something for you."

McGraw sets the suitcases down by the driver's door.

"I hope you like it". He hands it to him. "It's a leather bracelet."

Noah examines it. "This is super workmanship. Did you make this?"

"Whitey helped me."

"You guys really hit it off, didn't you?'

"Sure did. He's fun to be with."

"And he likes you, too," McGraw says.

"Will you wear it?"

"I would be honored to," McGraw says, as he slips it on his right wrist. "Now you and I will always be connected."

Dusty wraps his arms around McGraw's waist. "I love you, McGraw."

"I love you, too, Dusty," he says, rubbing a hand through his hair.

Dusty turns and darts into the house. McGraw grabs the suitcases and follows Holly and sets them in the hallway.

She heads into Dusty's room. He's on the bed crying.

"I don't like it here. I want to live on the Circle M."

"Dusty, you know that can't happen. This is our home."

She knows Noah is hearing this.

"Why not. You can marry McGraw. You love him. I know it. And he loves you."

"Oh, Dusty, honey…."

She hears the front door close.

Holly comes out of Dusty's room, knowing that Noah heard everything.

———•••———

McGraw returns to the Circle M, doesn't go into the house. Instead, he walks the property as he always does when he has something on his mind. He meets up with Whitey.

"Hey, Noah. It's too quiet around here since Holly and Dusty left us."

"I'm trying to condition myself not having them around," Noah says.

Whitey nods. "Me, too. I can say with certainty that I haven't seen you this happy since Lee Ann passed. Holly's good for you."

He nods and heads into the barn, stops at Majestic Lady's stall, the horse Holly fell in love with.

"What do you think about Holly, Lady?" he asks, stroking her.

Majestic Lady neighs when she hears Holly's name.

"So, you like her, too. What do you think about us getting married?" He chuckles. "Guess you can't answer that."

Can our work put a strain on us if married?

Chapter 14

Jack Carter pulls into a parking spot close to Trader Joe's in a strip mall in north Atlanta. The lot is almost full this Saturday morning. He enters the supermarket, removes one of the carts from the three rows at the entrance, and begins walking the aisles, checking the fruits and vegetables. He's feeling energetic today, being his day off. He might even go to the cabin if he has time and do a little fishing.

As he pushes the grocery basket through several aisles, he enters the frozen food section. Carter remembers that he needs some frozen veggies to stir fry. As he opens one of the many glass doors and reaches in for a bag of broccoli and cauliflower, a sudden sharp pain hits the back of his legs and lower back. He flips around. This woman, he guesses, is in her seventies, has deliberately run a shopping cart into him, and has him pinned against the glass door. "What the hell's wrong with you, lady? Move that damn cart back so I can get out of here."

"You're too damn slow. Why in hell are you shopping anyway? Men don't know how to shop. Get the hell out of my way," she shouts.

"Are you hard of hearing? Move the basket out of the way." Jack sees his mother's tongue waggling as the lady lashes out at him.

"Go to hell," she says.

He rages.

She's all dolled up, dressed to kill and her hair has been styled. Carter wonders why her servants aren't shopping for her? "What are you doing out shopping anyway, old woman," he says.

If it weren't for his sunglasses, she would be able to see his eyes narrowing with a stare that could pierce steel. "Thought a rich old bitch like you would have one of your servants do the shopping for you. Can't believe you even have a driver's license."

"'Old,' who in the hell is 'old?' You're the one that's hard of hearing. Get the hell out of my way." She shoves the cart at him again, but he blocks it with his hand and pushes it back into her.

You're a mean old bitch. It's time someone rips out that tongue of yours.

Carter looks around for cameras, none that he can see. He isn't concerned about them; knows it'd be hard to identify him. All they'd see is a tall man in a cap and sunglasses. He keeps his head down as he checks out, carries his groceries to his car, loads the trunk and hops in the Caddy. He knows there are cameras in the lot. He has a good view of the exit from his parking spot. As he waits, all he can think about is her wagging tongue chastising him, like his mother used to do. Carter fumes while waiting.

He has to play it smart. He knows the security cameras would record him following her out. He will take a different route.

After fifteen minutes, the old gal comes out with one of the teen-aged baggers pushing the cart behind her, loads the plastic bags in the trunk of her Mercedes. She doesn't say anything to the young man, not even a thank you; instead, she gets into her car, pulls out of her parking space, almost hitting the car behind her. Carter pulls out and drives in the opposite direction but watching her move slowly out of the lot in his rearview mirror. He goes around the block, out of reach of the cameras, and falls in behind her. He can barely see her head.

Ten minutes later, the woman pulls into the driveway of a ritzy house in the northern Buckhead neighborhood. He gets the name *Gail Murdock* off the fancy brick mailbox as he drives slowly around the block surveilling the neighborhood. The Murdock home sits far back from the street, partially hidden with trees and lush shrubs. He smiles. This he likes because it's hard to see much from the street.

He rubs his temples. His mother's voice is screaming at him.
Kill the bitch.

———•••———

Carter heads home, pulls into his driveway and drives to the back, parking in front of the two-car garage where he keeps his mother's black Tahoe. He flips the trunk of his Caddy and gets out, removes several plastic bags of groceries and takes them to his secret apartment. After putting the food items away, he sits at his desk working his laptop keys, maneuvering through his open source database. It's amazing how much information is out there in cyberspace. He's spent years studying open source information, searching databases with the help of a hacker he knows. Carter finds the skills he learned from this underground hacker paying off. He begins searching for Gail Murdock, finds she's a widow woman. Husband died five years ago. Has one daughter. While profiling Gail, Jack goes to one of the senior matching sites—women in their late fifties and sixties—looking for companionship. He gets an erotic exhilaration as he looks at these Atlanta women pictured on the site, thinking how easy it would be to entice them to their deaths.

He rises and goes into his bathroom, slips in green contacts.

Grabs his gear and heads out.

Chapter 15

Carter eases up to the Murdock home around seven and parks the black Tahoe across the street, watches for thirty minutes to see who comes and goes. Murdock still hasn't removed her Christmas decorations.

He waits.

The garage door opens.

Out comes the Mercedes, stopping long enough for the automatic door to slam shut. She maneuvers out of the driveway and heads north. Carter reaches for the car door handle to get out, but quickly changes his mind. A bright light flashes over his SUV from a patrol car that pulls up behind him with its brights on. An officer bails out, comes around to the driver's side, shining a light from his hand-held flashlight.

Carter's heart pounds in his chest.

"Shit."

He lowers the window and places his hands on the steering wheel.

"What are you doing here?" the officer asks, flashing his light on Carter, then peering in the back. "Car trouble?"

"No, officer, I'm trying to get up nerve enough to ask this girl I just met to go out with me. I'm expecting her to come home any minute."

The officer smiles. After a few minutes of starring at Carter, he says, "Well, good luck with that." Returns to his patrol car and sits for a few minutes, then pulls around the black SUV and heads out of the neighborhood. Carter fears the officer has run his plate and vehicle description into the Intel database.

"Shit, shit, shit!" he shouts slamming a fist on the steering wheel.

I can't kill the old bitch until I know if that cop ran me.

He could be recorded as being in this area. If something ever happens in the neighborhood, Carter's name and vehicle would show up as being here this day and time. Carter begins hearing his mother's voice screaming in his mind. "You screw up. Look what you've gotten yourself into. You must kill the old bitch now!"

"Shut up, shut up!" he screams. "I should have sliced out your tongue when I had the chance." He shifts into drive and races off. "I think I'll do it now." He flies into Pinelawn Cemetery, travels the road that leads to his mother's burial site, stops and bails out, darts up to the grave bearing the headstone inscribed with the letters, *John Dell Sunday.*

He drops to his knees. "I hate you! I've hated you all my life!" he screams, pounding the dirt. "I'm gonna shut you up permanently." Like a madman, he screams and starts digging the ground like a dog burying a bone.

The night watchman rolls up in his golf cart, jumps out flashing a light on Carter.

"What are you doing? Stop! You can't disturb that grave."

Carter looks up into the light. "Get the hell out of here. I gotta do this."

"What's wrong with you, man?" he says. "Do I need to call someone. You look like you're going off your rocker."

Carter jumps up, punches the man so hard he falls backwards and rolls a few feet away.

"You son of a bitch!" he shouts. "You're as loony as they come. I'm calling the cops." He runs to his cart and races off.

Carter takes off.

Back in his lair, Carter slams the door shut, knocks over a chair, inhales a deep breath and sits. Looking at the pictures of the murdered women on the wall next to his computer eases his rage. Minutes later, his thoughts turn to the guy who had explained computer coding to him. Code is the language used to talk to computers. It tells the computer what to do, how to do it and when to do it. The best thing about coding is creating things you want to create. A group of coders meet in the back of a coffeehouse in town. Jack went a few times to learn all he could. While it wasn't well known, a few coders were malicious hackers. Jack knows Big Sam can hack into anything, even the government, for a price. He didn't know where the name *Big Sam* came from. The guy is a little punk who needed a shave, bath, and clean jeans. He was told the punk was brilliant.

Carter got a brilliant idea. He'll ask Big Sam to infiltrate McGraw's computer systems. Once he has McGraw's codes, he'll be able to maneuver throughout the system; specially to learn if that patrol cop who pulled up behind him at Murdock's place ran his plates and vehicle. Carter smiles.

After work the next day, Carter heads to S.E. Atlanta to Moreland Avenue, pulls up to the curb in front of a black building with a twelve-pane glass window that covers the entire front. The Cat's Eye Coffeehouse. He ambles out of his caddy and walks inside. The large room has a black ceiling with round, white bubble lights of different sizes that give off a dim glow. On the rough plastered walls are unframed paintings of all sizes, attached in no special order. Many give the impression that the artist threw buckets of colored paints on the canvas. As he approaches them, he sees price stickers attached to the bottom.

Who would buy this shit? Carter thinks.

To his left is a counter where you pick up coffee specials and place orders for sandwiches, baked goods and healthy salads. Through an opening to the back is the kitchen. Farther down against the wall is another counter with T-shirts displayed for sale behind it. Several feet from it is a stand with several shelves containing an array of health food products.

Jack places an order for a Grande, skinny latte, half-caff. He takes it with him as he looks around the room and moves between a dozen round tables. It's difficult to see the homes across the street from inside because of the thick bushes and trees. The place has changed a little since he was here last, and he never paid much attention. He did remember that in the next room were square tables with wi-fi hookups where the geeks did their things.

He moves through the opening without a door into the next room which is dimmer than the one he came from. In the front, near the window are several students working their laptops with opened textbooks next to their computers. He turns and looks towards the back where the geniuses are. Even the little punk, Big Sam, is there working away at his laptop.

Carter eases up to the little guy and waits. He doesn't look up for at least a couple of minutes.

He knows I'm here, the little prick.

"Can't you see I'm busy?" he says.

Carter knew he's going to give him some grief. That probably increased the price. Jack's gonna find out how good this prick is.

"I got a job for you. Interested?"

Big Sam doesn't say a word, He keeps tapping the keys on his laptop. Carter doesn't like playing other people's games. Only he forces others to do that.

"Are you interested in making some cash, or not?"

"Depends."

"Bullshit! Don't play games with me. You interested or not. Cut the bullshit."

"Okay, okay. Don't get your blood pressure up. He motions for him to come around and take a seat behind him. "Keep your voice down."

Carter walks around the table and pulls up a chair behind the geek.

"What do you need?" Big Sam says almost in a whisper without turning around.

Likewise, Carter speaks softly. "I need you to infiltrate a system for me."

"Hack someone damn important?" he says, still working his computer screen.

"Yes."

"Who?"

"Detective Noah McGraw, APD Homicide."

"You mean Cowboy McGraw?"

Carter was surprised he knew McGraw. "You know him?"

"Who in the hell doesn't? Man, he's no one to mess with."

"C'mon. I know you've worked the government and other officials in high places."

"You don't know shit."

Carter rises. "I heard you were the best. I see now your nothing." Carter knows that if he rings this guy's bell, the punk will meet the challenge.

"Sit your ass down. Did I say I wouldn't?"

"Let's cut the bullshit and talk."

"It'll cost you. Big."

"How much?"

"Twenty big ones."

"You mean 2K?

He nods. "Cash only. I'll contact you."

"You know my number."

"That's not how I work. You'll hear from me. Make sure you have the cash."

Several days later, while Jack Carter's drinking his morning coffee in The Kitchen Door coffee shop, he ponders over a feeling he has. Someone's been following him since he left home. A tall guy in a tan overcoat dressed like a business man, white shirt and tie, enters and goes to the counter. Carter eyes him.

Could this be the guy?

The man gets a carryout coffee, goes to the side counter and adds milk to his cup, turns and heads toward Jack's table, taking a couple sips of his coffee. As he passes, he says, "The man will see you tonight at midnight in the parking lot. You know the place," and heads out the door. Carter knows he means Big Sam at The Cat's Eye.

Close to midnight, Carter drives into the unlit area of The Cat's Eye neighborhood with his headlights off and pulls into the north parking lot, which is pitch black. He eases along until he sees with difficulty the outline of a black car. *Is that a man or woman standing next to it?* he thinks. Carter brings the SUV to a stop next to the person and gets out with a package in hand. He stands by the door, not moving. The figure, dressed in a black overcoat and stocking cap, approaches Carter with his gloved hand stretched out, He said not a word. Carter knows what the person wants. He hands the person his package. In return, the mystery person hands him a package and turns and disappears.

An hour later, Carter arrives at his lair, opens the wrapped box and finds instructions on how to install the enclosed program to get into McGraw's systems without detection.

Let's see if this works, he thinks, as he opens his laptop and places the instructions next to it. Jack begins the stepwise process listed in the instructions. After thirty minutes, he's shocked how easy it is to get into McGraw's system. He maneuvers through the system to see if his SUV plates and vehicle have been entered for that day, time, and location.

Suddenly, he jumps up knocking the chair over and pumping his hands up in the air. "Hallelujah! No record," he shouts. When he calms down, he looks over at his kit and says with excitement, "It's your time, old woman!"

Chapter 16

The next evening Carter waits until Murdock leaves, opens his car door and walks across the street and up the driveway. He slips into nitrile gloves, black clothes, and shoe covers. He always slips in green contacts before he leaves his lair.

Moving to the door, he pulls out a small leather pouch, opens it, retrieves a pick, trips Murdock's lock and enters. This skill he developed when his dad taught him how to maneuver a lock to the open position as a magic trick. Jack knew it would become useful someday for slipping into victims' homes. He moves in and does his walk through. There's a tiled foyer that opens into a large living room with plush carpet, dining area with a beautiful dining set, table and eight high-back chairs, an open kitchen to the right with all the modern appliances and a marble island in the center. He moves down the white hallway, glancing into three bedrooms and a humongous bathroom with a hot tub. He retraces his steps back toward the entrance, determines that there is no sign of any relative living with Murdock. He slips out and heads home.

Leaving his sanctuary the next evening dressed in a black outfit, Carter guides the black SUV to the curb in the street behind Murdock's home. He steps out, rolls a dog-hair remover over his body, moves between the hedges carrying his forensic kit. The homes around Murdock's are pitch black; lights are on only in the house across the street. Gail Murdock's house is not visible from the street, obscured by heavy shrubbery. Traffic is almost nonexistent. This is too good to be true. Must be extremely careful. Carter removes the leather pouch from his pocket, picks the lock.

The door snaps open.

He inches it open, slips in, sets the forensic kit on the floor, eases the door shut. He waits.

Noise in the kitchen.

The old lady in a pink robe is preparing something at the stove. He inches in with the movements of a cat approaching its prey. Murdock's back is to him.

He grabs her around the neck, squeezing hard, air rushes out of her with a gurgling sound. She goes limp.

Falls to the floor. Dead.

Carter stares at the corpse at his feet, feeling elated. Grips her under the arms and drags her down the hall into the bedroom on the left, drops her on her back, and heads out to the foyer to retrieve the forensic bag. When he returns, he sets it next to his victim, reaches in for a jar filled with formalin, unscrews the cap, sets it on the rug. Reaches in for the forceps, clamps it on the end of her tongue, pulling it out as far as he can with his left hand. and with his other hand, reaches in for the scalpel and slices through her tongue—like a piece of steak—as far back into her mouth as he can reach. Blood flows. The mouth is very vascular, but blood doesn't gush. He drops the tongue in the jar, tightens the lid. Lifts it up into the air and gazes at his trophy. Replaces the jar back into the bag. Carter turns Murdock's head to allow some blood to flow out on the carpet. Pulls out his new Canon Powershot digital camera Megan gave him, shoots a couple of pictures of Murdock's face with her mouth open.

Carter gathers his things and slips out the front door, retracing his steps to the SUV, carrying the kit close to his body. A car approaches with its headlights on bright where he parked the Tahoe. Carter drops to his knees behind a hedge. The white Camaro passes by his Tahoe and pulls into the driveway next door. A woman gets out, stands by her vehicle for a few seconds eyeing the Tahoe, then goes into the house. Carter hops in his SUV and drives out of the neighborhood with its lights off.

Back at the hideaway, Carter places the kit on the floor, slides the bookcase to one side, opens the door to his former crawl space, which is now his trophy room, reaches into the kit for Murdock's jar and places it on the second shelf. He feels powerful, admiring his trophy. He reaches for the photo album on the top shelf and bends down to retrieve the Canon camera from the kit, walks over to his desk, removes the card, and slips it into the reader attached to his laptop. Murdock's pictures appear. He makes sure there's paper in his color printer, then prints Murdock's face and places it in the album. Carter returns it on the top shelf in the trophy room and closes the door, thinking how nice it would be to have had a picture of his mother and Hannah Clay, too, but he didn't take their tongues. He sighs, then slides the bookcase back into place. He feels safe in here with his trophies, free from the world. He's nothing without them. He can't believe how exciting and exhilarating it was killing Murdock, a defenseless mean old bitch.

He moves to his desk and opens the laptop, looking for his next victim. He revisits the match-making site for seniors—lonely, vulnerable women looking for a mate. He becomes excited thinking how easy it is to kill these unsuspecting souls. Not any woman. *She has to fit my code— women who are mean, selfish, and hateful to someone like a husband or children.* The women he hates the most are those who drink and abuse or abandon their children.

Chapter 17

Dressed in a starched white shirt, jeans, jean jacket and boots, and white Stetson, Noah McGraw is listening to Willie Nelson's CD, *Always on My Mind,* in his RAM pickup on the way to Holly's. This Monday morning in January will be their first day back at the precinct since McGraw was wounded in Mississippi.

McGraw drives into a middle-class neighborhood with brick homes, trimmed lawns—a little bare this time of year—trees lined up in military formation along the curbs. Mid-sized to full-sized SUVs are parked in the driveways. Holly's driveway leads up to the house with large front windows. This dwelling is part of her divorce settlement from her ex, a real estate developer, Joel Richards, who decided one day he had enough and left. Couldn't stand for her to be away so much doing police work when he wanted her around to show her to his clients.

Holly is waiting for Noah out front as he pulls up next to her white Jeep Grand Cherokee. She looks stunning standing there, hair gleaming in the morning sun. She had called earlier, said she'd wait outside for him, no need to come in. *Strange,* he thought. He always walked to the front door and Dusty would run to him even before he could knock. Ah, he surmises. *It's because she doesn't want Dusty to see me. Might stir things up a little now that he's almost back to his normal self, according to her.* She opens the truck door and hops in.

"Thanks for picking me up," she says. "I feel better if we both go in the bureau together, being this is our first day back." A silver Toyota Sequoia passes as he pulls out.

"It'll feel good getting back to doing what we do best."

She nods. "I miss Kramer and Gomez."

Noah turns to her. "Glad to hear my little red-headed friend is doing better. Dusty was really upset the day I took you guys home."

"He's doing much better now. He still talks a lot about Texas Rodeo."

"TR's easy to ride and to get attached to," he says, pulling into the precinct lot, parking in a slot next to the building.

A little red Fiat pulls in next to them. The M.E., Nora Philips, hops out. They clamber out and meet up with her behind the pickup. She and Holly hug. Nora, close to forty, was a brunette when they last worked with her, but now she's a blonde, hair cut close to a pretty round face with only a little makeup. She's slender built and smiles a lot. McGraw and Holly have talked about Nora being a health nut because as a pathologist she sees what bad eating has done to the organs of the corpses she cuts on.

"Well, it's about time you guys got back to work," she says. "We especially missed your harassing, Noah."

"My specialty," he says. "Missed doing it, too." He pauses, then says, "I see you're a blonde now. I like it."

Her face turns crimson, and she touches her hair as she says, "You guys really like it. I kinda wanted a change."

"I love it," Roark says. "You did the right thing."

"Oh, thanks," she says as she locks arms with Holly. They walk to the entrance, meeting up with two uniform officers.

"Glad to see you back, detective," one of them says to Holly, holding the glass door open.

"Thanks. Good to be back," she says as they enter the building.

"Heard you got the bad guy in Mississippi," the other officer says as he and McGraw follow in behind Holly and Nora. "You look good, lieutenant."

"Thanks. Never felt better."

As they walk into the lobby, a drunk is standing next to a uniform who is talking with the desk sergeant. The officers that came in with McGraw turn left and head down the hall to Burglary. Nora waves goodbye as she rushes to the steps leading down to the Morgue. McGraw and Roark walk through the hall to the Detective Bureau. He opens the door, and as they step in, they notice changes in the bureau.

Detective Gomez spots them. "Here they come!" he shouts to Kramer. They rise and rush over to greet McGraw with a handshake and hugs for Roark.

"Where in the hell have you been, boss? Goofing off?" Gomez says, laughing. "So glad to have you both back," he says.

"I'll second that," Kramer says.

Gomez goes to the coffee stand, fills McGraw's Braves cup, adds cream. Kramer leaves the room.

"Here's some coffee to welcome you back, boss," Gomez says, handing the cup to him.

McGraw smiles as he reaches for his favorite cup. He takes a drink. "Just what I need. Thanks."

Holly says, "Gomez, what the heck's going on here? Everything's been rearranged."

He shakes his head. "The Capt. thought we needed to look more professional. That the place needy sprucing up, so he had the room painted beige and our desks rearranged."

Kramer comes back into the squad room with a can of coke, Roark's favorite, and hands it to her. "Welcome back, sergeant."

"I like all this attention," she says. "Maybe we should go away more often, McGraw."

"I don't think so, sergeant," Kramer says. "Need you here."

"No way," Gomez says. "It's been like Dr. Philips's morgue in here.

They laugh, again.

"How do you like our new setup?" Kramer asks.

The homicide squad has the area up front in the detective bureau separated from the other detective teams by a metal divider. Homicide consists of McGraw and his three detectives. Their desks face his. A conference table has been placed in the space between them.

"Why the table?" McGraw asks.

"Capt. thought you'd like to sit with us and talk over the cases rather than standing all the time at the white boards," Kramer says.

"That's where the evidence is, but we can move the boards, if you guys get tired of standing."

They laugh. "No way," Gomez says.

McGraw's desk is in the same general area, just built up a little higher than the others, so he can look out over them and they can see him better from their desks. There's a long table against the wall with monitors connected to the interview rooms, and an area for tagging evidence.

Detective Sergeant Holly Roark's name plate is on her desk, which is closest to McGraw's, facing him. He sets his coffee cup down and removes his Stetson and sets it on the desk.

"Okay, everyone. Gather around," McGraw says, moving to the white boards. "We won't be using the table just yet," he says smiling.

The detectives move to the front of the room.

"Kramer?" McGraw says. "Whatta we have?"

"Nothing much, just a suicide we put to rest, boss," he says.

McGraw feels himself frowning.

Now Kramer's calling me 'boss'. Things have really changed. I kinda like the sound of it.

"So, no evidence of foul play?"

"Couldn't find any, boss," Kramer says. We considered everything as evidence until it was cleared."

Now Roark frowns when she hears Kramer call McGraw, 'Boss,' for the second time.

At that moment, Capt. Dipple, comes out of his office, the Lion's Den is what they call it, across the room and walks over to the pit with a folder in his big hand.

"Boss, here comes the Lion," Gomez says.

Dipple has a wide smile on his face.

Bulldog's lost some weight in the face, McGraw thinks.

"Welcome back, cowboy. You were missed." He turns to Roark. "You, too, sergeant. It's been too quiet around here without you guys. Kramer and Gomez were lost without you, too."

Roark smiles at McGaw.

"Now that you're back, things will become more orderly."

They laugh.

"Cowboy, you look good. Are you up to leading a murder case?"

"You know me, Capt., always eager to help the vics," he says. "Whatta you got?"

"A 78-year-old female named Gail Murdock," he says throwing the folder on McGraw's desk. "The decedent lives in the Buckhead district." He pauses. "You won't believe it." He pauses, again. "The perp cut out her tongue."

Silence in the pit.

"I'm aware of bone and skin collectors, but tongues?" McGraw says. "It'll be an interesting challenge to determine why this perp goes for the tongue."

"Everyone's on the site—patrol, M.E., and forensics," Capt. says. "I didn't want to go out on the radio with this one. Must be a slow day for the media. Been getting calls asking what's going on."

"Bet Gary Spencer at the Constitution has been on your case," McGraw says.

"Yep. Called for you first. Said you owed him."

"Glad you didn't, Capt. He can be a pain."

"Tongue?" Roark says, shaking her head. "These weirdos must have their trophies."

Capt. nods. "Sure thing, if he's serial." The big man starts to head back to his office, stops and turns back to McGraw and Roark, smiles, but says nothing.

"What's that all about?" Roark says. "Did you see that smile. It's like the Lion's up to something."

Gomez and Kramer look at each other and smile.

What's going on? McGraw thinks.

"Okay. Everyone, over to the table," McGraw grabs his Stetson and pulls out a chair and places a boot on it. "We might as well use this thing."

He opens the file and reads out loud through the information called in on Gail Murdock. When finished, he says, "Let's head out."

Outside, Captain Dipple and the Chief of Police are standing next to a black Silverado SSV (Special Service Vehicle). The Capt. motions to McGraw. "Lieutenant McGraw," the Chief of Police says, "Glad to have you back and to learn that you are doing well. I am pleased to inform you that your request for an SSV was approved by the higher ups and we are pleased to present these keys," he says holding them up, "to you in honor of your service to the department."

The SSV has no police markings and the police lights are recessed inside as McGraw requested. No citizen would suspect this is a police vehicle.

Everyone is smiling. "Thank you, sir. I am pleased. Never thought I'd ever get one. I've been turned down so many times."

Holly is pushing McGraw towards his prize.

"Well, it's your time now," Capt. says. "Get in it and see how it feels."

"Were heading to the Murdock home," he says.

McGraw goes to the driver's side and Holly slips into the passenger seat.

McGraw starts it, pushes his foot to the pedal and the black monster takes off. The APD mechanics have installed a computer and communication setup. Kramer and Gomez try to keep up in a black detective unit.

The Buckhead district is north of the precinct. Patrol cars are in the street and in the driveway. Uniforms have the house cordoned off with yellow tape. One officer stands guard.

McGraw and Roark bail out. Kramer and Gomez follow, begin checking with patrol for witnesses, then hit the neighborhood. The officer standing on the grass in front of the yellow tape greets them with a nod.

"Wow! What a special vehicle, lieutenant. Sure's fancy."

"Sure is."

"Please sign in, detectives," he says, handing them a pen and holding the clip board for them. He keeps staring at the Silverado.

"Thank you," he says, after they finish signing in.

McGraw notices several patrol officers are at his new vehicle looking it over.

"Where's the super?" Roark asks.

"She's inside." He lifts the tape. The detectives pass under and enter the house. Inside, the Sergeant-in-Charge meets them in the foyer. They slip into blue nitrile gloves. "Detectives McGraw and Roark," she says, nodding.

While examining the door frame and scanning the area, McGraw nods and says, "Sergeant."

The homicide crime scene is the most important crime scene investigators will encounter because of the nature of the crime. A careful examination of the scene requires investigators to consider anything and everything as evidence. Evidence can be physical, photographic, or eyewitness testimonials. It must be preserved and brought to the attention of the homicide detectives.

"Understand we have a seventy-something female without a tongue."

"That's right, sir. The M.E.'s in the bedroom with her now. Forensics is working the place over."

"Anything that stands out, sergeant?" Roark asks.

"Lot of prints and blood that's believed to be the vic's."

"Name of next of kin?" McGraw asks.

"One daughter, Karen Morgan, husband's name is John." She hands him a sheet of paper. "They live across town, address is listed."

"We'll have to see if she was the last person to see her mother alive?" McGraw says. "Your guys round up any witnesses?"

"None, sir. No one knows anything."

"That's the way it always is," Roark says."

She nods. "It's all yours, lieutenant," she says as she heads to the door.

A team of four forensic workers dressed entirely in white—coveralls with hoods, masks, gloves, and foot covers—are working throughout the house. Their eyes are barely visible. At that moment, a young woman in a forensic uniform comes out of the bedroom, removes her mask and introduces herself to McGraw.

"Lieutenant McGraw? You don't know me. My name is Megan Turner. I'm Jack Carter's assistant. I've seen you in the Crime Lab."

"Yes, I've seen you, too. Where's Alan?"

"Oh, he retired, sir," Megan says. "I've taken his place. Budget, you know."

"I see. Well, pleased to meet you. I understand there's not much for us here."

"Everything's been dusted. Lots of prints and blood. Most likely the vic's but hopefully something will belong to the perp, if he cut himself. No traces of anything that would lead us to believe anything else would belong to him."

"This perp is pretty sharp if he leaves nothing for us," Roark says.

Megan nods. "This one is."

"Find a cell phone anywhere?" Roark asks.

Megan shakes her head. "Nope. The vic probably didn't use one. Just a landline."

"Check the recorder, sergeant," McGraw says to Roark, as he turns to Megan and says, "Look forward to receiving your report."

"Yes, sir."

He walks into the kitchen, which is just to his right. Roark is looking for the landline phones. A forensic worker is moving about in the kitchen and apparently has just finished.

"Anything stand out?" McGraw asks as he walks around the marble-top island with his senses heightened, glancing over at the counter, cabinets, and sink.

"Only prints. Probably all from the vic. But we might get lucky."

McGraw squats. "What about this black fiber here on the floor against the island?" McGraw says pointing. It's almost invisible. The worker photographs it, squats with a tweezer in hand, lifts the black fiber, places it in an evidence bag and marks it.

"Don't know how we missed it, detective," he says with disappointment in his voice.

"No problem." McGraw walks down the hall to the bedroom. Nora, the blonde M.E. is with the body while Roark looks on. McGraw scans the room, then concentrates on the body.

"Howya doin', cowboy?" Philips says.

"Nora," he says tipping his hat. "Whatta we know?"

"Got a first for me. A vic without a tongue. The poor thing was strangled from behind. Bruises around the neck and capillaries in eyes are broken. We'll see if the hyoid is broken. She wasn't a match for the perp. Too frail."

"Time of death?"

"I'd say between nine and eleven last night."

"No tongue, you say? That is a new one. What kind of instrument would he use?" He shakes his head. "Seems a little unique on how he'd remove it."

"Wow! How perceptive you are, McGraw. Probably a scalpel, and forceps to pull out the tongue."

McGraw slips into investigative mode whenever he works a crime scene, opening up all his senses as he walks the grid, visualizing what has taken placed based on the position of the body, the artifacts in the room, what has and hasn't been disturbed. Often something will spark at the scene and perps always leave something behind and take something with them (Locard Exchange Principle.) Blood is a good witness. The perp may have sliced his hand while cutting out his victim's tongue, leaving some blood behind. Hospitals will be checked for anyone who came to the ER with a lacerated hand. Evidence gathered by forensics and taken to the City Crime Lab could provide some leads.

McGraw pushes the front brim of his hat up as he bends over the corpse. "Turn her," he says.

"Some scratches on her back, Noah," Nora says as she turns the body. Roark watches with interest. Philips holds the body against her with both hands; victim's back is exposed.

"Bruises on the back and front of the neck," Nora says. "The perp has large hands."

McGraw visualizes the vic being dragged from the kitchen into the bedroom. Her gown shredded, which is a sign it was scraped across the floor.

"This is not where it happened," McGraw says. "Killed in the kitchen. Probably making tea before hitting the sack. Marks on Murdock's back indicate she was dragged in here from the kitchen after the perp choked her. Some faint skid marks are in the hall. From all signs he removed her tongue in here. Anything under her nails?" he asks Nora.

She shakes her head. "Nothing. No defensive wounds."

"Found a black fiber in the kitchen," McGraw says.

"More likely came from the perp," Holly says.

"Anything more, cowboy?" Nora asks.

"That's it for now. You can take her."

"Thanks."

As McGraw and Roark enter the hall, they meetup with Kramer and Gomez. They've been canvassing the neighborhood looking for witnesses to anything unusual—a strange person in the neighborhood the last couple of days, strange cars cruising the neighborhoods, noise from the Murdock home. Anything.

"Whatta you got?" Roark asks.

"One neighbor saw a black car cruising the neighborhood for a couple of days, but couldn't identify it," Kramer says. "The way she described it, could be an SUV. A lady living on the street behind Murdock's saw a black Tahoe SUV parked a few doors from her house. It was there for over an hour."

"What time was that?" McGraw asked.

"Between eight-thirty and ten-thirty. She couldn't remember exactly."

"The lady across the street from Murdock said there was a black car parked by her curb several days before the murder," Kramer says. "A patrol car pulled up to talk to the person in the car and both left around the same time. But that was the last she saw of the vehicle."

"Ok. Good work. Forensics has finished. You guys take the bedroom apart. Roark and I will hit the kitchen."

Larry, the M.E.'s assistant, comes in from outside, pushing the gurney past them and into the bedroom. Minutes later he returns with Gail Murdock enclosed in a black bag, moving her through the hall and out the door with the blonde M.E. behind him.

Kramer and Gomez work the bedroom, going through all the drawers and closet—clothes, shoes, several boxes on the shelves. Pictures are removed from the dresser. Meanwhile, Roark and McGraw sort through kitchen drawers, cabinets, pantry, and trash. McGraw steps out the side door to inspect the tall green trash barrel. Nothing.

A receipt from Trader Joe's supermarket dated the day before Murdock's murder lies on the counter. Her check book, bank statements, and phone records are in a drawer by the landline phone under the kitchen cabinets.

Kramer and Gomez come out of the bedroom carrying several boxes.

"We found her canceled checks, old bank records, telephone and utility bills in the closet," Kramer says.

"And a copy of her trust," Gomez says.

When finished, they exit the home and sign out with the patrol officer. McGraw tells Kramer and Gomez to head out to Trader Joe's with the receipt found in the kitchen to learn if anything unusual happened on that day, and to get their video discs.

Chapter 18

McGraw pulls the black Silverado out of the Murdock neighborhood heading to Karen Morgan's home, the only child of Gail Murdock. The traffic is heavy. Takes thirty minutes to get across town. The area is a middle-class neighborhood with attractive homes and well-kept yards. He pulls up in front of the Morgan's brown brick house and stops. It appears Karen has just gotten home and has gone inside. The car's in the driveway with its back door open and so is the one at the main entrance. She comes out, goes to the silver Lexus and removes a bag of groceries from the back seat and slams the door with a knee. She doesn't notice the detectives.

"She must have a lot on her mind," Roark says. "She didn't look our way."

"Could have had a fight with her hubby. You know how women can get?"

Roark scowls. "Oh, so how's that? So, you're taking the hubby's side?"

"What side? You're a detective, right?"

"The last time I checked."

"Well, detect. Look at her. She's fuming. Women don't fume unless they're hacked off for not getting their way."

Roark almost rises out of her seat. "What! So, you're a psychologist now?"

"I don't like to brag, but I do have a degree in psychology."

She frowns. "Oh. I seem to remember that…but that doesn't mean you're always right."

"Ninety-nine-point ninety-nine per cent of the time," he says, bursting out laughing. He couldn't hold it in any longer.

She hits him on the arm. "Oh, you, dirty dog. Let's see if you're right."

Karen has closed the front door but now is watching them from a large picture window.

They slide out of the black monster with their ID's ready. They walk up the drive to the front of the house and before they can knock, the door opens. The attractive brunette, tall and slender, dressed well with a diamond necklace and a Rolex watch, is the woman they saw carrying in the groceries.

"I saw you out there at the curb and was wondering when you were coming in. What has my mother done this time. Are you with the police?"

"Yes, ma'am," McGraw says, tipping his hat. They hold up their ID. "I'm Lieutenant McGraw and this is my partner, Sergeant Roark. We are with the APD, homicide division

"Homicide?"

"You are Karen Morgan, is that right?" Roark asks.

"Yes. Has something happened to my mother?"

"May we come in, Ms. Morgan?" McGraw says.

Fear crosses her face. "What's happened?"

She steps aside and they move in.

Expensive perfume, McGraw thinks. *And watch. House well-kept.*

Karen leads them into a well-furnished living room. Two couches and two over-stuffed chairs and an ornate wooden coffee table.

"Please. Tell me. Has something happened to my mother?"

"When did you last see your mother?" McGraw asks.

"Two days ago, we had lunch. What's happened to her? Did she hit someone again?"

"I'm sorry to tell you.," McGraw says, watching for her reaction. "Your mother," He pauses for three seconds. "She was murdered last night."

"Murdered?"

"Yes, sometime between nine and before eleven," Roark says. "We'll know more when we get the autopsy report."

McGraw wonders why she doesn't appear to be affected by the news. That's strange. There may be a reason for her lack of compassion.

"She usually makes tea around nine and heads to bed unless there's a program she likes," Karen says."

"Where were you and your husband last night around that time?"

"Lieutenant!" she says almost in tears. "I can't believe you're asking such a question."

"Just routine. Please answer."

"Here at home going over our expansion plans. Our architect, Erik Allard, was with us. I can give you his phone number."

"That would be helpful," McGraw says. "We can get it on the way out."

"Were you and your mother close?" Roark asks.

"Not really," she says. "Mother is hard to get along with. Actually, she can be very hateful at times. We just tolerated each other."

"I see," McGraw says. "Does she have any other relatives in Atlanta or in the state?"

"None."

"How about friends?" Roark says. "We'd like to have their names and addresses."

"Detectives, mother didn't have any friends that I know of. Since my dad died, she just goes to bingo once a week and to church every Sunday. She may have some friends there, but I don't know them, if she did."

Roark looks over at McGraw. "We'll need the name of the bingo parlor and her church.

"Do you want me to get them now?"

Roark shakes her head. "When we leave will be fine."

"What does your husband do?" McGaw asks.

"We own a wholesale plumbing company together. His name is John. Like I said, we are expanding."

"Does he manage the place?"

"We both do."

"Did your husband get along with your mother?"

Karen frowns. "I can't believe you would think either one of us would harm my mother. John wouldn't hurt a flea."

Oh, those clichés, McGraw thinks.

"So, you don't know anyone who would want to harm your mother," Roark says.

"No. No one."

"Is your business doing well?" Roark says.

"Yes, very well; otherwise we couldn't expand."

"Are you and your husband on good terms?" McGraw asks.

"Lieutenant… I don't understand where all this is going."

"We noticed you were upset when you came home."

"Oh, that. Sometimes John can be such an ass to work with. He doesn't give in easily. We had a disagreement on the expansion. I wanted to go one way with it and he in another."

"Who won out?" Roark asks, glancing over at McGraw.

"John, of course. His way was less expensive."

McGraw looks over at Roark, who scowls at him.

McGraw stands. He reaches into his shirt pocket for his business card and hands it to her. "We'd like you and John to come to the station to give statements. Please call me at that number to set up an appointment. The sooner, the better."

She looks at the card. "I don't know what else I can tell you."

"Both of your statements are necessary in this investigation."

She frowns at him before saying, "Guess we can come in the morning around nine." She goes to the kitchen. "I'll get those names for you." At a makeshift desk in the counter, she writes on a pad, tears the sheet off and returns, hands it to Roark and leads them to the door.

"Thanks for your cooperation, Ms. Morgan," McGraw says, adjusting his hat as they go out the door. They walk to the black monster and slide in. Roark doesn't say a word. After he pulls away from the curb, McGraw glances her way but says nothing.

Several miles down the road, Holly says, "I know you want me to say you were right."

McGraw tilts his hat back. "Not really. Just wanted to make a point."

"And that is?"

"Always look at everything as potential evidence."

"Any other lessons of the day?" she asks, smiling.

"Never doubt yourself and don't ever believe anyone. Let the facts do the talking."

Chapter 19

Back at headquarters, Holly goes to the fridge for a coke. McGraw ambles over to the coffee stand. Earlier, Kramer and Gomez had placed all the evidence collected from the Murdock residence on the bench against the wall before going to Trader Joe's. Noah and Holly begin sorting the material in the boxes. They pay special attention to Gail Murdock's financial records, home line telephone calls—she doesn't own a cell phone or one of those prepaid ones many seniors like—insurance policy and her trust. Her phone records show very few calls.

The old gal really didn't have many friends, Roark thinks.

After an hour of examining the evidence, Holly goes to her desk, lifts the phone, calls the bank about the Murdock bank balance and asks if there were any large sums withdrawn. None. Calls the hospitals ER. No patients had come in with cuts on their hands the last couple of days. Murdock's pastor had nothing but good things to say about her. The bingo parlor didn't remember Ms. Murdock being with anyone, mostly stayed to herself. Very private.

Holly then runs the Morgans through the system. There are no records of outstanding legal actions against them, or any financial problems. As a matter of fact, they are well-off. No police records, no motor vehicle violations, nor any domestic abuse charges.

Kramer and Gomez return from Trader Joe's.

"There definitely was a confrontation in the supermarket between a man in his late thirties or early forties and an old lady," Gomez says.

"They could be the perp and that Murdock woman."

"An employee in the produce department reported it," Kramer says, "but gave a sketchy description of them both."

"Not all is lost. We have a disk, boss," Gomez says, holding it up. "It's from the day and time registered on the receipts."

"Great. Set it up."

Gomez walks over to the computers against the wall and sits.

Roark reports to the team that Murdock's daughter and son-in-law have a very successful wholesale plumbing business. No debt. No liens. No financial problems. The daughter is the sole beneficiary of Murdock's holdings. They didn't need the old lady's money. No other living relatives.

"Ready, boss," Gomez says.

They gather around gazing at the monitor. McGraw sits next to Gomez.

"Here we go," Gomez says. The scenes move along with the times clicking off at the top right corner. McGraw moves in closer to the screen.

"Stop it there," he says, pointing. "That guy. He fits the description."

"Tall with a strong built," Roark says, "dressed in a stocking cap and sun glasses. Probably has strong hands, too."

"Unfortunately, it's grainy but there are two people that appear to be going at it," McGraw says. "Kinda fits."

"The room becomes quiet. Everyone stares at the boss waiting for his analysis and assignments.

He studies the figures in the video for a few more moments, then says, "Here we have a perp that is fascinated with a body part. He's either a serial predator or could turn into one. It would be helpful to know the pathology dealing with his obsession for the tongue. Let's check our systems for missing elderly women. Maybe one was able to ward off her attacker and could give us a description of the guy." He glances at Murdock's picture. "Cutting out the tongue is an act of violence," he says, "which means the perp is a person subject to rage."

"The door to her entrance wasn't damaged or scratched," Holly says. "Maybe he's in control until he sees his victim."

"It could be that Gail Murdock knew her perp and let him in." Kramer says. "Which means he couldn't be the guy in the supermarket."

Roark shakes her head. "We have to I.D. this guy. I'd bet he used a special tool to get in."

All the while, McGraw is listening intently.

"The guy's a maniac, a psychopath. He ain't done," Gomez says.

"What about slipping a credit card through the crack?" Kramer asks.

"No way. Only with a special tool," Holly says.

Gomez nods. "We know some detectives carry lock pick kits that open locks. "How about that?"

"Are you suggesting the guy's a detective?" Roark says.

Gomez frowns but McGraw answers for him. "Gomez means that the perp picked the lock like our guys would in certain situations. Which tells me that he must have special training."

⸱⸰⸱

After running missing elderly women, Gomez calls out from behind his computer. "Boss, two seniors, both in their 70's left their homes and never returned. One had Alzheimer and got lost. She was eventually found. The other one hasn't been found. Another woman in her eighties was getting out of her car to go into her home when attacked by a male dressed in dark clothes, stocking cap. He was large and strong, grabbed her round the neck She fought him off screaming. He took off with her purse. She gave a description of her attacker to the police. He had a blue and yellow eagle tattoo on his neck. Our guys caught him coming out of a seven-eleven. His name is Neil Draper, a metal worker. Said he was looking for drug money."

"Good work." McGraw lifts his phone and calls the Burglary Division to talk to Lieutenant Green, learns Neil Draper is nothing but a junkie. McGraw knows she has his prints and has probably taken his DNA. He requests all she has to rule the guy out.

"No problem," she says. "Get it to you ASAP."

Chapter 20

McGraw enters the Capt.'s office. He's on the phone, raises a hand with two fingers in the air, meaning give him two minutes. After setting the receiver into its slot, he looks up and asks, "What do you have for me, cowboy?"

"Just a heads up on the Murdock case."

"Let's hear it."

"Our perp is sharp. Knows how not to contaminate the crime scene. We found only a black fiber in the Murdock home, which probably came from his wool outfit."

"What's your take on him?"

McGraw says. "He knows too much about crime scenes. I'm thinking he's got some type of forensic training, which makes him elusive."

"Think he's one of us."

McGraw shakes his head. "Naw. Could have some training or has taken special efforts to learn all he can about homicide crime scenes. That's what many serials do."

"I think the latter. Any witnesses?"

"None," McGraw says. "We've interviewed the daughter. She and her husband are here now to give a statement."

"Was the daughter the last person to see her mother alive?"

He nods. "Yeah, but a few days before her demise."

"What are you thinking?"

"They're not involved. No reason to be. The suspect is a strong male.

Neighbors have seen a black SUV driving around in the neighborhood. He could be our man."

McGraw turns to leave. "Like to keep the lid on this for a little while longer. Don't want Spencer to get a whiff of this just yet."

Capt. nods. "I agree. But we won't be able to much longer."

<hr>

The Morgans are seated in chairs in front of Roark's desk. McGraw played a little subterfuge to get them in, but now he has all he needs.

Karen stands when she sees him coming into the squad area.

"This is my husband, John, lieutenant," she says.

McGraw nods and they shake hands.

"Are we suspects, lieutenant?" John asks.

"Thanks for coming. We just need your statements for the record. Detectives Kramer and Gomez will show you to the interview rooms."

He had told his men before he went to meet with the Capt. that they should put Karen in interview room one and her husband John in two.

Kramer and Gomez return to the monitors against the wall to scrutinize the Martin's reactions during their interviews.

McGraw reaches in his drawer for his pocket recorder and grabs a yellow pad from his desk. "You available, Sergeant?"

"Just finishing," she says, working at her computer. She rises. "Ready."

"You take the lead," McGraw says.

They enter interview room one. Karen is seated in the uncomfortable, wooden chair facing the table with two bucket chairs behind the table for the detectives. She appears uneasy, crossing one leg over the other a couple of times.

Roark takes the seat closer to Karen while McGraw sits to Roark's right, places his pad on the table and slides the recorder next to it.

"Thanks for coming. Can we get you anything to drink? Water?"

"No, I'm fine. Can we get started? We have lots to do at the company."

"Of course. Lieutenant McGraw will be recording this meeting. Is that okay with you?"

She shrugs. "I guess."

"Good. Would you please state your full name for the record?"

She frowns. "Ah, Karen Morgan."

McGraw states the date and time for the recorder.

"Did you know that you will inherit all of your mother's assets?"

"She mentioned it once. To be honest, I thought she would write me out of her will." She pauses for a few seconds. "Detectives. I… I never loved my mother. I was a daddy's girl. No girl could have had a better father than I did. He was kind, loving, and thoughtful." Tears welled in her eyes. "Would do anything for me. My mother, well, she was the opposite. Never showed me an ounce of love." She looks at them and says, "I'm sorry, but I have no feeling for my mother. I'm not surprised someone killed her." She reaches in her pocket for a tissue and looks down at the floor, wiping her eyes.

Roark looks at McGraw. Giving him the eye to take over.

"Sorry to drum up bad feelings, Ms. Morgan," McGraw says.

"I understand…." She pauses. "Just had to tell the truth."

"We appreciate that." He writes something on his pad. "Sergeant Roark called your mother's church and the bingo parlor." He looks at Holly.

"Sergeant, what did you learn?"

Roark straightens up in her chair and says, "Yes. We learned that you were right. Your mother had very few friends. The Pastor said he enjoyed talking with her on the phone but that she didn't associate much with the congregation. She'd come to the service and leave."

"And the same thing with the bingo parlor, is that correct, Sergeant?" McGraw says.

"Yes, sir."

"Well, as I said, no surprise," Karen says.

McGraw turns off the recorder and stands. "I believe we have enough, Mrs. Morgan."

"That's it?"

"Yes," Roark says. "Let me show you out, Karen."

McGraw heads to Interview Room Two. Roark won't be joining him, she'll watch at the monitor. He enters to find John Morgan agitated.

"Well, it's about time, detective. I've been waiting nearly an hour."

"Sorry for your wait. We were with Mrs. Morgan." McGraw said. Sorry, he wasn't. It was his ploy to stall to see how John would react and he got his answer.

McGraw sets the yellow pad and tape recorder on the desk and sits.

"Can I get you water or coffee?"

"No, let's just get on with whatever you do. Some of us have to work for a living."

"Sure. I'm taping this interview. And for the record, please state your full name."

"Taping? I thought we were to give a statement. What's with the interview? I thought we weren't suspects."

"Everyone is a suspect until we clear them. This interview is a way to get your statement. Now, state your full name."

"John D. Morgan."

McGraw states the date and time.

"To start off, please tell me your relationship with your mother-in-law, Ms. Gail Murdock."

"Relationship?" he says in a harsh tone. "Hell, what relationship? We had no relationship. That old bitch hated my guts, didn't like anyone, not even her daughter, and I doubt if she even liked herself."

"So, you hated your mother-in-law?"

"I wouldn't say hate. I just didn't like the bitch. I rarely visited her. Mostly Karen saw her. I haven't seen Gail in six months. And that was because Karen's car was in the shop and I had to drive her to that old bitch's home."

That old lady maybe, McGraw thinks, *but isn't bitch a little harsh?*

"Did you know that your wife inherits all her mother's estate?"

"That's a surprise. I thought she'd give it to her church."

"How's your business doing? I understand you are expanding and her money would really come in handy.

John leans forward, staring into McGraw's eyes. "If you're implying that I'd kill the old bitch for her money, you better think again. I wouldn't take a dime from her. Anyway, Karen and I always thought Gail would give it all away."

"I understand that your wife loved her father and not her mother."

"That's definitely the case. Karen went to the house often until he died five years ago. Sad day for her."

"So, do you know of anyone that would want to harm Ms. Murdock?"

"How about most of Atlanta."

"You included?"

"Hell, no! How many times do I have to tell you. I don't need her money, lieutenant. We are doing fine, and I don't like your accusations."

"We're done here," McGraw says. Turning off the recorder. He rises, grabs the pad and recorder and leads John Morgan out of the room.

They meet up with Karen. McGraw has Roark escort them to the exit. When she returns, McGraw has his team gather around the white board.

McGraw is about to test his squad to see if they paid attention to the Morgan interviews as they watched on the monitors.

"How many times did John Morgan call his mother-in-law a bitch?

Gomez shakes his head and laughs. "Man, he said it four times."

Roark and Kramer frown at Gomez.

"You mean you actually counted, Gomez?" Roark asks.

"Sure, man, he's cool. Hated the bitch 'cause she was mean and had it comin' to her."

"Good work, Gomez," McGraw says. "Glad you were really paying attention to every word."

Gomez did the Groucho Marx eyebrow routine at his team members.

They couldn't help from laughing.

"Okay, let's get serious. What's your take on the Morgans?" McGraw asks.

"Felt sorry for the wife," Kramer says.

"Me, too," Gomez says.

"C'mon. We all felt sorry for her. But what about that husband?" Roark says.

"He's a bastard," Gomez says, "but I kinda like his gutsy attitude. No way he'd do the old lady, Boss."

"I agree," Kramer says.

"John Morgan has bottled up anger. Maybe it's stress from his business expansion, but I don't consider him a suspect," Roark says

"Whatta you think, boss," Gomez says."

"Crime scene was too clean. Our perp is clever. John Morgan doesn't have those skills."

"That's for sure," Roark says.

Chapter 21

Joel Richards drives up into Holly Roark's driveway around four this afternoon, slides out of his black Lexus and walks next door to the Martins'. He knows his son will be there. The Martins have always taken care of Dusty when he and Holly were together. Married, that is. That was some time ago. Joel feels a little anxious, which is unlike him. He's been poised in everything he's attempted. Real estate is a tough business and he has to be strong and confident. But this is different. He doesn't know how Dusty will receive him. This is no client of his, this is his boy. Joel feels it's time they reconnect, to get to know one another again. Holly and he have joint custody but it's been six years since he and Dusty spent a weekend together. Dusty was only four. They were never very close because Joel was never home. Surely Dusty would still remember him?

He knocks. Seconds later, a white-haired, round-faced woman about five-foot four, in her seventies, opens the door with her mouth wide open.

"Hi, Mattie."

"Joel? What a surprise. What are you doing here?"

"May I come in?"

"Oh, of course. I'm sorry." She steps aside.

He moves past her. "Is Dusty here?"

"He's in the kitchen playing checkers with Lloyd."

"I'd like to see him."

"You know the way," she says.

Joel has been in the Martins home only a couple of times. He remembers the kitchen being in back of the house, off the living room. He walks through the carpeted living room, filled with three couches and a recliner that form a square around a coffee table, a cabinet against the wall with a 42-inch TV sitting on it, and a piano covered with dozens of family pictures. The kitchen is a few feet away. He enters and finds Lloyd and Dusty at the table, concentrating on the checkers. Mattie is right behind him.

Lloyd looks up. Ole stone-face shoots him an ice-cold stare that pierces Joel innards like a lancet. They never got along after Joel and Holly divorced.

"What the—" Lloyd says, stopping in midsentence, apparently avoiding an expletive. "—do you want?" he croaks. Mattie scowls at him.

Dusty looks at his father but says nothing. He seems puzzled.

"I'm here to see my son. Lloyd."

"After all these years?"

"Now, Lloyd, is that a way to treat Mr. Richards?"

Mr. Richards? I guess I deserved that.

Joel moves to the table. "Dusty, you know who I am, right?"

"You're my dad?"

"That's right.'

"What do you want?"

Joel looks over at Mattie and then to Lloyd. Both of whom are waiting to hear his answer.

"I thought maybe we could get to know each other again. I know it's been a long time, but things have changed in my life and I'd like to spend more time with you. Would you like that?

"I don't know."

"Maybe you and your mother and I can meet and talk. Would that be okay?"

Dusty shrugs. "I guess so."

Joel doesn't know what else to say. The Martins are staring at him and his son won't look him in the eye. He feels warmth around his collar.

"Tell you what. I'll call mom as soon as I leave and talk with her and maybe we can all get together, or go out and eat somewhere."

Silence

Joel looks at Mattie. "I'll see myself out. Thanks for allowing me to see Dusty."

After Joel leaves, Dusty says, "McGraw's my father now."

Lloyd looks at his wife.

"But he's not your father, Dusty," Mattie says. "Joel is."

"I don't know him."

"That's why he wants to spend more time with you, son," Mattie says. "I know he hasn't been the best dad, but I believe him when he says he wants to make up for lost time. You need to give him a chance."

———•◆•———

That evening, Dusty tells Holly his dad came to the Martins to see him.

"I know, honey. He called me. Your dad wants to come into your life again but feels that you don't want anything more to do with him. Is that true?"

He shrugs. "It's just that I don't know him, mom. I like McGraw. I feel he's more like my dad."

"When your dad and I divorced we told you that I have sole physical custody but that your dad would be allowed to visit you. You remember that?"

Dusty nods. "That means you are still in charge, right?"

"Yes, why?"

"What if I don't want to see him."

"I understand how you feel, but your dad has the right to see you. You can even spend a weekend fishing or something."

He shakes his head. "I don't want to go with him. Why don't we ever go to the Circle M? I miss McGraw and Texas Rodeo and Prince and Tucker. Anna Marie said we could come anytime."

"You know I'm working a case with Noah since we went back to work. It has taken most of our free time. We have a serial killer out there."

"You're always working." He turns away. "We never have any fun."

"Now Dusty. We've been over this many times."

"I know. But why can't McGraw be my dad? You like him, I see how you look at him."

Silence.

Holly isn't surprised Dusty knows how she feels about Noah. When she's away from the station, her feelings show through whenever she's around him. She can't help herself. She's never forgotten their talk when Noah was in the hospital in Mississippi. She's about to say something to Dusty when the doorbell chimes.

"Maybe that's McGraw?" he says running to the door.

"That's your dad," she shouts.

Dusty opens the door to find his dad standing there with a box of pizza in his hands.

"Oh, it's you."

"Can I come in before the pizza gets cold?"

"I guess," Dusty says, stepping aside with disappointment in his voice.

"Your mother never told you I was coming, did she?" he says moving in. "We spoke after I left the Martins' and she thought we could have dinner together."

"I'm not hungry," Dusty says. He rushes off to his room.

"But your mother told me pizza is your favorite thing."

Holly walks up to Joel. "Thanks for bringing dinner. We can eat in the dining room. Come on in."

She leads the way to the kitchen. Joel hands her the box. She removes the pieces of pizza and places them on a platter. Takes a salad bowl out of the fridge.

"Grab the plates on the counter and the silverware," she says, "while I take the salad bowl and dressing."

"Dusty's not happy to see me. I can't blame him. Coming over, I thought he might warm up to me just a little. I'd like to talk to both of you, if it's alright." He pauses. "Or do you think I should go?"

She shakes her head. "No. That won't be necessary. Give him a few minutes. Let's set the table and I'll get him."

Holly goes to the kitchen to get glasses and Joel takes the pitcher of water and fills the glasses.

Minutes later, Holly goes to Dusty's room. She knocks and enters.

"Son, come on out. Your dad brought dinner and you must show him some respect."

"But I'm not hungry."

"What did I say? Come on. You can at least sit at the table and listen to what your dad has to say."

Dusty gets up and sits on the edge of his bed. "Okay if I don't eat?"

"It's up to you."

He gets up and follows his mother to the table. Joel is standing to the right of the head of the table, which he has apparently reserved for Holly. Holly and Dusty take their places and sit.

"Would you like for me to say Grace," Joel says.

Grace? That's a big change. Is this an act? she thinks.

"Can we join hands," Joel says.

Dusty resists at first until his mother gives him the dead eye. He knows when she gives him that look, he'd better do it or else there will be a price to pay.

After the prayer, Holly serves each one a slice of pizza. Even Dusty. Holly knows her son. It won't be long and he'll gulp down the slice and ask for more.

Joel serves the salad.

After everyone has finished their meal, Joel looks at Holly.

"Would it be okay if I said my piece now?"

"How about some coffee first," Holly says, rising and going to the kitchen.

Joel nods. While Joel and Dusty wait for Holly to return, Dusty looks down at his plate and Joel keeps his eyes on Dusty. He must be hoping his son would look him in the eyes.

Holly returns with two cups of coffee, one black and one with only cream, no sugar. The latter would be hers.

"Okay," Holly says after taking a drink of her coffee.

"Thanks. You remembered how I liked my coffee." He takes a sip and then looks at Dusty.

"Dusty? I know you are unhappy with me. And I don't blame you. I don't want to upset your life, I just wanted to see you again and to learn if we could have a relationship. It may not be a father-son relationship to you, but how about just being friends?"

Tears began forming in Holly's eyes.

"I know more about you than you think, Dusty. I've kept track of you ever since I stopped being part of your life. I watched you from a distance and through friends. I know that you are attached to Noah McGraw, who I think is a wonderful person. My life was so busy when your mom and I were married that my work became my idol. I neglected her and you. And for that I'm sorry."

He took a drink of his coffee.

Tears rolled down Holly's eyes.

"But now I'm a different person. No longer is work my idol. I have a new life now. I met this wonderful woman who brought me to Christ. Now Jesus is my Savior and I've turned over my life to him. I wanted this meeting to ask for your mother's and your forgiveness, Dusty, for the way I treated you both."

Holly wipes her eyes with her napkin.

"I don't plan on disrupting either of your lives. I just want to be friends with you both. This lady and I are planning on being married. She has no children and we thought that maybe once in a while Dusty might visit us. No pressure. Just whenever you feel like it, Dusty."

Holly takes a drink of her coffee to hide the redness in her eyes from her son.

"Dusty, if you would like me to attend any of your school functions, or if you need anything, I want you to know I'm here for you. Also, I've established a college fund in your name. That's another reason I wanted to meet with you both."

He drinks the rest of his coffee.

"Now, I think it's time for me to go."

He stands.

"Could we hug and if it's in your heart, would you please say you forgive me? I really need to have your forgiveness."

Holly is the first to stand with tears trickling down her cheeks.

She hugs Joel.

She whispers in his ear, "I forgive you, Joel. Wish you much happiness."

He smiles. "Thanks. I needed to hear that."

He waits for Dusty.

Holly turns to Dusty and motions for him to come hug his dad. This time Dusty is smiling. He comes around his mother with arms out, and embraces his dad, and says, "I forgive you, too, dad. I'm sorry the way I treated you earlier and at the Martins."

"Thank you, son."

Chapter 22

Jack Carter is in his office at the City Crime Lab scanning his personal laptop, stopping every fifteen minutes to look out over the lab to make sure no one walks in on him while he's corresponding with the women on the seniors' matching site. He looks up.

Megan Turner and other forensic scientists have just placed bags on the evidence table. She heads to Carter's office.

"C'mon in."

"Evidence from the Murdock case?" he asks.

"Yeah. Mostly latent prints, blood, vic's clothes, shoes, and a black fiber that Lieutenant McGraw wants checked out. He thinks it's from the perp."

"Well, let's give the lieutenant top priority."

"Didn't find much. This perp is pretty good cleaning up," she says.

"Is that right? Why do you say that?" Carter is feeling prideful at the moment.

Megan shakes her head. "Been at this for some time now and I've never seen a crime scene that clean. Whoever did the vic knows what he's doing. Didn't leave a trace."

"That's rare, Megan. You know killers always leave a trace."

"Some scenes are easy," she says. "We know the three S's in sex crimes: Sweat, Semen, and Saliva. But this is no sex crime. This perp knows how to clean up a scene." The criminalist shakes her head, again. "This is a new one on me."

Hearing those words from Megan has Carter feeling proud of himself. He can outsmart all of them, anytime, any day.

"Oh, by the way. Did you send Lieutenant McGraw the report on that suicide case?"

"You mean Hannah Clay?"

He nods.

"Yes. The report was brief. Found nothing. Open and shut."

Carter smiles.

Chapter 23

The sky is gunpowder gray this early Friday afternoon when Jack Carter and Megan leave the Crime Lab and drive over to Raymond Gardens Apartments to help Megan's cousin pack.

On the way, Megan tells Jack how excited she is about moving in with him. She has been pestering him since his mother left. Finally, he has given in. Only because he knows he can manipulate her more if they're together. She paid off the remaining balance of his white Seville and surprised him with a Rolex for his birthday. She will join him in house-sitting for his mother who is away in Charlotte taking care of a sick relative. That's what he told her. She knows nothing about his apartment in the back and he'll never tell her or let her near it. He'll kill her first.

The Raymond Gardens Apartment Complex is located in a middle-class area, with plenty of trees and a park across the street.

Jack pulls into the parking lot on the side of the building in southwest Atlanta. The lot is only half-full. As they step out of the Caddy, he spots an orange U-Haul truck in the back lot.

Appears Amy is getting things done, he thinks.

As they approach the front of the building, Megan points out the park across the street with its lush bushes, flowers, and trees. Mothers are sitting on benches reading paperbacks. In between turning pages, they watch their children on the swings, slides, and teeter-totters.

They enter the building and head to apartment 4A on the right side of the first floor. There they find the brunette Amy in shorts and blowing her hair out of her eyes as the sweat trickles down her face as she seals a box with packing tape. Megan hugs her cousin, Amy.

"Thanks for coming to help. There aren't enough boxes," she says. "We'll have enough for tonight, but I'll have to get more in the morning to finish up. Can you guys stay until dark?

"Of course, Amy," Megan says. "We're here to help you finish."

Got to finish by tomorrow afternoon. The manager is on my back. She wanted me out tonight."

"Okay. I'll call for pizza," Jack says pulling out his cell from his sport coat pocket.

"I got some drinks in the fridge," Amy says. "Haven't cleaned it out just yet."

"I'll get up early and get the boxes for you," he says, removing his sport coat and folding up his shirt sleeves. "Let's get to it until the pizza arrives."

After their meal, they worked until around eleven, headed to the Carter home. They showered and hit the sack.

During the night, Megan is awakened and frightened from the jerking motions coming from Jack. She looks over at him and sees him writhing and mumbling indistinguishable words.

She shouts, shaking him, "Are you okay, Jack? Jack, are you okay? she asks a second time, thinking he's having convulsions. He turns over and the convulsions stop. She watches him for several minutes and believes he's okay, and turns over and goes back to sleep. In the morning, she'll ask him about it.

The next morning, Jack notices Megan staring at him while he's eating a quick bowl of Raisin Bran cereal.

"Something is bothering you?" he says. "What is it?"

She slams her spoon down next to her coffee cup and sighs. "Yes.

You scared the hell out of me last night."

He feels himself frowning. "I did? How did I do that?"

"You woke me from a deep sleep, jerking and mumbling words that I couldn't make out. I thought for a moment you were having a seizure, but after a few minutes, you turned over and went back to slept. Are you having nightmares, Jack?"

"Oh, that. Sometimes I do. The psychologist said it was from my days being locked in the basement. It doesn't happen too often."

He can see the sympathy arising in her face. She bought it hook, line, and sinker.

"Oh, I'm so sorry, Jack," she says, placing a hand on top of his. She smiles. "I'm just glad you weren't having a seizure. I didn't know if you could still have one from that concussion."

"I don't have the jerking too often, I don't think. The doc said they should get less and less."

She nods, "I'm glad now that I know."

"Let's finish our cereal and get going to Amy's," he says. "Lots to do before her movers come."

She smiles, picks up her spoon and returns to her cereal.

Carter holds his head down, looking into the cereal bowl while he finishes his breakfast, thinking about the nightmares he really has. He's been struggling with visions of his mother's fluttering tongue urging him to kill. The nightmares are increasing. He can't stop her voice in his head. Killing Hannah Clay and his mother were out of necessity, but since then the killing of Gail Murdock has given him a new thrill, a new high. He's enjoying it so much, he takes his photo album at night to his desk and looks over the women he's killed, but realizes he has to be careful not to become too cocky and make a mistake. Serial killers kill their victims repeatedly. Never wanting to stop. He believes that if he removes his victims' tongues, the vision of his mother's tongue will eventually stop screaming at him.

"I'm done here," she says, rising and taking her bowl to the sink.

"I'll go get more boxes and I'll see you over there."

"Great," she says, and heads out the door behind him, to her silver Nissan.

Jack has been packing for about an hour when he hears a knock at the door. Someone is mumbling behind the door as he walks over to it. He opens it. A lady in her late sixties, attractive and dressed neatly with hair that would lead him to believe she just came from the beauty shop. He smells liquor on her breath.

"Can I help you."

"I'm the manager. Where's Amy?"

"Oh, hi, Mrs. Fox."

"You were supposed to be out." She steps in, staggering, grabbing hold of Jack's arm. "I mean, gone," she screams. She looks around. "Where is that damn cat? You know we don't allow pets in the apartments. You broke your lease." She turns to Jack. "I told that woman she had to be out last night. I have another tenant that wants to move in today. And this place better be clean. No cat piss smell. And don't expect any of your deposit."

"We'll be out by late afternoon, Ms. Fox. I told you that yesterday."

"Get out, and I mean now!" she shouts as she turns and heads down the hall.

Jack turns to Amy. "She's a mean one. Where's her apartment?"

"At the end of the hall. There's a sign on the door." She shrugs. Just let the old battleax be. We can hurry this up and get the heck out of here."

"I'm gonna calm her down and tell her we're here to cooperate and we'll hurry up and be out by four." But Jack had other things on his mind.

He finds the manager's apartment, the last door on the right, close to the exit that opens to the parking lot in the back. No apartment across the hall. The name plate has inscribed: *Elizabeth Fox, manager.*

It opens.

"Oh, it's you," she says, holding a glass of whiskey, neat, in one hand and a lighted cigarette in the other. Her eyes are glassy. The apartment is saturated with cigarette smoke.

She's blocking his entrance, but he pushes his way in.

"What the hell are you doing?! Get the hell out!"

"I wanted to apologize for my girlfriend's cousin for not being out on time. She got behind. We'll be out soon."

"Her problem is not my problem," she says, slurring her words. Staggering. "Go tell that bitch she better be out this afternoon or I'm calling the cops, to throw her ass out on the street."

You're the bitch, Jack thinks.

Seeing her tongue quivering as she lashes out at him causes his hands to ball into fists. He holds back from clubbing her. Calms himself and looks over the two-bedroom apartment. She lives alone. He watches as she takes a sip of whiskey and a puff on the cig.

"I'm sorry you feel that way. We will be—"

"—Get the hell out. Now!"

He moves to the door. She shoves him out and slams the door hitting him in the rear. He could hear her mumbling something behind the door.

While strolling back to Amy's apartment, Carter thinks how Elizbeth Fox is going down. She fits his code of conduct—a drunk, abusive, and a hateful battleax. *It's time.*

"What did she say?" Megan asks upon his return to the box-filled apartment.

"Amy has to be out this afternoon or she's calling the cops."

"We'll let's get at it," Megan says.

"We don't have much more, only a couple more boxes." Amy glances at her watch. "The guys will be here in an hour."

"We'll be ready," Megan says.

The last box was loaded at six o'clock. Amy returns from the driveway after paying the movers. They hug and Megan and Jack take off for his mother's home.

"What about dinner," Megan says.

"I can round something up from the fridge. I'm tired of pizza," he says.

"Great. I'm going to take a shower now and after having a bite I'm hitting the sack."

After finishing off a glass of Chardonnay, a meal of pasta and garlic bread, they clean the table off and Megan heads to one of the four bedrooms in the back of the house while Jack goes into the living room. For the next thirty minutes, he reads Jeffrey Deaver's, *The Bone Collector.* He reminds himself that now that Megan is with him, he mustn't bring such books into the house from his lair in the back. He rises, goes to the back to make sure she's asleep, hears only light snoring.

Jack slips out of the house and enters his hideout. He enters and immediately locks the door behind him. He promised himself he'd never make the same mistake as he did when his mother snuck in behind him. Sitting at his desk, he opens his laptop, runs Elizabeth Fox.

Fox is sixty-eight and has only one child, a son, David. Divorced years ago, she's had several DUI arrests and her driver's license has been revoked. Police were called to the home several times for domestic violence. The last time she tried to cut David with a knife, is what he told the police, "The drunken bitch tried to kill me." Currently, he lives in Phoenix.

She fits my code perfectly.

Chapter 24

The next evening around nine, Carter pulls the black Chevy Tahoe to the back of Raymond Gardens Apartments, close to the exit door leading out from hall in front of Elizabeth Fox's apartment. Only two cars are in the lot and there's no activity. Dressed in his full black outfit, he slips out of the SUV, grabs the forensic kit on the passenger seat, moves into the building wearing his disguises as he did for his first victim, except for the mask. He didn't want Fox to scream. Several TV's can be heard as he moves into the hall. A strong odor, probably a mixture of different dinners from several apartments, lingers in the hallway.

Carter puts his ear against her door. The TV is blaring. He sets the kit on the floor and knocks hard. He hears footsteps. The old gal opens the door, plastered from too much booze.

This is an easy one, he thinks.

She doesn't seem surprised to see him. "What is it this time?" she says with contempt in her voice and slurring her words. "Why are you dressed like that?"

In a flash, Carter grips his large, gloved hands around her neck and squeezes the breath out of her. She gasps, tearing at his gloved hands, eyes as large as half dollars, not able to scream. There *will be none of my skin under your nails, bitch,* he thinks. In seconds, she collapses in his arms and slides down his body like a snake to the floor. He grabs the kit, closes the door, sets the kit next to the body and straddles her, reaches in the case for a forcep and scalpel with his gloved hand. With his left hand,

Carter pulls Fox's tongue out and like a surgeon, slices across the back of the tongue until the front half flies out, turns her head to the side so the blood flows out on the floor. Carter removes a jar of formalin and a camera from the kit. He drops the tongue into the solution and recaps the jar. He positions the camera and snaps the picture after he squeezes open her mouth with the half-tongue exposed.

Before he leaves, Carter walks the crime scene. This is where his forensic skills kick in. Satisfied he hasn't left a trace of evidence, Carter says to himself, "the smartass cowboy McGraw will never find any evidence at my crime scenes." He laughs and slips out.

Thirty minutes later, he wheels the SUV to the back of the house and into the garage. Steps out of the Tahoe with the kit and goes to his hideaway and unlocks the door. Inside, he opens the kit on the counter, removes the jar with Fox's tongue in it. He pushes the bookcase to one side and opens the door. He moves Gail Murdock's tongue over and places Fox's next to it. They look the same. Feeling elated, he takes the photo album from the top shelf to his desk. On the first page is the photo of the open mouth of Gail Murdock. Carter fixes Elizabeth Fox's photo in the four-corner tabs, rubs his hand over the pictures and smiles.

And now there're two.

Proud that he has rid the world of women who don't deserve to live, he closes the album and returns it to the top shelve in the trophy room, closes the door and moves the bookcase back in place. Carter opens his laptop looking for email responses from the lonely women with whom he's been corresponding.

The following morning at the breakfast table, drinking coffee, Jack notices Megan seems perturbed.

She sets her coffee cup down and glares at him.

"Jack…where…where do you go at night? You're not cheating on me, are you?"

He laughs, then tells her sometimes he works a case with a private investigator friend and they usually spend days on a case. "I can't tell you much about what we do. Don't want to betray the confidence of my PI friend."

She nods as she lifts her cup to her lips. After a few swallows, she says, "I understand now. I guess I wasn't thinking. Have been wondering if you had another woman stashed away."

"I'm pleased you're jealous."

"Guilty," she says, as she finishes her coffee.

"Not to worry. I'm a one-woman man."

She smiles. "Nice to hear."

Must be careful, he thinks as he glances at her over the rim of his coffee cup. She is showing signs of accepting his explanation, but from now on he'll make sure she's gone when he works in his lair. Killing his prey, well, that's another matter. That would be when his PI friend needed him on a case.

"We'd better get ready for work," he says.

Chapter 25

Lieutenant Noah McGraw is reviewing the autopsy report on Gail Murdock in the murder book when he receives a call from dispatch. The com center is in the main precinct building in the basement. After 911, these centers across the country were placed in secure, bomb-protected structures where they can continue communicating during a city catastrophe or national disaster.

"Hey, Marlboro Man," dispatch says, joshing, "patrol needs you and your partner out at the Raymond Garden Apartments. Got a DB. ME and forensics are on the way."

"I know the place, Mahoney," McGraw says. "You've been drinking? I smell it through the phone,"

"My people only know that the DB is an old woman. Didn't want to screw up the crime scene. They'd leave that up to you, cowboy."

McGraw could hear him laughing, a muffled sound. Probably holding his hand over the phone.

"Just tell your people to stay out of our way, so we can do our job. They've probably contaminated the scene." McGraw knows that'll get under his skin.

Dispatcher hangs up on him.

McGraw turns to his team. "Dispatch called. Got a DB at the Raymond Garden Apartments. Patrol is there, ME and forensics are probably already there."

Roark shuts down her computer and rises.

Kramer and Gomez hop up and head to the exit.

Outside, McGraw and Roark climb into the Silverado monster and Kramer and Gomez slide into a detective unit and speed out of the lot. When they arrive, patrol cars are parked in front of the apartment building cordoned off with yellow tape and a uniform is keeping people away from the building. Other officers are questioning people around the building.

McGraw pulls the black monster in front of the patrol cars. He and his team sign-in and walk up the front steps. The patrol sergeant in charge meets them at the entrance and nods.

"Hello, lieutenant," he says. Turns to Roark. "Sergeant."

They nod.

"I understand we have an elderly female?" McGraw asks.

He nods. "Name's Elizabeth Fox. In her late sixties. Lives in the back apartment. Was the manager," he says. "Forensics is in there, ME hasn't showed up yet. And the vic is missing her tongue."

"You didn't touch the body, did you?"

"No way. You only have to look at her and you can tell she has lost some of her tongue."

Another one, McGaw thinks. "Thanks."

McGraw tells Kramer and Gomez to start knocking on doors. He asks the sergeant if there are any witnesses. None so far. They walk down the hall to the back of the building. "We'll take it from here, sarge," McGraw says as he looks into the apartment. A body is on the rug in the living room.

"She's yours, lieutenant."

McGraw and Roark do not enter. They wait for clearance from forensics who are dusting the door and room for latent prints, collecting evidence, and shooting dozens of pictures.

A technician moves into the living room after he finishes dusting the door and frame. McGraw notices there's no forced entry. No damage around the door.

Forensics is about to wrap it up, he thinks.

"If you move out of the way, Noah, we can go to work," Dr. Philips says, pushing her way in.

"Certainly, Nora," Roark says, as they move to one side so she and Larry can move past them.

A forensic tech comes to the door. "Lieutenant, you and the sergeant can come in now. We're done."

"Thanks," McGraw says.

As he walks into the room past Philips, who is on her knees, examining the corpse while Larry has a hand in the black bag ready to hand her what she needs.

"It's about time you made it," McGraw says. "Thought I'd have to do her myself."

"That'll be the day, cowboy. You better stick to the easy work."

Roark moves into the kitchen and looks over the counter and opens the cabinets above, one on either side of the sink and below. Nothing out of the ordinary.

McGraw glances at the victim, who is no more than ten feet from the door, head in a pool of blood. He studies the room. Begins visualizing the area around the body in concentric circles, moving away from the body out to the edge of the room, looking for anything that has been disturbed. Nothing.

"Vic has been dead about 36." Nora says. "Half of tongue is gone. Died of strangulation before he took it. The perp has large hands that are very strong. Hyoid broken. Easy for him to overpower his women."

"Perp is turning into a serial, taking his trophies," McGraw says. "But there has to be a reason for the tongue. I'm trying to figure that one out."

"The departmental shrink may help," ME says. "Sherri is very good."

McGraw nods. He knows her. He spent time with her a couple of weeks ago before he was allowed to return to work. "Think I will."

"You can look over the vic now, Noah. She's quite frail and osteoporotic."

McGraw squats down next to the body, pushes his hat back, stares at Fox for a few seconds, turns and stares at the door, visualizes the perp bursting in as vic opens the door, grabbing her around the neck. He's strong and big. She's like a rag doll, can't defend herself. Down she goes.

"Are we done here?" the ME asks, shaking him out of his reverie.

He nods. "I'll be down tomorrow."

Philips motions to Larry, who has been waiting at the door with the gurney. McGraw watches him push the gurney with a black body bag on it past him. Larry releases the gurney so it collapses to floor level so the bagged body can easily be placed on it.

McGraw walks over to Roark who is in the bedroom searching through drawers, night stands, and the one closet. She has several evidences bags on the bed.

"Found a life insurance policy, but no will or trust," Roark says. "Bank statements show just one bank, no investments, just direct social security deposits and canceled checks. Seems she was living off of her salary as manager and social security."

"Anything in the other bedroom?" he asks.

She shakes her head. "Don't think she ever used it. Kinda dusty."

"Another clean crime scene," he says. "Just like Murdock."

"I've been thinking the same thing. Who are we dealing with, Noah?"

"Someone that knows how not to contaminate a crime scene. And who do you think that can be?"

"Could he be a cop, ex-cop, or someone familiar with law enforcement?" She stares at him.

"Maybe a worker in the medical field who has access to medical instruments."

Just then, Gomez is calling for them.

"In here," McGraw says. "What's up?"

"Most of the folks in this building didn't hear a thing or see anything, except one lady that lives toward the front of this floor. Kramer has her in the living room."

They step out of the bedroom and go to the apartment down the hall close to the entrance. Gomez opens the door. A middle-aged, thin and mousey looking lady is seated in an overstuff chair.

"This is Ms. Caster," Kramer says. "Tell Lieutenant McGraw what you told me, ma'am."

"I don't know," she says, shaking her head, wringing her hands in her lap, "if I really should say anything." She looks around like she's expecting the killer to come in after her. "I don't know much. I just heard the backdoor close when I came home. Hadn't had time to take off my coat." She wrings her hands, again. "I peeked out my door, just enough to see this big guy dressed in black clothes like those special forces people in Afghanistan, except his shoes were covered up. He was knocking on her door. I snuck back in. Didn't want him to see me."

"What do you mean by 'big guy'?" McGraw asks.

"You know, big and strong. A little taller than you."

"Did you look at his face? Can you identify him if you saw him again?"

"No. It was covered."

"Why didn't you call the police?"

"I wasn't sure. I thought about it. Guess I was scared."

"Did you at any time hear anything coming from the manager's apartment," McGraw says. "A scream, loud voices?"

She shakes her head.

"Did you hear the man leave?"

She shakes her head again, but is now looking at the floor. "I was afraid to look out. He could come to my apartment."

"Anything else you can think of?" Roark asks.

"Not that I can think of."

McGraw hands her one of his business cards and tells her if she can think of anything, no matter how small, to call him. She reaches for it, but he knows he'll never hear from her again.

The detectives move out into the hall. McGraw tells them, "We'll need to learn who are the members of Elizabeth Fox's family, her friends, a list of previous managers, current tenants, and past tenants the last two years."

Chapter 26

Noah McGraw had made reservations for seven that evening. He enters close to six-forty-five, indifferent to the frowns and stares as the cowboy is ushered to his table near a large window that overlooks the street. The place is half full and the women are smiling at him in a flirting gesture. McGraw sits, removes his hat, places it on the chair next to him and orders iced tea and requests that wine be brought to the table at seven—a glass of Merlot and a glass of house Chardonnay.

In minutes, the waiter, who earlier was standing, back against the wall, gawking at McGraw when he came in, brings his tea. McGraw sips his drink while he watches for his friend, Drew Nelson, Supervisory Special Agent in Charge of the Atlanta FBI Field Office. McGraw has chosen this restaurant because it is at street-level with large windows, not far from the Bureau. Even though it's dark outside the sky is clear and the well-lighted streets provide a clear view of the Federal building. He finds this restaurant with its tables covered in white cloths an attractive venue; believes he made the right choice. He glances at his wristwatch, it's close to seven and the place is filling up. The waiters standing at the far wall dressed in tuxes, looking like penguins, are still gawking at him and whispering to each other. He wonders if they've ever seen a cowboy come into their restaurant. He guesses not.

McGraw and Drew have worked on cases through the years and have become good friends. The most recent was the Max Kingston case. Drew often makes resources of the Bureau available to McGraw without the typical red tape. He never has to worry about the Bureau bigfooting, that is, taking over his case, making it their investigation.

Noah has arranged this dinner meeting to seek Drew's help in utilizing the Bureau's Behavioral Science Unit where they study serial killers, develop psychological profiles, victim profiles, and give advice.

The tall, slim waiter, approaches a second time bringing menus, placing one next to the filled water glass across from Noah's and hands the second one to him.

"Shall I bring the drinks now, sir?"

"Yes, please."

No sooner said, Drew waves as he walks past wearing a dark suit which goes well with his graying temples. Noah waves back and notices the wristband on his right hand that his little friend Dusty gave him. It reminds him of that day Holly and Dusty returned to their home and how much he misses the little guy.

Noah rises as his friend comes to the table. They shake hands.

"Good to see you again, Noah."

"Same here."

Drew takes the seat opposite him. The waiter brings two drinks on a tray and places them on the table in front of the two men.

"I didn't think you drank, Noah," he says, reaching for his glass. "I thought you Southern boys only drank iced tea with lots of sugar.

"Only on special occasions, but I take my iced tea with lemon and not sugar, 'cause I'm sweet enough.

"I bet your mother told you that."

"Sure did," Noah says.

"Oh, well, then I understand."

They laugh and raise their glasses.

"I should have been the one to invite you to dinner," Drew says. "Remember, Noah, I was fool enough to bet you a week's pay that time we were waiting for that psychopath, Max Kingston, to show up at the drop to get Dudley Hamilton's money."

McGraw nods. "I thought you'd forgotten, but I'm letting you off the hook."

They laugh again.

"I hope this meeting is about what I think it is?"

"Afraid not. I love my job."

Noah can see the disappointment in Drew's face.

"So, you're not accepting my offer?"

"Thank you, but no."

"That's a disappointment. I thought we were going to get you, and that's what this dinner is about." He pauses. "The offer remains on the table. Whenever you're ready."

They hold up their glasses again, and take a drink and set them next to their water.

"So," Drew says, frowning, "if you aren't going to join the FBI, then how can I help the best top-notch detective I know."

"You're very kind. But I got a problem that requires your expertise. Afraid I got a serial killer on my hands, and I wanted to give you a heads-up. The perp has performed violent acts against two older women, and cut out their tongues. God knows how many he's killed. So far we've covered two homicides."

Drew frowns and shakes his head. "I've worked psychopaths before that were obsessed with body parts, but the tongue? That's a new motivation."

"I believe he'll strike again, and I need your help to stop him. The perp is smart and cunning."

"What have you learned so far?"

"You remember my partner, Holly Roark?

"Sure do. How is she?"

"Doing well."

"Good. Tell her I asked about her. Now tell me about the case."

"Holly has entered all we have into the databases, including VICAP."

Violent Criminal Apprehension Program (VICAP) is a unit of the FBI responsible for the analysis of serial violent and sexual crimes, situated within the Critical Incident Response Group's (CIRG) National Center for the Analysis of Violent Crime (NCAVC).

"I can take a look at what you have," Drew says.

"Can you run the perp through Behavioral Analysis Unit?"

"After a profile?"

He nods. "It would be very helpful."

"Send me all you have. I'll check it and send it to BAU. Then I'll let you know." He stares at Noah for a few seconds. "I see you're wearing a bracelet. Is that in support of a sick friend?"

Noah raises his arm and looks at the bracelet on his wrist. "My little ten almost eleven-year-old friend, Dusty, gave it to me. He's Holly's son and they stayed on the ranch while I recouped from my wounds received in Mississippi."

"Sounds like a wonderful young man."

"He is."

And I need to take my long overdue gift to him.

"I really need your help on this one, Drew."

"Anytime."

"Thanks," McGraw says as he motions for the waiter. "Now let's eat."

Chapter 27

Holly steps out of her Jeep Grand Cherokee and walks next door to the Martins' to collect her son from the retired couple that have been babysitting Dusty since preschool. She waits until they are in their home before she tells him that McGraw is coming for dinner.

Dusty runs to the front room, hops on the couch, pulls the curtains back from the window, and looks out. "I can't wait to see him. I hope he brings me another book. What time is it?"

"Hold on, young man. Come and help me set the table!"

"Whatta we havin'? You know McGraw don't like pizza."

"Dusty, do you hear yourself? "He 'don't' like pizza. You know better than that."

Here I'm acting like Noah, correcting my son.

"I know. I should have said doesn't. I'm just excited. Please don't tell McGraw I slipped up."

"Not this time, but don't let it happen again."

She bursts out laughing.

"Aw, mom. Stop teasing."

They laugh.

"You didn't say what we're having," he says as he sets the table with dinner plates, forks, knives, napkins, and water glasses.

"Salad in the fridge and the noodle casserole that Anna Marie taught me while we were at the Circle M is in the oven. Good thing I had made it a few days ago."

"Oh, man. I love that. Anna Marie is a great cook."

"Does that mean, I'm not?"

"Oh, no. You're about as good."

She smiles. "'About,' huh?"

"You're getting better. Do you think McGraw will like it?"

She smiles to herself the way Dusty changes the subject.

"Yes, anything made by his mother, he'll like." She pauses. "I know how much you care for McGraw. He's been your friend since you were little."

"I wish he was my dad."

"I know."

"I think I heard him pull up." Dusty runs to the window again.

"He's here. I see his blue pickup."

<hr>

Noah pulls into Holly's driveway and parks next to her Cherokee. He grabs the package on the passenger seat and slips out of the pickup. Before he can knock, the door opens and Dusty flies out to hug him.

"Howya doin' little buddy? I missed you."

"Me, too. How come it's been so long? I was worried you didn't like me anymore."

"Oh, you know better than that." McGraw raises his right hand. "Look, I'm still wearing the bracelet you made for me. How could I forget my best friend?"

Dusty grabs his hand and pulls him into the house.

"Mom, McGraw is here."

McGraw pushes the door with the heel of his boot to close it behind him.

Holly comes from the kitchen. She smiles at her boss.

"Hi, boss."

McGraw feels himself frowning. "Cut it out."

"Is McGraw your boss, mom?"

"She's just being playful," McGraw says as they head into the kitchen. "Everything's about ready."

"I hope I'm not late. Got stuck with the Capt."

"The Lion's after you again. He never lets up. What's it this time?"

"A minute-by-minute update on the perp. Things are beginning to heat up. The Chief may be riding him and wants this case solved fast. They think in terms of 48 hours. But it isn't going to happen. Not with this serial."

Holly turns to her son. "Where are your manners? Take McGraw to his seat. Dinner is being served."

He takes Noah's hat and places it on the coffee table.

"C'mon, you can sit by me," Dusty says. He pulls out a chair for his friend.

McGraw thanks him and sits, places the package to the right of his plate, so not to be too close to Dusty. The little guy sits at McGraw's left.

"Hope you don't mind eating in the kitchen. Got too much paperwork on the dining room table."

"You know that's where I eat at home. That way I can appreciate the aroma of Ma's cooking."

"Well you're in luck. We're having Anna Marie's noodle casserole. And salad."

"Now, that's what I like to hear after a busy day."

She removes the casserole from the oven and places it on the counter. "Dusty loves Anna Marie's cooking, too."

The youngster isn't paying attention to his mother. He's concentrating on the package that McGraw brought.

"I met with Drew Nelson. He's developing a profile on our serial. He needs all our info you put into the computer and our reports to do it."

"Good to hear," she says. "We sure need his help on this one. Did you tell him how clever the perp is?"

He nods.

Dusty looks at McGraw with a frown. "Did you just come to talk police work with my mom?"

McGraw realizes he's neglected his little friend. "I'm sorry. No, I really came to talk to you."

"Good." He looks at his mother who is placing the casserole on the table. "I set the table."

"And you did a professional job. Just like those waiters in the fancy restaurants."

"Thanks."

Holly brings the salad and rolls. "I don't have any wine. Sorry."

"That's okay. Don't need any."

She sits and reaches for her napkin and places it on her lap.

Dusty says, "Isn't McGraw going to say Grace?"

"Well, of course." She smiles at him.

"I'd be pleased," he says.

After a brief prayer of thanks, she serves the casserole and passes the salad and the rolls. Halfway through the meal, McGraw has been watching Dusty. "I know you've been wondering what I have in this package," he says, laying his hand on it.

Dusty's face lights up. "Yeah. I think I know."

"I want you to know that the only reason I came tonight is to be with you and to give you this present that's long overdue. I really missed you being on the ranch and so does TR (Texas Rodeo). You need to come and spend some time with him."

"Can I, mom! See, I told you we should go."

"We'll see, Dusty."

"Aw, mom. Can we?"

"What did I say?"

"Anna Marie asks about you two all the time. She's really gotten attached to the Roarks."

"How about you, McGraw?" Dusty says.

His question takes Noah by surprise. "What do you mean?"

Dusty springs from the table and darts to his room. McGraw feels himself frowning.

"Did I say something out of place?"

Holly shakes her head. "Oh, no. You said nothing wrong. It's just he misses you and hopes to live on the ranch. He's not happy here."

"I see."

Holly rises from the table and leaves the room. Noah drinks his coffee, thinking he knows where the conversation is heading.

Dusty and his mother return. His eyes are red.

"I have something for you, Dusty."

Dusty sits but doesn't look at him. Noah moves the package next to the young man's plate.

"Aren't you going to open it," Holly says.

He places his hand on it. "I know what it is," he says in a monotone. "It's an Ernest Hemingway novel."

"Why don't you open it and see," McGraw says.

He tears the paper off the hardcover book. It's Herman Melville's, *Moby Dick*.

Dusty looks at McGraw. "You know I like the books you give me. But I want more now than books."

McGraw looks at Holly, who raises her brow and shrugs.

"What's that?" He knows what's coming.

"I want to live with you. Mom says we have our own house but that's not all." He pauses looking at the book.

He's getting up his nerve, McGraw thinks.

"I love you and I want you to be my dad." He grabs the book and darts out of the room.

Noah and Holly sit in silence for a few moments.

Finally, she says, "I'm sorry. I know he can be pushy. But you know how we feel about you."

He nods. "I do. We will need to have our talk. And soon."

Chapter 28

The owner of the famous Pitcher's Mound Restaurant, former Braves pitcher Moose Johnson, Cy Young Awardee, is pictured throughout the best steak house in Atlanta. As eager customers enter his restaurant, the first thing they see is a large gold-framed painting of a forty-something, lean black man in a Braves uniform, poised in a pitching stance on the mound, and smiling, hanging on the wall in the foyer. The dining area is complete with tables covered with vanilla linen tablecloths, some are lined against soft gray walls over which hang beautifully framed pictures of this famous pitcher taken with politicians, movie stars, and other VIPs. The one that stands out in the center of this montage representing the passage of time is Moose accepting the Cy Young Award.

Several months ago, McGraw horsing around with Moose, gave him the nickname 'Satchel' after the great pitcher Satchel Paige. Satchel started out in baseball pitching in 1926 for the Chattanooga White Sox of the minor Negro Southern League. Ole Moose really like the comparison and the name stuck.

Noah McGraw and Zee have been seated at their table against the wall in the center of the room below the picture where Moose, with a big smile, is holding his award. McGraw is below the picture, with Zee facing him. The short pudgy waiter is aware that this table is retired detective Zee's whenever he makes a reservation. He's made certain that all is ready for the big Italian cop, or he would get an earful. He gingerly places a glass of scotch, neat, in front of Zee and a glass of Merlot for

McGraw next to his water glass. He steps back a few steps, smiles, and almost bows to Zee as he takes leave.

"What's with the waiter," McGraw asks.

"What?"

"He almost bowed to you? What did you say to him?"

"Nothin', man."

"You must have said something at one time or other that put the fear of God in the poor guy."

Zee shrugs. "No way, man. Can I help it if he respects me? More than I can say about you, champ."

They laugh.

"By the way, what's the leather bracelet on your wrist?"

McGraw raises his hand to display the bracelet. "This was given to me by my little freckled-face friend, Dusty. You know him. He's Holly's boy."

"Of course. He's the kid you challenge all the time about reading and remembering authors' names."

"He's the one. You knew they were staying with me at the Circle M while I was healing?"

Zee nods and takes a sip of his Scotch.

Noah rubs the bracelet with affection. "Dusty gave it to me the day I took them back home. It was a sad day for him. He loved the horses."

"I see," Zee says. "And from your eyes I see that you miss them, too."

McGraw takes a drink of his Merlot. "I guess I do."

The reason for this occasion is that McGraw owes Zee a steak dinner and he hasn't visited with Moose since he was wounded on the Ole Miss campus. But this interaction with Zee is really about the tongue collector case. Noah feels the need to run his ideas past his old partner, like they used to do when they were in homicide together. For his money, the old Italian was and still is a top-notch detective.

Noah spots the owner, Moose "Satchel" Johnson, talking to customers at the far end of the room, close to the kitchen. Moose likes to wander through the restaurant talking with people. Noah'd bet ten-to-one that Moose is going to bring up his need for Noah to cook for him again and to have Anna Marie and Holly help serve at his Home Plate Mission in east Atlanta. He would like to work the mission again, but the tongue collector case is a tough one and is going to take up all of his time. Maybe he'll drop off his mother and Holly and maybe even Dusty to serve lunch. Moose is coming their way.

"Here comes Satchel," McGraw says.

"You still calling him that?"

"Just for fun."

"Howya doin' Zee," Moose says, gently slapping him on the shoulder. Zee turns and looks up over his shoulder at the famous man. They knuckle punch. "Doing good, Moose," Zee says.

He turns to Noah and shakes his hand. "How's my cook? Heard you ran into some trouble down yonder in my neck of the woods."

"Doing well now, Satch. Back at work."

He smiles and winks when he hears the name Satch. "Zee tells me you've got a tough case."

McGraw nods. "Got a smart perp. Going to take some creative juices to catch him. It's like he's trying to outsmart me."

"That won't happen, my friend. I won't bug you about helping me out at the mission. But would like you to consider having that lovely mother of yours and that charming partner of yours to serve for me?"

"They'd love it," McGraw says.

"Well, you know the ropes. Give 'em my love," he says. "Gotta move about, but will be back." He moves to the next table and shakes hands.

"Let's get another drink and order that big steak you owe me before we talk about your tongue collector," Zee says.

He waves to their waiter, who is a few tables from them.

"Ready to order, sir?" he says.

"Yeah. We need another round of drinks and bring our usual steak dinner," Zee says as he hands him his empty glass.

"Yes, sir," he says, reaching for their glasses and hurring off.

"Okay, champ, let's hear it."

McGraw begins by describing the last two homicides involving two elderly women, a perp who the witnesses describe as a white male, tall, with strong body and hands. He has a morbid interest in the human body—the tongue, and he leaves no evidence at the crime scenes.

"The guy's smart, no doubt," Zee says, "and the tongue is his trophy. Choosing these elderly women can also be based on accessibility and convenience."

"He's too well organized, Zee to choose his victims randomly. And because he's so well organized, he's extra careful not to leave evidence at the crime scenes."

The waiter comes with their drinks.

McGraw takes a swallow of his wine. "I figure he does a thorough check on them and visits his kill sites before he strikes," McGraw says.

Zee is frowning, which means he's deep in thought. "Okay. What do we know as cops? We know the three motives for murder are: money, sex, and revenge. Doesn't appear the perp wants money and you haven't mentioned any molestation. That leaves revenge." He reaches for his glass and takes a humongous swallow of his scotch. "I needed that. Perps that hurt women get under my skin." He finishes off his drink. "Revenge relates to your perp's hate for women, maybe one that reminds him of his mother or grandmother, or some other woman that beat the shit out of him. That would tell you why he attacks elderly women. What it doesn't tell you is why he goes after the tongue. Determine that and it'll lead you to the bitch he hates so much."

"The mother could be the key to all of this," McGraw says.

"I believe so. Have you thought about talking this over with the department shrink?"

"You're the second person who asked that. We have an appointment with her."

Zee motions for another drink. "That will be your next step, champ. Find his motivation."

Chapter 29

While waiting for the APD's shrink, Dr. Sherri Frey, to come into the squad room, McGraw is at his desk thinking about his discussions with Zee and drawing on his knowledge learned in his psych degree program at Harvard. Thinking about the perp's obsession with the tongue nearly kept him up all night. An obsession with a body part doesn't develop overnight. Something had to have happened in the perp's past when he was young.

McGraw rises and goes to the Lion's den to escort the Capt. to the meeting. As they come out of his office, Dr. Frey is visiting with McGraw's squad—Roark, Kramer, and Gomez.

"Dr. Frey, thank you for coming," McGraw says. Of course, you know Captain Dipple?"

"Yes, of course. How are you, Captain?

"Good, doc." McGraw cringes as the Capt. says 'good.' "Thank you for coming," Capt. says, flashing his Ernest Borgnine smile. "McGraw and his team need your input on a tough case."

"Happy to oblige."

"This way, doctor," Holly says as she ushers her into the conference room. "Can we get you anything?" Roark asks. "Coffee?"

"Yes, black, that would be great." She chooses a chair with her back to the door. McGraw sits at the head of the table with the doc at his right and Capt. Dipple at his left, placing him facing Sherri Frey. Kramer and Gomez take seats down from the Capt. Roark enters with a cup of coffee and sets it in front of the doc, then chooses the chair next to her.

McGraw knows Frey is smart and he has great confidence in her. He begins, explaining the last two homicides involving a perp, who witnesses have described as a white male, tall, with strong body and hands. He killed two elderly white females, and interestingly, he has an obsession for the tongue. He leaves no evidence at the crime scenes, not even a trace, which indicates that he knows about crime scenes.

Frey takes a drink of her coffee. "The first thing that comes to mind is serial killer. Any sexual component?"

"No."

"Then it's not sadism, which is associated with sexual violence. However, if he enjoys inflicting pain for the sake of pain, then he has a social personality disorder."

"Does that mean psychopath?" Roark asks. "Is that because of these violent acts?"

She nods. "From what you're telling me, your perp is well organized, has much experience around a crime scene, and plans his attacks very carefully. There are two reasons for your perp's interest in tongue collecting: One, payback and two, his hate for women. Misogynist.

"Revenge?" Roark asks, "How does that play into it?"

"Someone did things to him when he was young, when he couldn't defend himself. Now that he's grown, he takes action against women who fit the person he hates the most. Could be a member of his family."

Sounds like Zee, McGraw thinks.

"Mother or grandmother?" McGraw asks.

"Or teacher or nanny," the doc says.

"But still, why the tongue? Why isn't killing enough?" Kramer asks.

"Let's go with the premise that your perp has this morbid interest in the human body. In this case, the tongue. Let's discuss the physiology of the tongue. It is used for mastication, aiding in digestion; for taste; and for speech. Of the three major uses of the tongue, speech jumps out at us. Did someone say something to the perp that hurt him? That wouldn't be enough to cause him to attack these women and remove their tongues. Then, what could it be?"

Gomez joins in. "How about someone beat the kid over and over when he was young? Turned him into a rabid dog and now he acts out when someone does something that reminds him of the bitch that beat him?"

"That could be part of it, but that wouldn't be why he goes for the tongue," the doc says. "Something about the tongue that sets him off. Maybe cutting out the tongue he feels he's getting even for the verbal abuse. He's more than likely killed that one person who first mistreated him, found he liked inflicting pain, and that has turned him into a serial killer."

"And the vics he kills now, they must set him off in some way that reminds him of that family member," McGraw says.

The Capt. has been listening with narrowing eyes and lowering brow, raises a hand and says, "The stimulus must be something other than verbal. He could walk away, but the tongue does something to him."

"Very good, Chief," Frey says.

Kramer interjects, "He sees it in a threatening way,"

"Yes," the doc says. "The killer is enraged not only by what is said, but what the tongue reminds him of. These two go hand-in-hand."

"But he just doesn't kill for the sake of killing," Roark says. "Don't psychopaths use some sort of code that attracts them to their prey?"

"Excellent point," doc says.

Holly looks over at McGraw and raises her brow.

"A code of behavior," Frey says. "I'd say it's that family member who caused him to develop his code."

"Okay," McGraw says. "Let's for the moment consider the facts.

1. The perp attacks and kills women over sixty.

2. The two vics were tough old birds.

3. They didn't get along with their children, divorced their husbands, and either deserted or had nothing to do with their kids.

"These factors could be the basis on which our perp developed his code of behavior."

"Excellent," the doc says.

Now it was Noah's turn to look at Holly and raise his brow. They smile at each other.

"Who do these factors point to?" Frey says.

"His mother," Gomez says. "I've seen it in my family, but not me. I had a wonderful mother. My aunt's children ran away as soon as they were old enough. She drank and beat the shit out of them. My uncle left her."

The Capt. shoots a stern look at Gomez.

"Oh, sorry for the language, but I hate my aunt even today," Gomez says. He raises his hands above his head. "But, don't get me wrong, I wouldn't kill her."

Doc Frey smiles. "Of course not." She takes a drink of her coffee. "So, we've narrowed it down to the perp's mother. She must have beat him and done other things to him. She probably even ridiculed him for wetting the bed. He probably killed animals when he was about 8. Maybe the perp's father left his mother. She could have been an alcoholic or prostitute."

McGraw says, "I like the idea of the perp killing women that fit the code he developed from his experiences with his mother. But the code only tells us why he kills women around his mother's age. What would her tongue remind him of?"

"I see you're on to something, lieutenant. What is it?"

McGraw answers. "We said the tongue is used for speech. And his mother lashed out at him. Maybe he sees her tongue flapping—for the lack of a better word—as she lashes out at him, and maybe even sees it fluttering in his mind or in his dreams. Could it be he cuts out their tongues thinking it would silence her?"

"I'd say you have it," Dr. Frey says. "He still sees her wagging tongue and it hasn't stopped."

"That accounts for his mother," Kramer says, "but what about our vics? They never knew him."

"But they fit his code," McGraw says. "When a woman berates him for some reason, probably some kind of confrontation, his mind plays tricks on him and he thinks it's his mother's voice and her tongue berating him. His rage causes him to check the woman out to see if she fits his code, then he proceeds to set up his kill. When he attacks her, he cuts out her tongue with the hope that his mother's berating will stop?" McGraw stops for a second, frowning. "So, the berating is the stimulus that brings out the image of his mother's tongue—his motivation for cutting them out."

"That makes more sense, McGraw. I like that," Frey says.

"Does that mean we now know why he does what he does, doc?" the Capt. says.

"I believe so, sir."

The Capt. rises as does the others. They tell Dr. Frey how much they appreciate her help.

"I believe we've made progress here," Capt. says, as he leads the doc out of the room.

McGraw summarizes what they know so far: a white male; strong body and hands; kills elderly white females who berate him—the stimulus; has an obsession with the tongue due to mother's flapping tongue; killed two females, possible serial killer; he's careful not to leave evidence at the crime scenes; and he's smart.

Chapter 30

While Megan is away shopping, Jack Carter is at the desk in his secret hiding place, working his laptop in search for his next victim on the senior matching site. His mother's voice is getting stronger in his dreams and is driving him to kill. He's found his next victim.

Alice King.

His heart pumps fast and his blood is racing through his veins, as he reads the latest email from her. To get Alice to open up about herself, he writes lies about his drinking and leaving his family—that which fit his code of behavior for choosing his victims. And of course, he's not using a picture of himself, but one that he took from his database.

The lies worked.

Alice writes back that her life has been similar to his. The stress of family life drove her to drinking. Becoming an alcoholic tore the family apart and she abandoned her husband, leaving him with two pre-teen girls to raise. She didn't want the children and took out her anger on them. Stayed as long as she could, felt it better to leave the home in Missouri, and never look back. Alice, now in her late sixties, dates men with the understanding that she has no plans of ever becoming serious in a relationship.

Carter runs her through public records and finds Alice King has a police record. Two DUI's in Missouri, lost her driver license, and police were called to the home on several occasions for domestic abuse against the children. She fired a shot at her husband once but missed. He didn't press charges. In Atlanta, she has been working with a house-cleaning company. Her picture matches the one she uses on the matching site. There has been a loitering charge. Police affidavit states she was drunk on a park bench in the Kirkland area. The officer kept her in jail overnight to sleep it off.

Carter is writing to her under the name of Alex Sawyer. She wants to rendezvous at Jimmy's neighborhood bar in southeast Atlanta to see if they hit it off, then maybe they could date. He sets up their meeting for eight this evening. He'll tell Megan that he's going out on a case with his PI friend.

Around seven thirty, Carter comes out of his lair this cool evening dressed in a black suit, white shirt, but no tie, carrying a forensic kit and gym bag filled with clothing he'll wear for the kill. He goes to the garage and backs out the black SUV. Fifteen minutes later, he arrives in the Kirkland area of dimly lighted streets, fifty-year-old framed houses in need of repair, and late- model cars parked at the curbs. He moves along at five miles per hour, spots Jimmy's on the corner to his left, nearly passes it, backs up to make sure. A curved metal pole with a single bulb attached at the end bends down over the front of the place, giving off little illumination. Other than that, it's hard to determine if it's a bar. At least a sign with Jimmy's name painted in red letters on a white background is visible above the door. No mention of it being a bar. There's only street parking. Carter finds a spot across the street where he can keep an eye on the entrance. He pulls into the space; his headlights flash on cars with dents and in need of paint. No porch lights are on, making the neighborhood even murkier—his cup of tea. Jack Carter looks at his watch. Seven-fifty. He doesn't move. He waits.

Ten minutes pass. He slides out of the SUV.

No street lights are on.

Jack glances over at the single light; *it can't escape the black hole*, he thinks. He strolls in the darkness, finds the curb and steps into Jimmy's bar, closing the door behind him. The cigarette smoke chokes him. He clears his throat while looking the place over. The bar is in front of a mirror and an ancient cash register. A woman is the only patron at the bar, sitting on a stool. Several round tables are spread throughout the room.

Two single lights are over the bar and two in the center of the ceiling above the tables. Still, the lighting is so poor he sees only the silhouette of the couple at the far end of the room. The clientele is low class. Three tables are occupied with couples dressed in crumpled clothes, drinking beer, eating burgers and fries. Many appear to need a shower. Men need a shave and the women's hair needs scrubbing. They pay no mind to him as he walks across the room to the bar.

He recognizes the brunette from the Internet, sitting on a stool smoking a cigarette. She's dressed in a sweater, blouse, and dark skirt. She's not bad looking up close, for a woman in her late sixties. Her face has those spider wrinkles around the eyes and leathery skin from too many cigs and too much booze. The bartender is slender, under six foot, probably in his early thirties, handsome, with blond hair and smooth skin.

Whatta hell is he doing in a dump like this? Carter moves to the end of the bar. "What'll you have?" bartender asks, placing a napkin in front of him, which surprises Carter that in a dump like this the bartender would place a napkin on the bar.

"Scotch, the best."

"Look around. Do you see any Scotch drinkers? Only Bud on draught."

"I'll take a Bud."

He nods, reaches under the counter for a stein, pulls down on the large white handle in front of Alice to fill it, then sets the glass on the bar and slides it down to Carter. It stops in front of him.

Pretty damn good, Carter thinks. He takes a long pull on the cold beer and wipes his mouth with his handkerchief. He doesn't trust the napkin. *Not bad.* Jack likes his beer very cold.

Alice has been watching him. Lights another cig, tilts her head back and blows smoke in the air, then turns and looks his way.

Carter moves to the stool next to her. "You Alice?"

"Who wants to know?"

"Mr. Sawyer. He sent me."

She takes another drag on her cig. "I'm Alice. Did the bum stand me up?"

"He sends his regrets. His father died, and he had to leave town."

"That's a new one," she says, laughing. "Just doesn't have the guts to face an old hag, huh?"

"Sorry, but it's the truth." Jack Carter finishes off his drink. Throws a twenty on the bar and tells the bartender to give her another. Outside, he breaths deep draughts of air to clean his lungs. He walks over to his black Tahoe and slides in the back to dress for the kill.

He waits.

An hour passes and out she comes, alone, ambling across down the block heading south, weaving as she walks. Carter pulls away from the curb with his headlights off, advancing just a few miles per hour. In her condition, Alice's going to be easy to take down. After three blocks, she turns to her left and disappears into a black hole. Carter eases the SUV to the curb across from the house and parks. He unzips the gym bag. Pulls out a wool cap with face mask. Slips them on. Reaches for the forensic kit and leaves the vehicle. On his way around the house with no lights, he makes it to the back, finds a small building. A dim light flips on. He cases the place, peers in the window that once was the front of a garage, and finds her back in a small kitchen off from the living room. She leaves the light on and moves into the living room carrying a bottle of beer. The place can't be more than 600 square feet. She flips on the TV and sits in a rocking chair in the dark a few feet away. Jack Carter looks at his watch: ten o'clock. He moves to the door on the side of the building, sets the forensic case down, removes a small tool from his pocket, works the lock until the tumblers click and the door opens.

It's time.

Ten o'clock news is on. Alice is fixed on the TV. In rapid succession, Carter slings the door open wide and darts in. She only has a millisecond to turn his way before Carter slams a fist into her throat, knocking her to the floor. He pulls the shade down in the only window in the place, goes to the door for the forensic kit and closes the door. Straddling Alice, he strangles the life out of her, reaches into the forensic kit for his tools.

Close to eleven thirty, Carter pulls the black SUV into his garage, reaches for the forensic kit and gym bag and slips into his hideaway.

Inside, he throws the bag on the bed and sets the forensic kit on the counter. He quickly removes his gloves, outer garments, and shoe covers, opens the kit and removes the jar with Alice King's tongue, then opens his secret trophy room, places the jar with the others.

And now there are three.

He removes the card from the camera, inserts it into the reader, prints off Alice's picture, and places it among the other victims in the album.

———•◦•———

Jack Carter awakens from a wrestling dream, sweating and groaning. This one is like the others. His mother screaming, "Yes, Yes! Don't stop. Don't stop!" as he removes the tongue from his victims. Jack sneers at his mother. Tells her he loves what he's doing but becomes saddened because she can't hear him. He really wants to tell her that he feels good ridding the world of useless women, and that she was one of them.

He kicks the covers off and turns over. Megan's not there. She sleeps in the spare room, couldn't stand his jerking and groaning during the night. He rises, goes into the bathroom, and looks over his body in the mirror. Healthy and strong and built to take on more victims. He takes out the green contacts. Like most serial killers, he's drawn to his victims for a reason. He's going to become even more famous than his idol, Ted Bundy.

I'm smarter than him, he thinks.

Chapter 31

It's after six. Second shift of detectives has settled in.

McGraw closes the murder book on Elizabeth Fox. His phone rings. He picks up. "Lieutenant McGraw."

"Noah, it's me, Holly."

"I recognize the voice."

"Ha, ha. What're your plans for this evening?"

"Nothing really. Have dinner with ma and talk to my horses."

"Would you rather talk to me? Dusty is with his dad tonight. Thought I'd grill something and we can have our talk. Haven't done that since coming home from the Circle M."

He'd been wanting to talk to her since his last visit with Dusty, but the serial killer has kept them busy 24/7. "I've been wanting to talk, too. Can I bring something. A bottle of Chardonnay?"

"You bring the wine; I'll grill some steaks. Come as soon as you can."

"On my way." He stops by the Circle M and darts up to his room. On the way out, Anna Marie meets him.

"Is this the night, son?" she asks. "You're smiling."

"It is."

She hugs him. "Holly's a jewel."

When Noah arrives with the bottle of Chardonnay, Holly meets him at the door, wearing sweats like she did when staying with him. Standing in the doorway, her black hair is catching the light from the living room and her smile brightens those beautiful soft eyes. He can smell her body lotion as he enters. *An orange or peach scent*, he thinks. The door to the patio at the back is open and the lights are on. Aroma from the steaks sizzling on the grill is traveling inside. Holly grabs his hand, shuts the door, and leads him into the kitchen. "You certainly know how to make a salad."

"Of course." He sets the wine bottle on the counter.

"Well, we'll see. I seem to remember that Anna Marie did all the cooking."

"Ha, ha."

"There are knives in the wood block and cutting board on the counter. All the veggies have been washed and are in a colander in the sink. The bowl to mix everything is there, too. Go to it. When done, bring us a drink." She rushes out the door and flips the steaks.

He finds it amusing the way she's ordering him around. Turnabout is fair play. Guess she has enough of him at work. Noah fills himself a glass of wine and sips it slowly before tackling the salad. He looks around the kitchen. The table is dressed with plates, napkins, glasses, and candles. Oh, oh. Candles? He read somewhere that candles mean something different for women than men. He tries to remember. He thinks it is her signal for lovemaking. Is it true?

Fifteen minutes later, Noah carries two glasses of wine out on the partially enclosed terrace with one of three ceiling fans circulating overhead to swirl the smoke away. Holly is putting sauce on the steaks. Noah hands her a glass of wine.

"Have a seat, they'll be ready in a jiffy." She takes a drink. "Hmm good, I needed that."

McGraw chooses the beige metal chair with a blue cushion, takes a swallow of his wine as he looks around. "I like your outdoor furniture. The dinner table and chairs are beautiful."

"My ex, the real estate mogul, chose the furniture. I have to admit, he has good taste."

"Sure does," Noah says, finishing his wine. "Are you ready for another?" he says holding up his glass.

"Let's wait. The steaks are done," she says placing them on a platter, "and the potatoes in the oven should be ready, too, if not charred."

They laugh.

He grabs her glass and opens the door for her. She moves in and sets the steaks on the counter next to the salad, removes the potatoes from the oven. "They're done," she says. "You did a nice job on the salad. Looks edible." She laughs.

"That was my intent. Can I help with anything?"

"You can fill the wine and water glasses while I put everything on the table."

A few minutes later, she says, "There, I believe we're ready. Would you mind lighting the candles," she says as she dims the lights. He uses the lighter on the table and glances at her as he lights each one.

"When Dusty and I were at the Circle M you said grace before every meal, and when you were here last. Shall we continue the custom?"

"I would love too," he says, as he sits. They bow their heads. He says the prayer, ends it by thanking the Lord for their time together.

"That was sweet," she said.

He raises his glass in a mock toast and then takes a drink.

"I hope your steak is how you like it,"

He cuts into it and takes a bite. He nods. "Just right."

She smiles and nods back.

Noah realizes he has been holding back since he lost Lee Ann to cancer, but now knows she would want him to move on. He likes the feelings he's had for Holly for some time and now he's ready to make a commitment. During their meal, they smile and gaze at each other as they sip their wine. He wonders what is going through her mind. He thinks he's about to find out.

"I don't have any dessert to offer," she says. "Oh, that's right. You don't eat sweets."

He smiles, thinking about what he told her once: *that he's sweet enough.*

"Shall we clean the table and wash the dishes?"

"She waves a hand over the table. "No. I'll put them in the dishwasher later. Would you like some coffee?" she says, rising.

"Would love some. How about us having it out on the Lanai and have our talk," he says.

"Agree. I've been wanting to for some time. Go on out, I'll bring the coffee."

Noah chooses to sit on the large couch.

Holly comes with two cups and places them on the glass coffee table and sits next to him. They sit in silence for a few moments savoring their coffee. The aroma from her cologne is stirring him.

"Would you like to go first?" he says.

"No, you first. Please."

"Okay." Noah takes his time to choose his words carefully. "I don't believe it's any secret how we feel about each other."

She nods and takes a sip of coffee.

"What you said to me in Mississippi has stuck with me, and I'd say we have even growing closer from our interactions during the time you and Dusty stayed with us at the ranch. Would you agree?'

"Very much so."

"I realize now that I've been reluctant to commit because of Lee Ann. I know she'd want what's best for me."

He knows Holly's been waiting to hear the words. He reaches for her hand. "No other way to say it," he says, "but to just say it. I'm in love with you."

She nearly jumps on him, wrapping her arms around his neck. "I've been waiting for you to say those words since our time in the ER at Ole Miss."

"There's another reason I've been slow to express my feelings," he says. "I'm deeply concerned about us working together. It would devastate me if anything ever happened to you while we were on a case. Anna Marie…" He pauses. "Well, we were talking. You've made a big impression on her. She said that you'd know what to do, that you'd follow your heart. Is she right?"

Holly nods. "Now, it's my turn," she says. "I fell in love with you soon after we started working together and especially when I realized how jealous you were when I dated Max. You acted like a big brother, pretending you didn't care. Knowing that made me love you more. When you were hit at Ole Miss, my heart shattered and I was scared to death that I was going to lose you. I knew in the ER that you were mine and no one was ever going to get you."

Noah smiled. "You loved me that much?"

"What did I say?"

They laugh.

"Do you like hearing it?" she says.

"I like the part where you said 'no one else was going to get me.'"

She gives him a love tap on the shoulder. He grabs her and kisses her for several seconds.

"Wow!" she says, straightening up. She inhales a deep breath. "There's no need for you to worry about me," she says. "We're partners and partners have each other's backs."

"But—"

"—no buts."

"What about our future?" he asks.

"You mean marriage?"

"Yes. You know we couldn't work together as partners, married," he says.

"Are you proposing?"

"What would you say, if I did?"

"Yes, with one condition."

"What's that?"

"We not marry right away until we figure out what's best."

"Agreed." Noah reaches into his pocket and removes a small white ornate box. He opens it and takes out a ring with seven diamonds. *One for each day of the week*, he thinks.

Tears begin to well in Holly's eyes.

"This ring belonged to my grandmother. She left it to me in her will."

"Was that the ring Lee Ann wore?"

"No, of course not. Grandma was still alive when Lee Ann and I married."

"Let's keep it in the family," she says.

"Grandma would be so pleased." He takes her left hand and as he places it on her ring finger, he asks, "Will you marry me when the time is right?"

"Yes, yes, of course I will."

Chapter 32

The next morning at sunrise, McGraw strolls the Circle M, then goes into the barn to visit his equine pals, TR and Majestic Lady. He rubs a hand down the side of Majestic Lady's neck and tells her that he and Holly are engaged to be married. Majestic Lady neighs her approval, hearing Holly's name. "Glad you approve, girl."

On the way out, Noah bumps into Whitey, as he comes to do his chores.

"Wow! Noah? Sorry."

"I'm the one who should be sorry. I wasn't paying attention."

"No wonder. Anna Marie just told me the good news. Congratulations!"

Noah shakes his head. "It's finally happened."

Whitey pats him on the shoulder. "It's about time, man. I was worried you were going to lose her."

Anna Marie calls out from the porch. "Noah, there's a call from Holly."

McGraw never carries his cell with him when he takes his morning strolls. He walks to the porch and reaches for his cell.

"McGraw."

"Dispatch has called. We got another vic," Holly says.

"On my way."

At the station, McGraw slips in behind the wheel of the black Silverado monster and flips on the recessed strobes. Holly is in the passenger seat. When they arrive in the southeast Atlanta area, patrol cars are parked on the street with strobes flashing and officers standing around. They gawk at McGraw as he pulls the black SSV into the driveway of the house given by dispatch. He couldn't have missed it with the patrol cars, uniforms, and rubbernecks waiting for the cowboy detective to appear.

McGraw and Roark clamber out.

"Oh, oh. There's Gary with his crew across the street," Holly says. "And here he comes." Gary Spencer, an investigative reporter for the Constitution, and McGraw go way back to the time he was on patrol. Gary's always looking for a story, and doesn't care how he gets it. He's six foot, in his early fifties, with bushy white hair, white mustache, chin whiskers—French style. He's wearing a blue crew T-shirt under a black sports coat.

"Howya, Noah," Spencer says, staring at him through hard-rimmed glasses

McGraw tips his hat up with his thumb, puts his arm around Gary and walks him over to the Silverado.

"Wow, man! You're coming up in the world. A Special Service Vehicle?"

It wasn't really a question. Noah doesn't respond, instead he says, "Gary, I need a favor."

The frown on Gary's face reveals he knows what's coming. "You want me to hold this one, right?"

Noah nods. "We may have a serial and we don't want to tip our hand. This guy's sharp. I need for you to hold off for just a little while."

"Does that mean I get the exclusive? I know there are two other women vics."

"You know you can trust me, Gary."

"Okay, Marlboro Man. You know me. I'll be a'calling." He turns and walks across the street and tells his crew to pack things up. "We're out of here for now."

Holly says, "We won't be able to hold him off for too long."

"We can feed him like we always do," he says as they walk past the M.E. and CSI vans. The area has been cordoned off with tape and a uniform is standing guard. He nods. "Your fans are out in numbers, lieutenant," the officer says, looking out over the crowd that has gathered.

"All the police cars make the neighbor folks come a'running to see what's up, Jimmy," McGraw says.

He nods and laughs. "They came to see the cowboy lieutenant. I heard 'em say, 'there's the cowboy.'"

They laugh. McGraw and Roark sign in and duck under the tape. Kramer and Gomez are standing outside the door talking to the sergeant in charge.

"Whatta we have?" McGraw asks his detectives. The sergeant nods and leaves.

"A sixty-five-year-old woman vic named Alice King," Kramer says. "She has a state ID but no driver's license."

"Boss, the doc says the old gal's been strangled," Gomez adds. "She's definitely one of our perp's vics. No tongue," he says as he makes a slicing motion across his tongue. "And she stinks of booze."

"Witnesses?" Roark asks.

"Folks in the house in front never heard or saw a thing," Kramer says. "We're on our way to knock on doors."

"Go for it," McGraw says.

He and Roark step inside, which opens into the living room where doc Philips is kneeling over Alice and the forensic team is working the place. He spots Megan. To their right is a narrow kitchen. In the back, two doors are open: one leads into a small bedroom and the other opens into a bathroom only large enough for a small person.

"Gomez was right," Roark says, "the place stinks of booze."

"Hey, doc," McGraw says.

She glances up at them, and smiles. "Got another one. This makes three." She stands. "Definitely got a serial on your hands."

"Any defensive wounds?" Roark asks.

Nora shakes her head. "The poor thing didn't know what hit her. Too much booze, cigs, and not enough protein."

"That's what our perp likes. Alcoholics. Probably because of his mother or someone else in his family," McGraw says.

"The psych stuff, I'll leave for you guys. Not in my pay scale."

"Detective McGraw," Megan, the forensic lead says, "It's all yours, we've wrapped up."

"Okay, Megan," McGraw says. "Thanks."

"Ready for me to flip her?" Nora Philips says.

He nods. "Probably nothing but you never know when he'll make his mistake."

Philips turns the body on its left side. McGraw squats and scans the body and the area under it. No trace evidence that he can see.

"This perp is a planner. He knows what he's doing," McGraw says. He tips his hat and says, "Thanks. You can take Alice now." McGraw likes to show respect for the victims by using their names rather than using pronouns.

After doc Philips and her assistant Larry remove Alice's body, McGraw and Roark walk the crime scene, as they always do, in a fashion he learned from his old partner, Zee. They move in deliberate steps, evaluating and assessing what has happened, even though they know the works of their serial killer. By walking deliberately across the scene, crisscrossing—forming a pattern of intersecting paths on the floor—they have found traces of evidence that other detectives have missed, which always pleased Zee.

McGraw plays the scene in his mind: *The monster dressed in dark clothes, cap, mask, gloves, booties, attacks swiftly, driving her to the floor in a flash and strangling her. He straddles her, reaches into some bag for forceps and a scalpel. Clamps the tongue in the forceps, pulling it out, slicing his trophy out of the vic's mouth with the scalpel.*

Fifteen minutes later, their search doesn't reveal fibers, hair, or footprints. McGraw knows trace evidence can be transferred from the perp to victim and vice versa. Hopefully, forensics has found something, but a background on King also will run through the system.

Chapter 33

McGraw enters an empty squad room close to seven the next morning, walks over to the coffee stand and brews a pot. While waiting, he goes to his desk, sits, and begins reviewing the reports on Alice King. Minutes later he opens the murder books (loose-leaf binders) on Gail Murdock and Elizabeth Fox. He's been through them twice.

What am I looking for? Something to tell me how to catch this killer would be helpful.

Nothing jumps out at him.

What am I missing?

Witnesses.

This perp is causing McGraw to have sleepless nights. He rises, grabs his Braves cup and takes it to the coffee stand. With a full cup, he heads to the crime boards a few steps behind his desk. He stares at the pictures of his three victims as he sips his coffee: Gail Murdock, Elizabeth Fox, and Alice King.

What are you ladies not telling me?

He returns to his desk, sets his cup down, and opens the file from the FBI Behavioral Analysis Unit containing the profile on his serial killer, that Drew Nelson faxed over to him.

"Have you solved it?" Holly asks as she enters and throws her purse on the desk.

He jumps, but lets it pass.

"Oh, sorry. Didn't mean to sneak up on you."

"Just going over the profile on our perp Drew faxed over."

Kramer and Gomez enter and walk over to their desks.

"I see you have your coffee," Holly says. "I need some before I can be of any help."

"Me, too, boss," Gomez says.

McGraw meets his team at the table in the middle of the room.

"I have copies of the FBI profile on our perp," McGraw says passing the report out to each one. "Take a moment to read it."

What's this FBI B-A-U?" Gomez asks.

"Behavior Analysis Unit," Roark replies.

"Roark sent him the evidence we have on the three cases and asked Drew Nelson to profile our serial. What you have in your hand is what they came up with," McGraw says.

"It reads: 'From the evidence you provided on your serial killer, our Behavioral Analysis Unit developed the profile described below.'"

Serial killers are psychopaths, but not all psychopaths are killers. Besides their childhood driving them to be the way they are, they characteristically are more driven by their inability to feel guilt, accept love, or empathize with others, which makes them perfect candidates for murderers. Nothing seems to shock them. Your Atlanta serial killer is a white male between the ages of thirty and early forties. Probably raised by a single parent. Possesses charm, good intellect, but is unreliable, and lacks remorse and feelings. His arrogance sets him up against others where he feels they are not worthy of his friendship; hence, he chooses not to be very sociable. He's capable of adapting to new situations with ease when necessary, makes friends easily, using his charm to overcome his victims, as Ted Bundy did to lure his victims. He keeps people at a distance. He does things alone: shopping, eating out, and going to entertainment venues. He would be hard to pick out of the general population as a murderer. Your serial chooses his victims very carefully. Probably does a thorough background check on them before he moves on them. He loves the nighttime and would generally do his killing then.

McGraw, holding the report in his hand says, "Let's move to the boards. He begins writing under the vics' pictures.

"This is what we have on our perp so far," he says going down the list of five.

    1. Kills elderly women

    2. Removes tongues as trophies

    3. Drives a black SUV?

    4. White male, tall, and strong.

    5. Serial killer.

Looking at the FBI report, he says, "We need to add:"

    6. Between thirty and early forties.

    7. Psychopath without feelings or remorse.

    8. Well organized.

    9. Kills at night.

    10. Loner.

    11. Can be charming and deceiving to kill his vics.

    12. Does background checks on his vics.

    13. Educated – degree.

    14. Extremely organized.

    15. Dysfunctional family.

McGraw says. "Reports so far from Megan in forensics haven't been helpful." He sighs. "This perp may be the smartest we've ever faced."

"How's that?" Kramer asks.

"He has a thorough knowledge of a crime scene, and I believe he's competing with us."

"I've thought that, too," Roark says. "Not leaving a trace of evidence means he has advanced skills and is organized around a crime scene. Could my original hunch that the perp may be an ex-cop with some medical experience or someone in the medical field be dead on?"

Staring at the boards, McGraw doesn't say a word. Minutes later he says, "Good thinking. I would only add that our perp has some forensic experience. He could be a CSI cop or someone who's worked forensics."

"Then it's gonna be tough to get a drop on this guy," Kramer says.

The boss nods. "We've never seen a perp this clever." He pauses. "One thing's for sure. Alice King is not his last victim."

"Because he's becoming more confident?" Roark says.

He nods, again. "This means he's bound to make a mistake sooner or later. All psychopaths in history have made them due to their extreme arrogance. They think they're invincible and begin to take chances. Like them, our perp's arrogance is going to bring him down."

Turning to Roark, he says, "What did you find on King?"

"She's originally from Missouri, been divorced for years. Had a couple of DUIs but nothing since she moved here. Was detained for loitering on a park bench, but other than that, she's clean. Her only sin seems to be the bottle."

"How about children?"

"Two. Fully grown by now. Do you want me to try and find them?"

"Don't think it would help."

McGraw turns to Kramer and Gomez. "What did you learn from canvassing King's neighborhood?"

Kramer answers first. "Nothing much. The people in the house in front, the ones that rented that garage apartment to Alice King, said she didn't list any relatives on her application and told them there's no one she cares about. She never had visitors and they know of no one that would want to kill her."

"Boss, I think we might have a lead," Gomez says. "The landlord suggested we go to a bar called Jimmy's, where Ms. King hung out. It's only a couple of blocks from her apartment."

McGraw looks at the wall clock.

"You guys get over there and find out all you can on her. Shake the bushes. Bring me something, anything. This guy is going to kill again. And soon."

"Will do, boss," Gomez says.

Roark frowns at McGraw. "Wow. You're really into it. 'Bring me something, anything.'"

Gomez pulls out of the station in a detective unit with Kramer in the passenger seat, drives to the Hispanic section in the east end and swings into the lot in front of Velasco's Mexican bar. He had told his partner earlier that they'd stop off somewhere to get a bite before going to Kirkland.

"Hey, I remember this place," Kramer says, as his partner pulls in. "This is where you brought me a couple of months ago and introduced me to tequila and your informant friend, Marco. I liked the tequila, once I got used to it."

"Thought we'd come here for eats and kill some time before heading out to Jimmy's bar," Gomez says. "Anyway, it's in this part of town. Your friend Marco will be glad to see you," Gomez says, bursting into a belly laugh.

"I bet. I know what he's gonna do, hit you up for cash. I'd bet money on it."

They step out of the car and walk to the red brick building. Inside, the place is quiet. The last time they were here, Mexican music was blasting so loud that they could hear it outside. Gomez is thinking something here isn't right. The same smell of tacos and beans is still floating throughout the place from the kitchen, but half the tables are vacant and only two men and one woman are sitting at the bar sipping tequilas. The dark-headed woman that was waiting tables the last time they were in is now tending bar. Gomez leads the way to the bar.

"Hey, Rosa, Qué pasa?

She shakes her head. "Bad things, Juan."

"Whatta you mean? Where's Marco."

"He's sick."

"Anything serious?"

She motions for him to walk down to the end of the bar by the kitchen door. A tall, thin Mexican man in his late twenties, wearing a white apron, shoots out of the kitchen with a tray of tacos and burritos, causing the door to fly open and hit the wall.

Gomez leans in and Rosa whispers, "Two goons beat the shit out of him."

"Can't be Johnny Parino's boys. They're all in the pen."

She shrugs. "No Parino. Gang."

"What gang? Mexican?"

She shrugs. "Drugs. People are scared."

"So that's why only a few people are here."

She nods. "Si."

"Is he gonna be okay?" Gomez says.

"He says back in a couple days. All okay then."

"Tell him to call me."

She nods. "What can I get you?"

"We're gonna find a table. Bring coffee," Gomez finds a couple coins in his pocket and goes to the juke box.

This place is too damn quiet, he thinks.

Immediately the place is blasting with Mexican music. Heads turn. He goes through a few body gyrations in sync with the music on his way to a booth in the back. The patrons smile, begin singing and clapping along with his body movements. This's what he likes, excitement.

"Living it up, are you?" Kramer says.

"Man, this place is dead, we gotta liven it up. Mexicans like hoopla and good eats."

An hour later, close to seven o'clock, the detectives leave Velasco's under a dark sky. The streetlights come on as they pull out. It takes fifteen minutes to reach the Kirkland neighborhood.

Jimmy's bar is on the corner in a run-down neighborhood. Gomez finds a space across from the bar and pulls in next to the curb. They clamber out.

"Man, this area is a shit hole," Gomez says. "No wonder this zone is known for its gangs, robberies, and rapes."

"We're not going to get much cooperation here," Kramer says.

The area is dark around Jimmy's, only one light above his entrance. The suits enter. The bar is smoky, dingy, and can be rated a hole-in-the-wall. Only a couple of tables are empty and most of the bar is full. Blues is playing on the box and the lighting is so poor it's hard to make out the couples hanging on each other in the small dancing area in the back. Heads turn as the suits walk between the tables to the bar. It's obvious these blue-collar patrons aren't the hospitable types.

Kramer finds a slot at the bar and elbows his way in to make room for him and Gomez. The blond bartender is slender, about five-eleven, in his early thirties, "Oh, no. Cops"

They pull out their ID's and Kramer says, "Homicide detectives, Atlanta PD. We'd like to ask you a few questions."

"Can't you see I'm busy here?"

"We can do it here or at the station. Your choice," Gomez says.

He looks around. "Give me a few," he says as he heads to the back. Thirty seconds later, out comes a burly guy with bushy hair and a scruffy beard, looks like he needs a shower. The bartender says, "Jake will take over until I'm done with you guys."

Gomez looks to his right at the end of the bar. No one is there.

"Let's move to the end of the bar," he says.

Kramer starts the questioning. "What's your name?"

"Blake Williams."

"Do you know a lady by the name of Alice King?"

"Sure. She's a regular. Haven't seen her yet tonight. Why? She'd done something?"

"Why do you ask that," Gomez says, "Is she in the habit of getting into trouble?"

Blake frowns. "No, I meant nothing by it. When the cops come in here asking questions about someone, they've generally done something."

"You haven't heard?" Kramer asks.

"Heard what?"

"She was killed last night."

"Alice? No way. Who'd want to hurt Alice?"

"That's what we'd like to find out," Gomez says. "Any ideas?"

He shakes his head. "She never bothers no one."

"What can you tell us about her?" Kramer says.

He shrugs. "She comes in here nearly every night and sits here at the bar. She was in here last night."

"Was she with someone?"

"Well, not at first. She didn't walk in with anyone. There's this guy, he came in about fifteen minutes after she did. He sat at this end of the bar where we are. She was sitting in the middle over there where Jake is standing," he says, pointing in that direction.

"What'd this guy do, hit on her?" Gomez asks.

He shakes his head. "He was something else. He asked for 'the finest Scotch in the house.' I told him, look around, does this look like a place that serves Scotch?'

"I can understand that," Gomez says. "Go on."

"I didn't pay much attention at first when I served him a Bud on tap. When he moved over to Alice, I got interested. She never gives anyone the time of day. She just sits, smokes and drinks. No one pays her no mind." He pauses. "The guy got my attention for sure when he told her someone by the name of Alex couldn't make it to meet her. At first, I thought he was feeding her a line but she acted like she knew who he was talking about."

"You think she was going to date someone?" Kramer says.

"Seemed like it. That's why I listened. That's a new one on me, if she dates."

"Like you bartenders never listen," Gomez says.

The guy shrugs again. "Man, you can't help it sometimes."

"Did you hear a last name for this Alex?" Kramer asks, as he removes a small notebook and pen from his suitcoat pocket.

"Something that sounded like sin. I believe Sinclair." He frowned like he was thinking hard. "That's it. Alex Sinclair."

Kramer writes in his notebook.

"What did he say about Sinclair?"

"The guy said Sinclair's father died and he couldn't meet her."

"Did this messenger guy tell her his name?"

He shook his head. "No."

"Describe the guy," Kramer says with pen in hand.

"I'd say educated with good tastes. Don't know why he'd come into a dump like this, so, maybe he really was just the messenger."

"Stop giving your opinions, just stick to what he looked like and what he said," Kramer says with some disgust in his voice.

"Okay, man. Don't get your dandruff up." He pauses for a couple of seconds. "Let's see," he says looking away as if in deep thought. "He had short black hair. I believe it had a little gray in it, dark eyebrows and scary green eyes that could stare a hole in you. His appearance gave me the creeps, like a guy that could tear you apart if he got mad at you."

"You mean the guy was big?" Gomez asks.

"Not fat but strong looking."

"How tall was he?" Kramer asks.

"I'm not good with height. I'd say just a little taller than you, detective."

"Was he white or black?"

"White."

Blake turns to look at Jake. "Give me a minute," he says as he goes to the scruffy old guy who's slopping beer on the bar. It takes a few minutes for Blake to get the situation under control. "Sorry, Jake's not with it tonight. Where was I?"

Reading from his notes, Kramer says, "You said the guy had short black hair, maybe some gray, black eyebrows and piercing green eyes that could stare a hole in you, and a little taller than me. Now, go on."

He shrugs a third time and gestures with his hands, as if to help him think. "The only other thing…the guy smiled a lot, not a good smile. It's one of those where he thinks he's got you by the balls."

"A conceited bastard?" Gomez says.

"You got it. Kinda made me mad the way he was treating Alice. Like she was nothin'."

"Doesn't seem like he was just a messenger," Kramer says.

"Hell, no. He wasn't a messenger," Gomez says. "He's our killer."

Blakes eyes widened. "Whatta you mean? A killer was sitting right here at my bar?"

"You're lucky you didn't piss him off," Gomez says, smiling.

Kramer turns and frowns at his partner.

"How was he dressed?" Gomez asks.

It took Blake a few seconds to get his wits about him. "In a black coat to the waist and a white shirt of some kind underneath. I get the chills just thinking about him. A killer?"

"Do you think you could ID this guy again?"

"Damn right! A killer in my place? You betcha."

"How did he talk?" Gomez asks. "Any dialect. Maybe an Englishman?"

"No, plain English. An all-around American guy."

Kramer looks around. "How'd this place get the name, Jimmy's. Is Jake the owner?"

Blake looks over at Jake.

"Jimmy was his partner. He made this business, for what it's worth. He died a few years ago. Jake is a lush and depends on me to run the place. I'm his grandson. He was in the back the whole time when Alice and that guy was here."

"Did they leave together?" Kramer says.

Blake shakes his head. "No way. He threw down a twenty on the bar and told me to give Alice another drink, and he left."

"Did she leave right after him?" Gomez asks.

"No. About an hour later. Left by herself."

"Was she drunk?" he says.

"She can handle the booze but was weaving a little when she left."

"So, no one in here is a friend of Alice King?"

"King? I didn't even know her last name," Blake said. "Always called her Alice." He looks at his hands. "She had no friends that I know of."

This guy is our only witness. The boss will be thrilled, Gomez thinks.

"Don't leave town," Gomez says. "Lieutenant McGraw will want you to come to the station. You'll be hearing from us tomorrow."

"I'll be here."

Kramer turns to Blake. "You wouldn't have a video installed in this place, would you?"

Blake twisted his face like a dried prune. "You gotta be kidding me. In a dump like this? Who'd we video, a robber? He'd be wasting his time and he'd know it. That's why we've never been robbed."

Heads turn again in this crowed musty, dark hell-hole, as the suits walk between tables to the outside. They take a couple of deep breaths to clear the smoke from their lungs. Kramer and Gomez look around Jimmy's building. I bet the bastard was parked over there where we are, watching her as she comes out, follows her home, and does her."

"Sounds about right to me," Kramer says. "She was crazy as hell to walk home by herself."

"And no one here gives a shit," Gomez says, "except Blake Williams."

Gomez punches Kramer on the arm, "Man, do you realize this guy can ID our killer. We have our witness."

"The boss will be thrilled," Kramer says. "Let's knock on some doors and see what turns. Wonder if anyone saw a black SUV."

"It'd be nice if they did," Gomez says. "We'd know for sure this was our man."

"Let's see if we can get one person that saw the car," Kramer says.

"Look at this neighborhood," Gomez says. "These folks are scared shitless. They won't answer their doors."

After forty minutes, Kramer and Gomez realize they're at a dead end. The two residents that opened their doors a crack saw nothing.

"No one sees or hears anything these days," Gomez says.

"You know witnesses lie and no one ever sees anything," Kramer says.

McGraw and Roark look up from their desks early the next morning when Kramer and Gomez come in.

McGraw says, "Grab some caffeine. Want to hear what you guys learned at Jimmy's."

They all move to the front of the room and stand around the white boards.

Kramer starts.

"We learned that Alice King had no friends. She was a frequent visitor to Jimmy's just to sit and drink beer all night. Night before last, a guy comes in. At first, he drinks a beer then moves over to Alice. Tells her that he has a message for her from Alex Sinclair. The message was that Sinclair couldn't meet with her because his father died, and he sends his regrets."

"You think she was involved in something?" Roark asks.

Kramer shakes his head. "No. Alice only went to Jimmy's to drink and smoke. Wasn't a talker or mixer."

"That fits with what I found when I ran her," Roark says. "She's alcoholic."

"What else did this guy do?" McGraw asks. "There's definitely something here."

"Boss," Gomez says, "this guy's definitely our killer."

"What's your hunch?" McGraw says.

"If you heard how the bartender described him and how he treated Alice, like she was nothin', a piece of shit," Gomez says. "He was no messenger. No way."

"Okay. Describe the guy," McGraw says as he picks up a black marker and glances at what's already up on the board.

1. Kills elderly women

2. Removes tongues as trophies

3. Drives a black SUV?

4. White male, tall, strong.

5. Serial killer.

6. Between thirty and early forties.

7. Psychopath. Without feelings or remorse.

8. Well organized.

9. Kills at night.

10. Loner.

11. Can be charming and deceiving to kill his victims.

12. Does background checks on his vics.

13. Educated – degree.

14. Extremely organized.

15. Dysfunctional family.

"Let's have it," McGraw says.

"The bartender described him a little taller than me," Kramer says. McGraw says, "That fits with what we have."

"Has short black hair with some gray, thick eye brows, green eyes. He's athletic built and a little over six."

McGraw adds to the list:

16. Short black hair with some gray.

17. Thick eyebrows and green eyes.

"He had a strong build," Gomez added."

"We have tall, but good to know he's around six-foot." McGraw stands back and looks at what's on the board, and says, "We've got a serial killer who is tall, strong, with short dark hair, some gray, green eyes, has killed three elderly women, cuts out their tongues, and drives a black SUV."

"Not enough there for a sketch artist," Roark says. "Don't know the shape of his head, forehead, nose, ears, jaw, and so forth. We need a witness."

"You mean we need a miracle," Gomez says with a smirk.

She frowns. "For sure, we do."

"Well, you got it," Gomez says looking at the boss.

"The bartender, the boss says. "What are you guys waiting for? You've found our first witness. Get Blake in here and get a sketch on that guy," McGraw says.

Mutt and Jeff take off.

McGraw says to Holly, "Even with a sketch, we have to be damn sure this guy is our man. We won't release it to the public until we're certain."

An hour later, Blake Williams is brought into Homicide, where they have made prior arrangements for a sketch artist to meet with him in one of the interview rooms.

Chapter 34

The next morning, Holly Roark rolls into the precinct, hops out of her white Grand Cherokee and rushes to the entrance, where she connects with a middle-aged woman in a light blue suit and purple hat who's about to enter.

"Are you a police officer?" lady asks.

"I'm a homicide detective. Are you wishing to report something?"

"Yes. Someone broke into my home, knocked me out and took my keepsake and jewelry."

"I see. Well, you'll want to talk to someone in the Burglary Division. Come with me, I'll help you find someone," Roark says, guiding the woman into the lobby of the station. Roark heads to the desk sergeant and asks him to get Detective Lillian Green in Burglary on the phone.

After a few minutes, he hands the phone to Detective Roark.

"Lillian, this is Holly Roark. Listen, I have a lady here who wants to report a burglary." A pause. "Yes, she says she's been robbed. Okay, I'll tell her." Roark turns to the pretty lady in blue with white hair standing next to her and says, "I never got your name."

"Oh, sorry. I'm Bea Kunz. Everyone calls me Aunt Bea."

"Okay, Aunt Bea. Detective Green will be down in a minute."

"And what's your name, honey?" Aunt Bea asks.

"I'm Detective Holly Roark."

"Why can't you help me? You seem so nice, and pretty, too."

They smile at each other.

"That's sweet of you, but I'm a homicide detective. It has to be someone in Burglary. Detective Green is a friend and she's a great person."

"But I kinda like you."

"I'm sorry, honey. I don't have the authority. Oh, here she comes now." Detective Green is a black lady, tall and slender with a pretty smile. She walks with straight posture and with confidence. She's coming to them through the hall from their left and smiles. "I'm Detective Green."

"This is Bea Kunz," Holly says.

Aunt Bea smiles and thanks Green. Holly notices Green staring at the purple hat and the pretty white hair.

"Come with me, Ms. Kunz, and let's see what we can do for you."

"Aunt Bea, please."

"Of course, Aunt Bea."

The two head back down the hall to the left. Roark hurries through the hall to her right and into the Homicide Division with just a few minutes to spare before she and McGraw meet with the Capt.

———◦◦———

Gomez has the squad room to himself. Kramer has left for his doctor's appointment, and the boss and Roark are in with the Capt. discussing the serial killer. He kind of enjoys the stillness of the place. He hears footsteps behind him and turns. A lady in a purple hat, blue suit, and pretty white hair comes into the bureau with Detective Green.

"Ms. Kunz would like to speak to Sergeant Roark before she leaves. I'm leaving her with you." She turns to Bea and says, "I'll be in touch. We'll do all we can."

"Thank you, honey," Aunt Bea says.

All the while, Gomez can't take his eyes off the purple hat and white hair that surrounds it. "I'm looking for that pretty detective with the gorgeous brown eyes."

"Well, I know it's not me," he says, bursting out laughing.

The hat lady frowns at him. "You're right. She's much prettier. I think she said her name is Dolly."

"Holly. That's Detective Holly Roark."

She points a white gloved finger at him. "You're right, young man. She did say, Holly Roark. I want to see her, please."

Gomes takes a drink from his coffee.

"I'm sorry, ma'am. She and the boss, Lieutenant McGraw, are in with the Captain. They're having a meeting." Gomez looks up at the wall clock. Ten-thirty. "They should be out in about thirty minutes. Can I take a message?"

"No way. I'm here to see Holly. Where can I wait?"

Gomez sets his coffee cup down on his desk. He knows this lady is not going to give in.

"I'll take you to the waiting area. I didn't catch your name."

"Bea Kunz. Everyone calls me Aunt Bea. You can, too, Sonny."

"My name isn't 'Sonny', it's Gomez, Detective Gomez."

"So, it says on your desk." She follows Gomez out the door and to an alcove. Couches and leather chairs fill the small room.

"I'll be back to get you," he says.

"Don't forget me, Sonny."

Gomez fakes a smile. *You're a tough old bird, aren't you?*

"Yeah, of course, 'Aunt Bea,'" he says.

Twenty minutes later, McGraw and Roark come out of the Lion's den. Gomez tells Roark about the lady in a purple hat who wants to see her.

"I met her earlier. What does she want?"

"Didn't say. I'll go get her."

"Who's that hunk of a man with Holly?" Aunt Bea asks as Gomez leads her back into the department.

"That's the boss, Lieutenant McGraw."

"He's sure a handsome one. He reminds me of a country-western singer."

Gomez feels a big smile coming on his face.

"I'm from Tennessee and we love our country music."

"He looks like George Street, doesn't he?" Gomez asks, making sure he said the last name wrong.

"You mean, George Strait," she says.

"That's what I said. Guess it's my Yankee accent."

"Man, he's a handsome one," Bea says.

Gomez is quick to change the subject. "The boss's already taken, ma'am."

"Married?"

"No, ma'am, but he and Detective Roark just got engaged."

"They make a beautiful couple," she says

* * *

As McGraw and Roark head to their desks, the boss says to Holly, "What do we have here? A woman in a purple hat is coming down the aisle with Gomez."

"I met her this morning coming in and got her connected with Lillian Green in Burglary."

"What's she doing here?" he says.

"I believe we're gonna find out."

"Hello, dear. I'm sorry, but I need some advice. I didn't get much help from Detective Green."

"I don't understand. Please, sit," she says, directing her to the chair next to her desk.

They sit.

"Can I get you anything, water or coffee?"

She shakes her head no, then stares into Roark's eyes. "My grandson… he was killed in Afghanistan two years ago."

"Oh, I'm sorry."

"He was honored posthumously for his bravery and I've kept his medal with me ever since. It hasn't been out of my sight. Someone broke into my home, knocked me out and took it with some of my jewelry. Like I told Detective Green, I didn't see who it was. I'm afraid I wasn't much help to her. She said I should have reported the break-in immediately to the police after it happened, and not to get my hopes up of ever finding it." Aunt Bea opens her purse, removes a tissue, and wipes her eyes. "It means so much to me."

"Just give me a minute." Holly goes to Noah, who is studying the crime chart. She tells him Bea's story and asks him if they can help her.

"May be stepping on Green's toes," McGraw says. "Don't want that."

"Lillian and I are good friends. I feel if I explain to her how Aunt Bea has taken to me, she wouldn't mind me helping out. How about that approach?"

"Give it a try. But if there's the slightest resistance, let it go." He turns back to the whiteboard.

"Will do." Roark goes to her desk and phones Lillian. When she hangs up, Roark tells Aunt Bea that Detective Green has agreed to allow her to participate as long as we cooperate with her division."

"That's what I like to hear, honey. I knew you'd be the one to get it done."

"Please call me Holly." Before she can ask Bea for some information, she says, "You're very sweet, Holly." She rises and hands Holly a sheet of nine-by-eleven paper. "It's a copy of all the information Detective Green recorded during her questioning me."

Roark looks it over. "Besides your phone number, home address, when the burglary occurred, there is the description of the medal. All this info will be very helpful in our investigation." She stands. "Do you need me to show you the way to the parking lot?"

"No. I can find my way. Look forward to hearing from you."

"Just a minute." Holly reaches in her drawer. "This is my card. I'm writing my cell number on the back in case you need me."

"That's so sweet of you to be concerned," she says reaching for the card, and turning to walk out.

Aunt Bea smiles at Gomez, who has been listening the whole time. "Detective Gomez," she says with a slight nod and smile as she goes by, "You behave yourself."

Gomez laughs. "I'll try, ma'am. But it's hard." He ambles over to Roark's desk. "I heard your conversation. Want me to check the pawn reports?"

Roark smiles. "You just read my mind. About to ask you. Let's split them up."

"Can do," he says, as he returns to his desk.

———◆———

Holly has just gotten home and is about to kick off her shoes and have a glass of red wine to unload the day's burden when her cell phone vibrates on the dining room table.

She doesn't recognize the number, but answers: "Detective Roark."

"Detective Roark, this is Aunt Bea. I hope you haven't had dinner yet. Have you?"

"Not yet, just relaxing with a glass of wine."

"Don't drink it. I'm inviting you to join me for dinner at my favorite restaurant. I want to thank you for helping me."

"I've not done much just yet. We are working on it."

"I know you'll find my grandson's medal. Please, I want you to join me for dinner. Whatta say, dear? We can talk more."

Holly doesn't really want to go. She's acclimated to enjoying the evening alone.

"Dear, please!" Aunt Bea says.

"Okay. Where do want to meet."

"My home at seven thirty. You have my address."

Click. Aunt Bea hangs up.

Holly looks at her cell phone as if she expected the motherly woman to make more demands.

At seven-thirty, Holly arrives in the Buckhead area and pulls into the driveway of a multi-million-dollar home.

Chapter 35

Jack Carter steps out of his white Caddy and makes his way into the City Crime lab. Megan is an early bird and has left the house at six-thirty. He's the director, so arriving at eight is not unreasonable. But the real reason he left an hour later is to check his emails from the women he's been corresponding with on his laptop in his lair. The last couple of days his urge to kill has become stronger, so much so that he has had to calm himself by admiring his trophies and staring at the photos of his victims.

Inside, he opens his office, then makes his rounds, visiting with his criminalists and discussing their results. Standing at the evidence table, Megan tells him they got a fiber. It's one like we got before, from the perp's black outfit he wears."

Carter feels his ego inflating. "Well, it's something. The perp is pretty elusive."

"I'd say so."

Carter loves hearing that.

They laugh.

The office phone rings. "Gotta get that."

He hurries to his office and closes the door.

Sally Crane is on the line. She is concerned. Hasn't heard from his mother nor has she been able to reach her. Wants to call the police without delay. She believes something terrible has happened to her.

No way in hell can he allow that. The friggin' cops would learn he was the last person to see his mother, and they'll want the names and the phone numbers of the relatives in Charlotte, who do not exist. He would become their chief suspect, and with warrants, they'd go through the house, his den, and the garage. In his secret hiding place, they'd find his photo album, and trophies, which they would confiscate. The black SUV in the garage would tie him to the victims. From the photo album, McGraw would eventually figure out his mother's grave and that he killed Hannah Clay. It would be all over, and he'd face the friggin' death penalty. No way is that happening, he tells himself. He convinces her to wait. They must talk because he has something to tell her.

Sally Crane has become a liability.

Carter tells Megan he has a meeting and leaves the lab, hurries to his Caddy, races out on the street, wheels screaming, making it home eight minutes off his usual time, flies into the driveway. Sally's sitting in a chair on the porch. He jumps out and dashes to her.

"You haven't called the police, have you?" he says, almost out of breath.

She shakes her head. "No, but you said Laura would be back by now. I knocked and there's no answer. You lied to me, Jack."

"I haven't lied." He looks down for a few seconds, feigning embarrassment. "Mom didn't want me to tell you. She's...she's in a treatment facility for her alcoholism. She's not with family. I took her up there at the advice of her doctor."

"Why not here? We have good treatment centers."

He could see she's not buying his story.

"You're pretty sharp, Sally. Here's the story: Mom thought if she were admitted here everyone at church would find out and worry about her and pester her by praying over her. She thought being in Charlotte we could say she was taking care of a sick family member. She has a friend up there that has been visiting her and taking her things."

She shakes her head. "Well, I don't know. I'd feel better if I can talk to her."

"Certainly. Let's go inside. I'll look up the number and you can talk to her. How's that?"

She nods. "That'll be fine. Let's just do it."

He opens the door and allows her to enter ahead of him. With her back to him, he grabs her around the neck and squeezes so hard she can't scream, only flail and gasp for air. Seconds later, she collapses on the floor. He turns her over and straddles her, like he does all his victims, and strangles her until she's dead. Should he cut out Sally Crane's tongue or not? He has to. It's his trophy. He carries Sally Crane's body to his hideaway, where he drops her body on the floor and walks over to counter to remove his forensic kit. He kneels next to the body, opens the kit, removes forceps and scalpel, and goes to work on the tongue. He holds the jar up in the light to admire his new trophy. After placing the jar in the trophy room, he gazes at Sally Crane on the floor. Where will he dispose of her body? Under a bridge, in a ditch, in the woods? *No*, he thinks. *Too many bodies are found in the woods. That's the first place the cops would look. I'll take her to the cabin and tie weights on her and dump her in the lake. That's it. I'll do it.*

There's no way he can let her be identified.

He kneels by the body, reaches for clippers, extracts her teeth, clips off her fingers and then her toes. The body parts are placed in a heavy bag and sealed to go into the lake.

Carter waits until about nine that evening to load Sally Crane's body in the SUV and heads to his cabin.

Two days later, Carter decides it's time to throw detective McGraw a curve with a stunt he has planned for some time. The barrel in his garage was picked up from a river bank for that purpose. What better way to irritate the cowboy than to place a barrel with some animal tongues on his property. He'll know that the perp that's been taunting him knows about the Max Kingston case. That'll throw him for a loop. *What a genius I am.*

Chapter 36

McGraw swivels his chair around to face the evidence chart as he does most days. He and the whiteboards are close friends. Physical evidence never lies. Witnesses lie. Evidence reveals motivation, means, and opportunity. He stares at the pictures of the three victims.

His cell vibrates on his desk. He backs his chair up and reaches for it. "Lieutenant McGraw," he says.

"Noah, you gotta come."

McGraw jumps up. "What's wrong, Whitey? Is it mom?"

"No. It's déjà vu. We got another barrel on the back forty."

"What?"

"Just like before."

McGraw lifts his desk phone and calls dispatch to have patrol and the Crime Scene Unit meet them at the Circle M, then grabs his Stetson. "Everyone. Your attention." He meets them at the table. "We may have a body."

"Where?" Holly says.

"At the Circle M. Another barrel."

"You're kidding," Holly says.

"Afraid not. Let's see what the perp has for us this time," McGraw says as he and Holly head out of the bureau with Kramer and Gomez in tow.

McGraw pulls the Silverado behind a patrol car. Whitey is waiting in the red jeep at the edge of the driveway. Noah and Holly step out and hop into the jeep from both sides. Kramer and Gomez pull up in a detective unit.

"I'll be back for you guys," Whitey says to Kramer and Gomez. The sun is bright and the crisp air flows over them as he races to the back forty, flying through a grove of trees, shooting out into an expanse of greenery and stopping twenty yards from the fence, where a black 55-gallon metal drum sits, almost in the same spot as the last one. McGraw turns to Whitey.

"You didn't disturb anything, did you?"

Patrol has cordoned off the area and forensics is working the scene.

Whitey shakes his head. "I always do what you taught me. Didn't disturb a thing." He inhales a deep breath. "Someone knows about that Guthrie fellow being in a drum, don't they, Noah," he says.

Noah nods, staring at the barrel.

They clamber out of the jeep and Whitey turns around and races off.

McGraw theorizes that this is the work of their serial predator, using a barrel as did Max Kingston to taunt him. *Killer thinks he's got me over the barrel.* He laughs to himself, *over the barrel.*

"Are you thinking the same thing as me," Holly says.

"As 'I'," McGraw says.

"I thought you weren't correcting me anymore. That you've changed."

"I get that way when I'm in deep thought, sorry."

"It's him, isn't it?" Holly says. "Oh, I mean, it's 'he.'"

He smiles. "It is he, indeed, my good lady."

She bows.

"Need Nora out here. Call it in, stat." He smiles.

"'Stat?' You've been watching too much ER."

Whitey pulls up with Kramer and Gomez. They hop out.

"Nora's on her way," Holly tells McGraw.

The CSI team, dressed in white, are working, snapping pictures and looking for prints, footprints, and tread marks. They work the outside of the barrel but won't open it until the M.E. shows.

Kramer and Gomez know their routine. Walk the property, look for evidence, tire tracks beyond the fence, don't disturb the crime scene until forensics has cleared the way. They'll walk the perimeter, then have Whitey run them to the ranchers nearby.

Dr. Philips and Larry, her assistant, dressed in white garb with long sleeves, arrive. Larry is carrying a black bag as they walk over to the barrel.

Nora turns to McGraw. "Another barrel? Seems your perp knows a lot about you and the Max Kingston case."

McGraw only nods.

Nora looks at the CSI analyst, who tells her he's done working the outside of the barrel. She removes the lid and finds the barrel filled half way with a solution. No body. "Hand me my rubber gloves," she says to Larry. He pulls them out of the black case. She reaches for them and pulls them on up to her elbows.

"What's this?" she says, reaching deep into the barrel, pulling out a large waterproof package.

"Well, open the damn thing," McGraw says with impatience in his voice.

She removes the outer layer of paper. "There's wording on the inner package," Nora says. "A gift for the Marlboro Man."

"Oh my gosh. The perp definitely knows the Kingston case," Holly says.

Nora raises her brow, then turns it over to forensics for prints before opening the brown paper package. Two tongues.

"Human?" McGraw asks.

"They're animal." She grabs one at a time with forceps and examines them before turning them over to forensics.

"Noah?" She hesitates. Probably wondering how he's going to take the news. "Noah? One's a cat's tongue. The other belongs to a dog."

Silence. Everyone is gazing at McGraw.

"This is getting personal," McGraw says walking around the barrel, stops and gazes at it. "The killer…he's telling me, 'screw you, detective, I'm smarter than you'."

He reads Holly's expression. "What is it?" he asks.

"The bastard is mocking us."

McGraw says, "To say the least."

"Writing Marlboro Man on the tape is just like the last guy," Nora says.

McGraw nods. "The perp is challenging me, thinking he's got the upper hand."

"Since there's no body, we need to wrap up and take off." she says.

"Thanks," McGraw says.

Holly says, "And forensics is through. They're removing the barrel."

Back at the precinct, McGraw goes to the evidence board, picks up a black marker and writes: *prep possibly in law enforcement.*

Copying Max Kingston reveals his knowledge of the case that wasn't released to the press. Finding someone in law enforcement would be tough.

———◄►———

Jack Carter has spent much of the morning in his office. He looks up at the clock. By now, McGraw has found the barrel on his property. A feeling of elation comes over Carter as he thinks about how this stunt would upset the great cowboy detective.

Chapter 37

McGraw rises early the next morning after a restless night. Thoughts about the killer and his stunt with the barrel kept his mind active most of the night trying to figure who he could be. *Nothing worse than a dirty cop killing helpless women*, he thinks. He skips breakfast and heads off to work. Holly is at her desk. Kramer and Gomez haven't come in yet.

"Hi, Noah. You look like crap."

"Up most of the night trying to figure out who in the hell is our killer," he says removing his hat and placing it to one side on his desk, away from the aisle, He grabs his cup and heads to the coffee stand.

"I know you too well, Noah. Once you get something in your head, you don't let go until you've solved it."

"This is a tough one." He adds milk to his coffee and sips it as he walks back to the evidence boards.

"Patrol got a call from a lady who hasn't seen her neighbor for two days," Holly says.

Silence.

"Did you hear me?"

"She's probably on vacation. You know how it is. People leave town without telling anyone. Do you tell your neighbors when you leave town? In this day and age, we hardly know who our neighbors are," he says, sipping his coffee.

"No. I don't but patrol questioned the neighbor and interviewed several others who told them that it was unusual for this lady to be gone overnight. What's weird is someone returned her car during the night two days later. They're worried something happened to her."

"It's not our case."

Chapter 38

Jack Carter is running errands around town in Megan's silver Nissan while his white Caddy is being serviced at the dealer. He's motoring along on Peachtree Road heading to Phipps Plaza where he intends to go shopping when suddenly a blue Lexus darts out from a side street. Carter has the right of way and has no stop. He's able to brake enough to prevent major damage, but runs into the back fender on the driver's side. Both vehicles are in the middle of the street. A couple of drivers stop, hop out of their cars to check on him and the lady in the other car. An elderly woman in a purple hat is behind the wheel and is the only occupant. She doesn't appear hurt. Carter really did little damage. His air bags didn't go off, so he's not suffering from burns or bruises. He's okay physically but is pissed, and clambers out and asks the two drivers if they'd help the lady get her car off the road and he'd follow. They agreed.

Carter pulls in next to her and gets out, thanks the men, and heads over to the woman's blue Lexus, with fists in a ball. "Are you okay, lady?" he asks, keeping his voice smooth even though he's steaming and would like to clobber her.

She motions for him to get away from her door, which she pushes open with her shoulder, slamming it against his knee and steps out. "Get the hell out of my way." She begins berating him. "Why weren't you watching where you were going. Bet you were texting on your phone, and you don't have insurance, either."

Carter's anger is shifting into high gear. No one berates him and gets away with it. There are consequences. He inhales to calm himself before speaking. "I had no stop. You had one, and shot out in front of me. You're lucky I wasn't going faster or you could have been killed."

He wanted to tell her how he really felt—that she shouldn't be allowed to drive at her age, and why in hell did they give her a license in the first place, but he didn't want to irritate her further. She'd want to call 9-1-1. No way is he going to exchange personal information with her or the cops. They would take his driver's license and put him in their database. So far there is no record of him in any of the databases. He has to get her off his back.

"We don't want to report this to our insurance companies," Carter says, "they'll raise our premiums." He reaches for his wallet. "How about if I just give you two-hundred dollars. That would more than pay for such minor damage."

She looks over the fender like a used car salesman. He wonders if she is going to kick the tires, too. "Whatta you say, ma'am?"

"I don't know. I think we should report the accident."

"But, ma'am, you're at fault. See that man over there, parked close to door with a coffee in his hand?"

She nods. "I see him."

"Well, he could be a witness and he says he saw everything. That you pulled out in front of me and that he'll tell the police that and even be willing to come to court." Carter studies her. "I don't want that. By the way, what's your name?"

"Bea Kunz, what's yours?"

He extends a hand, "I'm Ed Kramer," he says, taking one of McGraw's detective's name. "Do you live in Atlanta? I noticed this isn't a rental."

"What a stupid question. Of course, I live in Atlanta."

"I thought so. You're a sharp dresser and looker, and I bet you come from money." He's laying it on thick.

"Well, I try to look my best. My husband, bless his soul, has been dead ten years, was an attorney with a big practice back in Tennessee. He had five partners. Tennessee is where I come from."

"I can see that, you have that good ole southern charm. I hope I haven't offended you."

She nods. "I guess you're a nice boy after all."

"Do we have a deal, Ms. Kunz?"

She nods. Reaches for the two one-hundred-dollar bills. "But you better be more careful how you drive. You don't want to put people in the hospital."

"Thank you, Ms. Kunz. I will be careful. I promise."

Carter gets back into the Nissan and waits until she drives off. He writes down her license plate and follows her. His anger has reached its peak. The old bitch is lucky they weren't on a country road. She'd be dead in the woods.

Fifteen minutes later, she pulls up into her driveway. Carter is half a block away, watching. The lady in the purple hat gets out of her car and goes inside.

Jack's seen enough. Back at his hideaway, he opens his laptop and navigates through Noah McGraw's APD system that his hacker arranged for him and runs Bea Kunz. Learns all he needs to know about the woman from Tennessee.

It's time.

Chapter 39

Around eight the next evening, Jack Carter, dressed in dark clothes and cap, leaves his lair with the dissecting kit, slides into the black SUV and heads to the Buckhead district. He hops out of the SUV a block away, moves cautiously through the neighborhood with his leather kit. At the door he sets the kit down, reaches in his pocket and pulls out a tool to pick the lock, then slips in. The woman is in the kitchen. He inches his way up to her and grabs her around the neck and chokes her. His anger flows through his fingers as he squeezes.

"I'm going to cut out that tongue of yours for what you said to me."

But as he's strangling her there's a knock on the door. She faints from the lack of oxygen, he drops her, and rushes to the window. It's Detective Roark. He grabs the old lady's purse and darts out the back to the block behind Bea's house ending up at his SUV. He races off.

Aunt Bea regains consciousness. She hears pounding on the door and a voice that sounds familiar. She staggers to the door. Opens it. It's Holly. "Someone tried to kill me," she tells Holly as she's guided to a recliner.

"Are you okay. Can I get you anything?"

"A glass of water."

"Sure."

After Holly returns from the kitchen and hands the glass to Aunt Bea, she reaches for her cell and calls McGraw.

"Is there anyone you'd like me to call?"

"No, I'll be fine. Just need to sit a little while to catch my breath."

When McGraw arrives, Holly meets him at the door. They sit with Bea. "Tell Lieutenant McGraw what you told me," Holly says.

Aunt Bea says, "As this punk is strangling me, he said he was going to kill me and cut out my tongue. I tried to turn to see what he looked like, but he had a tight grip around my neck."

Holly looks at McGraw with raised brows, and he nods, knowing what she's thinking. *This perp is our killer.* "Do you know of anyone who would want to harm you? McGraw asks.

"Not really."

"I know you said you didn't see him, but is there anything at all you can remember about him?" McGraw asks. "Take your time."

Seconds later she says, "It's not that I didn't see him. I meant that I didn't see his face. I don't know if this would help, but I caught a glimpse of him in the mirror I keep on the rack next to the stove. He was wearing a black wool cap, face mask with holes for eyes and mouth, dark clothes, gloves. He was tall. Kinda had a physique like the man that ran into me."

"Ran into you?" Roark says. "Who ran into you?"

"This jerk hit my car on the driver's side. Dented the back fender a little. He was adamant about not having the police come. The name he gave me was Ed Kramer, and we settled on the spot. He gave me two one-hundred-dollar bills."

McGraw glances at Holly, who raises her brows when the name Ed Kramer comes up.

"Do you have the two-hundred dollars?" McGraw asks.

"It's in my purse over there on the table," she says pointing toward the living room.

"It's not here," Holly says, as she looks at McGraw. "A robbery?"

"No. It's our guy. Didn't want us to find his fingerprints on the bills."

"What did he look like?" Roark asks. "Was he white or black?"

"White. Do you think he could be the one?"

"Don't know," Roark says.

"Would you be able to recognize him again?"

"Without a doubt."

McGraw asks, "Did he speak with an accent?"

"No."

"How was he dressed?"

"Sporty. Nice clothes. He wasn't mad when we parted," she says. "Unless he was putting on an act."

"What kind of car was he driving," Roark asks.

"A silver Nissan. He acted like it was his baby."

"Thank you," McGraw says. "You've been very helpful."

"I hope you catch the bastard."

"We will," he says as he heads to the door, motioning for Roark to step outside with him. Roark doesn't wait for Noah to say anything, instead she says, "I'm worried about her safety. She's in danger now. This guy could come back. She's now a big liability to him."

"I was thinking the same thing. She's become target number one for our guy. I'll call narcotics and have her moved to a hotel for a few days with undercover protection 24/7."

"I like that," Roark says.

"But first we need to get a sketch of the guy that ran into her."

"I'll get her ready," Roark says entering the house.

Kramer and Gomez approach McGraw from canvassing the neighborhood. "Boss, a lady two streets over saw a black SUV parked by the curb in front of her house earlier," Kramer says.

"It left thirty minutes ago," Gomez adds.

"Black SUV? That's no surprise," McGraw says. "Take Aunt Bea to the station and have an artist draw a sketch of the guy that ran into her. Roark is getting her ready. After the sketching, narcs are moving her to a hotel and will guard her 24/7."

"Gotcha, boss," Gomez says.

Chapter 40

That evening, Aunt Bea leaves with the narc detectives and Roark brings the sketch and places it on the board.

McGraw and his team study the face of the man in the drawing. Next to it is the sketch of the man Blake Williams described to the division artist.

"Anything stand out on these two sketches?" McGraw asks.

"They look like the same guy," Kramer says.

"Why the frown?" McGraw says to Roark.

"The guy looks vaguely familiar."

Kramer and Gomez shake their heads.

"Never saw the guy," Kramer says.

"Never, boss," Gomez says.

"Well, we have our man. I mentioned earlier that we wouldn't send the sketch to the newspaper until I was sure Blake Williams' guy was definitely our man. Well, with this sketch from Aunt Bea, I'd say we have our guy." He turns to Holly. "Make some copies and send a sketch to Gary Spenser at the Constitution".

"Gary?"

"Yeah. I owe him one for staying out of our way. I'll get the Capt. to get us help setting up stations to answer the phones. Any word from our trace on the numbers on the barrel?

"Not yet, boss," Gomez says.

McGraw turns back to the evidence boards. "What do we know about our guy that's not up here?" he says more to himself than to his team. He ponders for a few seconds.

"Don't forget the disguises he wears," Holly says.

"Didn't Aunt Bea say the guy that hit her had brown eyes?"

"She did," Holly says.

"Well, our guy has green eyes," McGraw says.

Silence.

"What are you thinking, boss?" Holly says.

"Contact lenses. Criminals have been known to wear eye contacts."

"Smart move on his part," Holly says.

They scan what's on the crime board.

1. Kills elderly women

2. Tongues removed as trophies

3. Drives a black SUV?

4. White male, six-foot, strong.

5. Suspected serial killer.

6. Between thirty and early forties.

7. Psychopathic- without feelings or remorse.

8. Well organized.

9. Kills at night in special gear.

10. Loner.

11. Can be charming and deceiving to kill his vics.

12. Probably does backgrounds on his vics.

13. Educated – degree.

14. Extremely organized.

15. Dysfunctional family.

McGraw picks up a marker and moves in close to the board. "We can add the following."

16. Short black hair with some gray.

17. Thick eyebrows and green eyes.

18. Animal tongues – screw the cops.

19. Interrupted murder attempt on Aunt Bea—witness.

McGraw adds "possible green contact lenses" to number 17. "We have to step up our investigation."

Chapter 41

The night watchman at Pinelawn Cemetery is having coffee at the breakfast table with his wife, reading the Atlanta Journal- Constitution as a downpour belts the windows above the kitchen sink. Bobby Moses tries to concentrate. The APD picture in the article catches his eye. The police are asking if anyone has seen this man in the above picture to call in.

He turns to his wife.

"Hey, hon, I seen this bum here," he says, pointing to the picture in the newspaper as he lays it down in front of her.

Sitting next to him, she holds the paper up close to the light. "Where'd you see him, hon?"

"In the cemetery while on my shift. This guy was at the grave of Congressman Sunday."

"What would he be doing there at that time of night?"

He shrugs. "Beating his hand on the ground and screaming."

"Screaming," she says. "What?"

"I hopped out of the cart and ran to him. I thought he was having some kind of seizure. He was screaming, 'I should have cut your tongue out when I had the chance.' He said it over and over."

"Do you think he had something against the congressman?"

"It seems like it."

"Maybe the congressman did something to him that he couldn't let go and it made him crazy."

Bobby shrugs.

"Why didn't you just call the cops?"

"I thought I could help him but he screamed at me, called me names and told me to get the hell away. Then he hit me and knocked me for a loop. I ran to the cart and shouted back at him that I was calling the cops."

"What'd he do?"

"He took off like a jackal. Raced out of the place in a black SUV."

Bobby drinks some of his coffee.

"Do you think I ought to call the cops at the number in the paper?"

She stares at the sketch for a few minutes. She nods. "You should. He might be a killer."

Bobby Moses reaches for his cell and makes the call. He's told to come through the front entrance to the desk and an officer will take him to the Homicide Bureau to meet with Lieutenant McGraw.

Bobby turns to Helen, "They want me down at the station in an hour. Shit!" He shakes his head. "I don't know. What if the guy finds out I ratted on him? He could find out where we live and—" He stops in mid-sentence. "He...he could hurt you, baby," he says with tears forming in his eyes.

"Oh, honey." She places her hand on top of his. "That won't happen. It's your duty to cooperate with the police. Anyway, how will that guy know? The police won't put your name in the paper."

"You're forgetting those freaken reporters. They have ways. They'd come here to ask questions. Maybe even bring a camera crew." He pauses. "Can't let that happen, Hon. I'm afraid for you."

Helen stands up next to her husband and puts an arm around him. They hug. "You're sweet, baby. But you gotta go. He killed those women. He could kill again. You don't want that, do you?" she says.

"I... I don't know."

"Think about it. He likes older women. I believe I'm safe."

"But this's different." He pauses. "Okay, only if you think I should, then I'll do it." He kisses her. "You're a good person, Helen. Love ya."

They embrace again. "Love you, sweetie."

Bobby Moses leaves the house thirty minutes later, feeling shaky, travels across town to police headquarters. He keeps repeating to himself that Helen thinks he's doing the right thing. He slips out of his car and heads to the entrance. The desk sergeant looks at him.

"You Bobby Moses?"

"Yes, sir. I'm here to see Lieutenant McGrou in Homicide."

The sergeant jumps up, takes him by the arm. "That's McGraw. You better not let him hear you call him anything else. Come along. I'll take you to the lieutenant."

They move down the hall about thirty yards. The desk sergeant is more than a head taller than Moses. He pushes though the doors into the bureau, Kramer meets them.

"This is Mr. Moses to see the lieutenant."

Kramer nods. "Thanks. The boss is expecting him." The sarge nods and leaves.

"Lieutenant," Kramer calls out, "Bobby Moses is here."

The Cowboy Detective stands, sticking out his hand. "Lieutenant McGraw," he says, shaking the little guy's hand. Bobby stares at him as all first-timers do when they meet the cowboy. They're thinking, *a cowboy detective?*

"You're that cowboy detective? Likes in them movies?"

"Thanks for coming in." He takes Moses to interview one. "We're going to meet in here to take your statement."

As they get seated. Sergeant Roark comes in and is introduced. McGraw and Roark face the little guy. Kramer and Gomez sit at the monitors against the wall, observing.

Roark says, "We're going to record this session. Is that okay with you?"

He shrugs. "I guess. Haven't done this before." He pauses long enough to sit up straight and leans in to the table. "Before we talk. I want it said that I don't want no damn newspaper people to know about me. If they find I'm the rat, they'll hunt me and Helen down. I don't want to put my wife in danger. That understood?"

"Certainly. There's no way they'll find out who our source is because the information we get from you will be used only to confirm and apprehend the killer. That's all," McGraw says.

"Then fire away."

Roark turns on the recorder and states the date, time and who is in the room.

"Please start off by telling us how you know the man whose picture is in the Atlanta Constitution," McGraw asks.

"I'm driving around the property in my golf cart when I hear this man screaming."

"What was he screaming?" Roark asks.

"He was kneeling at Congressman Sunday's grave, beating a hand on the ground shouting: 'I should have cut your tongue out when I had a chance.' He said it over and over."

McGraw looks over at Roark before asking Bobby, "Had you seen him there before."

He shakes his head. "No."

"What did you do then?" McGraw asks.

"I hopped out of the cart and ran to him. Asked if I could help. He shouted for me to get the hell away, and socked me, knocking me down. I ran to the cart and shouted I was calling the cops. He took off and raced away in a black SUV."

"How is it you were able to recognize him in the paper?" Roark says.

"He had on a black cap pulled down over his ears, but I saw his face. Just like the one in the Constitution."

McGraw looks at Roark and raises his brow to indicate that this interview is over. She speaks the time the interview ends into the recorder.

"We're done here, Mr. Moses," McGraw says, as they stand. "You've been a great help." he says as he leads him out of the interview room.

"Sure thing, cowboy. Oops, man, I'm sorry. It just slipped out."

McGraw smiles. He likes it.

After Kramer returns from walking Moses to the parking lot, McGraw gathers his team together.

"Okay. Our guy," he says, pointing to the sketch on the board. "Why was he ranting and raving over Congressman Sunday's grave?"

"Maybe he and the congressman hated each other," Kramer says.

"But why? That's the question," McGraw says.

"Then who?"

He turns to Roark. "Do you recall what Moses said our guy was screaming?"

"Yeah. He said he should have cut his tongue out when he had a chance."

"Our guy said about the same thing to Aunt Bea," McGraw says. "I don't believe it was Sunday he was ranting about."

"What are you saying, boss?" Gomez says.

"Our perp had no beef with Sunday. Could someone else be buried with him in that grave?"

"What? Who and how?" Roark asks.

Chapter 42

McGraw has just entered the squad room, sets the Atlanta Constitution on his desk, reaches for his Braves coffee cup, and walks over to the coffee stand. He says nothing while filling his cup. Roark sees McGraw frowning. He goes to the evidence board and removes the composite drawn by the artist from the descriptions of the character given to him by three persons: Blake Williams, the bartender, Bobby Moses, and Aunt Bea. McGraw takes it over to Roark, places it in front of her. "Take a good look at this composite. Whom do you see?"

She lowers her head to stare at the drawing more closely. She looks up shaking her head. "I don't know."

"See any resemblance to Jack Carter?"

She shouts. "O my gosh! You don't mean the director of the forensic lab?"

He nods.

She frowns. "But he's so friendly and helpful. I really like him," she says.

"I know the bureau thinks highly of him, too."

"A man in his position has the means and opportunity but what would be his motive for killing these older women?" she asks.

"His demeanor could fit that of a psychopath," McGraw says.

She shakes her head. "Jack a psychopath? I can't believe it."

"There had to have been a reason he was at Congressman Sunday's grave."

"Jack being at his grave does throw me a little," she says.

"Last night I couldn't get Jack out of my mine," he says. "I researched his family and found his father Nick was a cop killed in line of duty. Guess where he's buried?'

"Don't tell me. Pinelawn?"

"Yep."

"Oh, so that's why he knew about that particular cemetery. But that doesn't tell us why he was at the Congressman's grave."

McGraw says. "What did we conclude from our meeting with the psych doc?"

"You mean your hypothetical psychopath?"

He nods. "Maybe not so hypothetical now."

"I remember your summary," she says. "Let's see if I can repeat it. Looking up at the ceiling, she says, "The perp develops a code from the way his mother treats him, and the tongue removal is due to the image of her flapping tongue when she berates him. He sees that image over-and-over in his mind or in his dreams.''

"Excellent," McGraw says. "You have a good memory."

"Well," she says with some theatrics, raising her shoulders and cocking her head to one side, "Thanks for the compliment. It's not often the boss gives out praise."

He smiles. "Only when deserved."

They laugh.

"Jack killed someone close to him is the only logical explanation."

"All the other vics were found inside their homes," she says.

"Then who would be the likely person Jack would bury in the Congressman's grave?" he asks. "If his mother berated him when he was a youngster, wouldn't she be the likely candidate?"

She shrugs. "I guess. But I find it hard to believe," Roark says.

"Not one-hundred percent," McGraw says, "but pretty close."

McGraw places the sketch on the white board. "For now, Jack Carter is a person of interest."

"Jack Carter?" Gomez says, frowning as he comes into the pit.

Kramer is with him. "You gotta be kidding. Not the director of forensics?"

"Yes. Just hear me out. Here's what we have. Jack's father, Nick Carter, was buried in Pinelawn years ago. Nick was a cop killed in the line of duty. That means, Carter knows the cemetery and there's a reason he was there."

"He could have killed his mother and buried her in the cemetery."

"That's all speculation," Gomez says. "How could he dig a hole and drop her in it? That caretaker would have seen him or seen a fresh pile of dirt."

McGraw doesn't say a word.

Roark turns to him. "I know that look of yours, boss," she says. "Tell them."

"Would he need to dig a fresh grave?" McGraw says. "How about burying her under someone?" McGraw says.

Kramer says. "Just a minute. To open a grave, pull out the casket, dig a hole deep enough to drop her in, and then drop the casket back on top of her would require more than one person."

"Certainly not a one-man job," Gomez adds.

McGraw says, "Okay, how about this. A grave had to be opened the day before burial. The caretaker wouldn't think anything of an open grave, that's why he never mentioned it. Carter could have read the obit on Congressman Sunday in the Constitution, then went to the cemetery to search for the open hole. Carter then took his mother to the spot, where he dug enough at the bottom of the open grave to put her in, and covered her up—"

"—and," Holly interrupts, "the next day, the casket of the person to be interred is lowered on top of her."

"Boss, that's brilliant," Gomez says.

Kramer and Roark glance at the Mexican.

"What?" Gomez says, raising his hands, palms out. "It is."

Kramer rubs his index finger against his nose to signify Gomez is brown-nosing the boss.

"Don't be too hard on him," McGraw says, "even though he's right."

Gomez shrugs and smiles at his colleagues.

They laugh.

He turns to Roark. "Call the Evans home. Find out who answers. I bet it won't be Laura Evans. I'll assign a couple of detectives to take shifts surveilling the home."

He heads to the Capt.'s office. "Gotta brief the chief."

Chapter 43

The Chief of Detectives' door is open. Dipple is scanning through a file on his desk. He looks up. "Paperwork."

"I know what you mean, Capt."

"What's up, cowboy?"

"Got a problem."

He points to a chair. "Have a seat. Let's hear it."

McGraw chooses the chair facing his boss. "I'm afraid we have someone in our system that is a person of interest in the tongue collector case."

Dipple almost rises up in his chair. "One of our own?"

"No."

"Then who in the hell is it?"

"Jack Carter."

The Capt.'s frown is so tight, his eyes almost shut. "Jack Carter?" he says with emphasis.

"Yep."

"How in the hell—?"

"—We have witnesses, and a sketch that you are familiar with."

"Has anyone actually identified the person in the sketch," the chief says.

"Three people. The bartender at Jimmy's, Bobby Moses, the caretaker at Pinelawn Cemetery who had that confrontation with whom we know is Jack, and you remember that lady who calls herself Aunt Bea?"

"The one with the purple hat."

"That's the one. She said when her attacker had a strong hold on her neck, he said he was going to 'kill her and cut out her tongue'. From his voice, she tied him to the guy that ran into her with his car earlier that day."

Silence while the Chief stares at McGraw.

"Chief, the FBI report fits our perp—*he has special forensic training.* Jack has that."

"What was Jack doing in Pinelawn?"

"We have proof that Jack's father, Nick Carter. is buried in there."

"I remember him," the chief says, "I was at his funeral years ago with many on the force. Where are you going with this?"

"I believe the only reason Jack was in Pinelawn was to bury his mother in there."

Silence. The Capt. stared hard at McGraw, again. "You're saying Jack killed his own mother and buried her there? How is that possible?"

"The caretaker didn't see any disturbed graves, so that means he buried her in an open grave of the person who was to be buried in it the next day."

"The Chief's eyes widened. "You believe someone is buried on top of her?"

"I do. We are trying to find out who that person is." McGraw believes it's Congressman Sunday, since Jack was beating and ranting over his grave, but McGraw feels it isn't time to bring it up with the chief just yet.

"Have you tried to locate Jack's mother?"

"We're on it. I have detectives watching the house."

"Cowboy, we have to be very careful with this. Can't put Jack on administrative leave as a person of interest without more evidence. You'll need more to get a warrant to check the Evans property." He pauses. "Listen. I'm friends with Jack's boss, Deputy Chief Sturgeon. We don't want to jump the gun and set him off. Let's see what you come up with on Laura Evans and in your Pinelawn investigation."

McGraw rises. "Will do, Chief."

Chapter 44

Megan has just gotten out of her car carrying two small bags of groceries. On the way into the house, she picks up the Atlanta Journal- Constitution from the lawn. She walks into the kitchen, sets the bags on the counter by the fridge and throws the newspaper on the table. It flies open. While putting the groceries away, she notices the picture on the front page. She reaches for the paper and looks at the sketch of a man. Atlanta PD is asking the public to call the special number under the picture if they know or have seen this man.

OMG. The guy looks like Jack, and he's wearing a hunting cap just like his.

Megan pulls her cell from her pocket and calls him at the lab.

"Jack, have you seen the morning Constitution?"

"Haven't had a chance. We're pretty busy."

"Well, on the front page is a picture of a man dressed in a hunting cap, sorta like the one you wear. His face is so much like yours. The article says the cops are asking for help from the public, to call in if they've seen this guy."

She sighs.

She's praying Jack's not the guy. Lately she's been bothered by the strange things that have happened since she moved in with him. He disappears often, but doesn't think she knows.

"Jack, you got to be honest with me. Are you involved in anything?"

"Of course not. We have to talk, but not now. Tonight."

"They say this man has killed elderly women."

He doesn't answer. His phone goes dead.

"Jack?" Megan flips off but isn't convinced. She heads out to the garage. *Jack comes back here, but where*? She never asked him where he disappears to. She figures it may be a workshop that men like to tinker in. Inside the garage, she finds nothing. Outside, she looks around for an entrance to the building next to the garage. No windows. *Strange*, she thinks. *This could be his secret hiding place.*

Anxiety overcomes her, thinking about what she might find inside, if there's a way in. Instead, she heads back into the kitchen, makes a cup of tea. Leaning against the counter, sipping it, she thinks about how Jack's been so interested in the crime scene evidence she and her forensics crew have brought into the lab the last few months.

Was he looking for something? Why didn't he distribute reports of our findings like in the past?

She's known from the beginning of their relationship that he was narcissistic, exhibited an inflated sense of his own importance, but she enjoyed doting on him. He sought her praise and attention like an addict seeking a fix.

She turns around to set her cup in the sink when she notices two men in a black car across the street.

They're cops?

The landline phone rings in the kitchen. She goes over to the wall phone and answers it.

"The Evan's residence," Meagan says.

"Laura Evans isn't here," she says. "Who is asking, please? Detective Roark? Oh, hi, detective. Remember me, Megan Turner from forensics? I'm doing ok, thank you. How about you? No, Laura Evans is still in Charlotte taking care of a sick relative. Is there a problem, Detective Roark?" She pauses, staring out the window. *They know something.* "No, I don't have a number for her, but I can get it for you when Jack comes home. I can call you back. Yes, Jack Carter, her son." She writes on a pad by the landline phone the detective's number.

———•••———

Sitting in the passenger seat of an unmarked black car outside Laura Evans home are two detectives assigned by McGraw.

"Hey, lieutenant, it's getting dark and all we have on the Evans' home is a Silver Nissan parked in the drive, and a gal in her thirties walking back and forth by the kitchen window, putting groceries away, and staring at us from time-to-time."

"Hold up, lieutenant," the detective behind the wheel says. "A white caddy has just pulled into the drive. A tall, well-built guy just stepped out and is going into the house."

"Stay put."

Chapter 45

Megan, at the kitchen sink draining water off cooked pasta, glances at the car across the street. Jack slips into the house.

"Hey, Megan," Jack says in a friendly tone, like nothing is wrong. He removes his coat and hangs it in the mud room. "What's got you so upset? That guy in the paper?"

"Partly. That black car across the street has two cops in it. Why are they watching this house?"

"I saw them when I pulled in. I don't know why they're there."

"I'm no dummy, Jack. Something's going on here, or they wouldn't be sitting out there watching us."

He goes to the wall and dims the light, then edges his way over to the sink next to her to peer out the window so as not to be seen. "How do you know they're cops"

"Who else would be watching the house?"

"Burglars. Watching our comings and goings. Have you seen this car before?"

She shakes her head without saying a word but continues staring out the window, wanting the cops to know that she's aware they're there.

"See, they're pulling away. There's nothing to worry about. If they were cops, they'd come knocking."

"Not really. They're shrewd. They want us to know that they're keeping an eye on us. It must be about that picture in the paper. You have to admit, that guy looks like you."

"Can't be me. Why do you keep insisting it is?"

"You're trying awful hard to convince me you aren't the guy, and that you aren't involved in anything."

Jack knows he can't fool me, she thinks. *I know him too well to fall for his bullshit.*

"You can't really believe I'm that person in the article?" he says. "He kills old women. You think I'd do such a thing?"

She shrugs. "You've been acting pretty weird lately. I barely know you anymore."

"How can you say that?" He moves in closer and puts his arms around her. "I'm more than fond of you. I'm falling in love with you."

"For real?" She goes limp in his arms, looking up into his eyes. "But things seem different since I moved in here."

"What do you mean?"

"You disappearing at night when you think I'm sleeping."

"I told you I'm working on a case to help a friend. I didn't want to wake you."

"Who's the friend? You won't tell me about him or what you two do."

"Baby, it's part of the deal. He wants to remain anonymous, and I honor that. He pays me under the table."

"And what about those times you slip out at night and go to the garage. You're in there for hours. Then there's your mother. I got a call from Detective Roark this morning asking to talk to Laura Evans."

Fear fills Jack's face. "What did you tell her?"

"What you told me. Laura's in Charlotte taking care of a sick relative."

"And that's the truth."

"They must have gotten inquiries about your mother? Detective Roark wants me to call in the number where your mother can be reached. Maybe that real estate women, Sally Crain, went to them."

"I doubt that. The last time I talked with Sally, she was okay with what I told her."

"And what was that?"

He sighed. "I guess I better level with you."

"The truth would be helpful."

"Mom is in Charlotte but isn't looking after a sick relative. She's in alcohol rehab and didn't want people to know. So now you have our secret."

"I'm sorry for her. But you could have confided in me earlier."

"I know. I guess I just wasn't thinking."

"But there's something else."

"What?"

"Why have you taken such an interest in all the evidence coming into our lab from those crime scenes involving elderly women without tongues?"

"Oh, that. Those are Lieutenant McGraw's crime scenes. He's one of the best detectives in Atlanta and I take a special interest in his cases to provide him the best analyses. Giving him special attention helps me with the Capt. and the mayor. You've become aware of it since you were promoted to my assistant."

"That's true, but lately we never see our reports you send to Homicide. Are you deliberately keeping them from us?"

"Of course not. I'll be happy to show you all the reports tomorrow."

"McGraw wants the phone number to your mother."

"No problem. I'll go visit with Lieutenant McGraw in the morning. I need to talk to him anyway. I promise I'll straightened everything out. Then I'll call you. How does that sound?"

She shrugs. "Okay, I guess."

He walks into the kitchen and glances out the window. The cops have left for now. *I have a brilliant plan. They'll never find me.*

"Good. Now let's have a glass of wine and fix a relaxing meal."

Chapter 46

Holly looks out from behind her monitor.

"Noah?" she calls out. "Megan Turner from the forensic lab answered the phone at the Evans home."

"And."

"And she said Laura Evans is in Charlotte taking care of a sick relative. She didn't have a phone number but Jack did and he's coming to talk with you, she says."

"Don't believe it," he says. "Laura's in the cemetery. Anything on the barrel?"

"The numbers were registered to the Eastern Chemical Company in New York, which is now defunct."

"Jack must have retrieved it from some river bank," McGraw says. "I'm sure of that."

"Yep. Polluted river banks."

McGraw walks over to the two evidence boards, picks up a marker.

"Let's assume Carter killed his mother and she's in Pinelawn."

He adds the following items on the board.

1. Carter's confrontation with caretaker at congressman's grave.

2. Races out in a black SUV.

3. Kills mother. Chooses Pinelawn where father is.

4. Mother under Congressman Sunday.

Holly says, "Witnesses saw the black SUV in the neighborhood of each tongue victims and Moses saw it race out of the cemetery. It's all tying together. We need to find that SUV. Still no word from Megan about the phone number to Charlotte. She can't get hold of Jack."

"There's probable cause and circumstantial evidence linking Jack to the alleged crimes with our three witnesses."

"Bobby Moses is our strongest witness, since he caught Jack at the grave," Holly says. "Chances are Jack never even met the congressman. So why was he at the gravesite?"

"Because he buried his mother there?" McGraw says.

"Exactly."

Chapter 47

The phone vibrates on McGraw's desk. He picks up. "Lieutenant McGraw."

"Lieutenant, this is Cotton Hargrove, the manager of Pinelawn. I have verification of the information you requested."

"Thank you, Mr. Hargrove."

"Cotton, please. The person interred that you've probably figured out is Congressman John Dell Sunday."

"Yes, thank you, Cotton. Bobby Moses told us about his confrontation with our suspect at the congressman's grave. We saw on your list the congressman was the last to be buried. I'd appreciate another favor."

"Certainly."

"I'd like the names of his living relatives and their addresses."

"Do you know who John Dell Sunday was, lieutenant?"

"I know that name from what Bobby Moses told us about the incident at Mr. Sunday's grave. Other than that, I never knew the gentleman."

"Former member of the House of Representatives from Georgia's 9th Congressional District."

"You're trying to tell me something?"

"Yes, sir, I am. It may be difficult to get the Sunday family to open his grave, if that's your intent."

"Why is that?"

"The Sundays had the ground consecrated to respect their loved one, and they don't believe in having it disturbed after interment."

"On religious grounds?"

"Don't believe so, but I don't know. We have families now and then that have ceremonies to consecrate the ground before and after the burial."

"Is Mrs. Sunday still living?"

"Yes."

"Any children or other members of the family?"

"Only a brother. The Sundays didn't have children."

"Could you email me all the information you have on them?"

"Sure thing, lieutenant."

McGraw gives him his email address.

Cotton hesitates for a few seconds. "I can tell you this. In my dealings with the brother, William Sunday, an attorney, he can be tough. But Mrs. Sunday is as sweet as they come."

Cotton doesn't know McGraw doesn't need the family's permission since this is a murder investigation. It's up to the court.

"Thanks for the heads up, Cotton. I look forward to getting that email."

McGraw hangs up the phone. Looks over at Laura Evan's picture on the board. Ponders over what to expect from the Sunday family when he tells them he has to have John Sunday's casket lifted off Ms. Evans.

Mrs. Sunday could be more reasonable than her attorney brother-in-law. Got to talk to the Capt.

McGraw has Holly prepare a petition for a court order to exhume Mr. Sunday's casket and remove the body of Laura Evans, and make an appointment with the Sundays for two p.m. The State of Georgia regulates exhumation and requires:

1. Petition to exhume.

2. Must have a valid reason.

3. List place of burial and date.

4. List of names of heirs and places of residences.

5. Decision to exhume is left up to the decision of the court.

McGraw steps over to Dipple's office. The door is closed. He knocks and enters. "Capt., we need to talk."

He waves McGraw in. Noah sits facing him.

McGraw explains in detail his theory about Laura Evans being buried below the casket of John Dell Sunday, and whose family, who he names, would probably resist opening the grave to exhume Laura Evan's body from underneath Sunday's casket.

"Of course, the family may resist, Cowboy, but since this is a murder investigation, we don't need their permission."

McGraw's has never been able to determine from Dipple's tone if he calls him 'Cowboy' out of respect or if it is a condescending gesture.

"Capt., I'm told the Sunday family is a powerful force in this community. They may put up a fight, especially the brother of the deceased, William Sunday."

Capt. rubs his chin for a few moments. "I know William," he says. "Guess you didn't know I play golf with him."

McGraw could feel his brow rise again in surprise. He never thought Dipple ever got involved with politicians. But now he knows. "So, what is your opinion of William? Could he be approachable and reasonable if we explain that we'd only lift John's casket out and not disturb it, and that we're only after the body under it?"

"Reasonable is the key word. William could be if you approach him with respect. He has to feel he has the upper hand. Go prepared and be very clear about what you want."

"Since the ground was consecrated, I'm hoping the Sunday family wouldn't want a body buried underneath their loved one," McGraw says. "I will have clergy there to show respect. It should seem sacrilegious to them with his body on top of one that's not even in a casket, rotting away."

"That's the right approach to take with William."

McGraw rises. "Thanks, sir. You've been a big help."

"Anytime, Cowboy."

———◆◆———

McGraw directs the big monster Silverado to the curb at the bottom of the drive that circles up to the majestic home located in the Buckhead district. The area is lush with magnolias, dogwoods, Southern pines, and magnificent oaks. A canopy of woods spreads from the city skyline into the Buckhead district. Sunday's mansion is on an incline surrounded by a manicured lawn, tall evergreens, and a large oak tree. Entrance to the home has a canopy extending out towards the grounds.

Roark, in the passenger seat, sits in silence for a few minutes. McGraw looks at his watch. Almost two. The detectives seem to be spellbound by the beauty of the place.

Finally, Roark says, "Breathtaking. I wonder what Silvia and William Sunday are like?"

"We're about to find out," McGraw says as he rolls up the drive and stops behind a black Mercedes parked next to a white caddy under the canopy. McGraw adjusts his Stetson before they step out. He takes the lead as they walk up five steps that widen across the front. He taps the door several times with the ornate knocker. Moments later, a maid dressed in a black and white uniform and head band opens the door. There it is again: that look of surprise when first-timers see McGraw's Stetson and his cowboy outfit. She stares a few seconds at his boots.

"I'm Detective McGraw and this is my partner, Detective Roark. We're here to see Mrs. Sunday."

She nods. "Detectives. She is expecting you. Please. Step in. May I take you hat, sir?"

McGraw removes his Stetson and hands it to her. She closes the door. They step into an atrium. She turns, asks them to follow her. The first floor is spacious. Everything is white: the walls, the drapes, the furniture. The open space has a checkerboard marble floor, black and white squares. Two huge staircases with red carpet become visible, one on the left and another on the right, both rising and meeting on an open second floor. Like the first floor, all is white and visible—furniture, windows, drapes, flowers, except for the antiques. Antiques are numerous on both floors and McGraw dodges them as the maid leads them to another open area to the left.

Don't they have walls in this place? he thinks.

Two persons are in what could be called a room without walls. The lady is seated on a white couch and the tall man, dressed in a black suit and red tie is standing by the fireplace. A gold-framed mirror is above it. The maid leads them in and announces: "Detectives McGraw and Roark are here, Mrs. Sunday."

"Thank you, Maria." She stands. "I'm Sylvia Sunday and that tall gentleman over there is my brother-in-law, William Sunday."

William has a strong narrow face with a dark mustache and hair to match. Oddly enough, he reminds McGraw of Walter Pidgeon, the actor, famous in films from the 20's through the 70's. McGraw loves movies of that era. Influenced by his mother.

William comes forward, stone-faced, extends a hand to them, and breaks a smile. His dark eyes are like drill bits looking where to drill holes into McGraw. William releases Noah's hand and returns to his place in front of the fireplace. A tray with pots of tea, coffee, and milk in the center, cups surrounding the pots, rests on a large glass coffee table framed in black metal. A plate of delicate white cookies and white cloth napkins are on the table.

Mrs. Sunday introduces herself as Sylvia, likes to be called by her first name, she says. She tells them to please sit. Both McGraw and Roark choose the other white coach that is at right angles to the one Sylvia is sitting on. Two large, white overstuffed cloth chairs face them at the edge of a thick white rug.

"Thank you for seeing us, Mrs. Sunday," McGraw says as he sits. He doesn't feel comfortable calling her by her first name. She's a tall, stately woman dressed in an ivory gown, moves so gracefully that McGraw feels the respect she richly deserves. Her smile warms his heart and her green eyes are inviting. He seems drawn to her.

She could be another Greer Garson, he thinks. *Not many of her caliber in the movies anymore.*

"Oh, please. Sylvia. Mrs. Sunday sounds so formal. Wouldn't you say, William." She looks over at him. "Yes, my dear."

"Yes, Sylvia. Of course. We'll get to the point," McGraw says.

"Please," William says.

Sylvia says, "You didn't say on the phone what this is about."

"It's about your husband's burial."

"What about my brother's burial," he says, moving next to his sister-in-law.

"You had no way of knowing this, but Congressman Sunday was buried in a grave with a body underneath his casket." McGraw waits a few moments before uttering another word, to allow the gravity of his statement to take effect. Sylvia looks stunned.

"You mean there's another casket under my husband," she says.

"That can't be," William Sunday says. "We had a ceremony in which the grave was blessed. We would have known if another casket was in the grave."

"There's no casket," Roark says.

"No casket?" he says. The tightness in his jaw is visible.

A hand flies up to cover Sylvia's mouth. "You mean just a body?"

"The person buried under your husband is the mother of our perpetrator," Roark says.

"You mean someone killed his own mother?" Sylvia says.

"Yes, Sylvia," McGraw says, "and she is naked under Congressman Sunday's casket."

Sylvia jumps up. "Oh, my," she says, ambling around the coffee table to the fireplace, where she stands with her back to them, head down, bracing herself with both hands on the mantel. William makes his way over to console her.

It becomes obvious that she's sincerely upset, but the truth has to be told. Jack Carter is responsible, not the detectives.

Sylvia turns around. "What upsets me is that a son would kill his own mother and bury her in such a manner. How could he?"

If she only knew how serial killers think and act, she'd understand. "He feels no remorse, mother or not," McGraw says.

William turns to the detectives. "I assume you're here to tell us about your plan to exhume John's casket. Correct?"

"Yes, sir. This is a murder investigation and as you know, we don't need permission to exhume the Congressman's body. It's up to the court. We're here as a courtesy and out of respect for the Congressman to tell you of our plan. We believe you wouldn't want a naked, decaying body in a sacred grave."

"I see," William says.

"Clergy of your choosing would be present. The M.E. would not open Congressman Sunday's casket. It would be set aside until the female body underneath is removed."

"Would you excuse us, please," Sylvia says. "We'll be back in a few minutes," she says wiping her eyes with a tissue. They leave the area and disappear across the way. Maria comes in and goes to the coffee table.

"Would you like coffee or tea?"

"Coffee, please, black," Roark says.

"Same for me, Maria," McGraw says.

She looks up at him and smiles. "We also have other refreshments."

Alcohol is prohibited while on duty. "Coffee will be fine," McGraw says.

Maria removes the platter of cookies and carries it over to Roark and then McGraw. They take one with a napkin.

"We also have fruit if you'd like," she says.

"This's enough. Thank you," Roark says.

McGraw nods in agreement as he bites into his cookie, which melts in his mouth, and takes a swallow of his coffee.

"Please make yourself comfortable. Mrs. Sunday and Mr. William Sunday will be returning shortly," she says, smiling, then departs.

Roark finishes her coffee and sets the saucer and cup on the table. "Do you think they're scheming to resist the exhumation, Noah?"

"I'm counting on Sylvia not wanting a decaying body under her husband. But we'll see what influence William has on her."

Fifteen minutes later, the two return. Sylvia is in the lead, moves gracefully to the couch and waits until William joins her. This time he sits next to her. Sylvia's eyes are red but she seems to have regained her composure. William keeps his eyes fixed on his sister-in-law, who is holding a wrinkled handkerchief in her hands, resting on her lap. Apparently, she has an announcement.

"We have discussed the matter at hand and have decided—"

"—Decided that we will not interfere having my brother's casket exhumed, but we request that there be no news people and no photographs. We want our clergy present, and that we will be present during the exhumation."

Maria comes into the area.

McGraw glances over at Roark. She raises her brows a couple of times to signify it's his call. They never allow families at the crime scenes of loved ones, but removing a casket is different and how much trouble could William cause if he approves of the process beforehand?

"I think your conditions can be met, but I'll have to run it by my Chief first and get back with you."

"Certainly."

They stand.

Sylvia holds up a hand to stop them for a moment.

"Detectives," she says but hesitates, looks down for a few seconds, then glances up. Innocent eyes. "A son killing his own mother, burying her like a piece of diseased meat is too dreadful for me to contemplate." She wipes her eyes. "We believe that the mother deserves a decent burial and we will cover all expenses when the time comes, Lieutenant McGraw."

"Yes, ma'am."

Chapter 48

The wind has slowed and the sun breaks through the clouds, which should make it easier on the Pinelawn Cemetery workers, digging Congressman John Dell Sunday's grave for the exhumation of his casket. Thirty yards away at the edge of the blacktop road that circles the northern portion of the cemetery, the hoisting crew have been waiting since seven-thirty, parked until it's time for them to lift the vault containing the casket of Congressman Sunday from his grave.

The cemetery workers drive a John Deere backhoe in front of the crew, up a path between the graves to the Sunday gravesite. The Environmental Health Officer, Funeral Director, and Mr. Cotton Hargrove, the manager of the Pinelawn Cemetery, and a clergyman are waiting for the detectives and Sunday family to arrive. Minutes later they all pull up in front of the hoisting crew and roll out of their cars.

Once all are in place, Mr. Hargrove turns to William Sunday and asks, "May we begin?"

"Yes, indeed."

Hargrove instructs the workers to begin digging the earth away from the huge marble headstone.

Nora Philips and Larry arrive with a couple of lab assistants. Nora greets and stands next to McGraw, Roark, and a couple of Georgia State Police forensic techs as they watch the digging. The grave is opened and Hargrove instructs the backhoe driver to back away. Two workers with shovels hop into the hole and begin digging the dirt away from the vault and around it as much as they can. When one worker calls out that they're done and ready for the hoist crew, everyone moved to the edge of the grave to gawk inside. Nothing but the top of a gray concrete vault.

William Sunday looks over at Hargrove. "How are you going to lift it out?"

"The hoisting crew will put heavy straps through the handles on the sides of the vault to lift it out. Then they will set it on the ground next to the grave."

"Could those straps break?" William says.

The funeral director says. "Mr. Sunday. I can guarantee that those straps can bear the weight to raise your brother's vault out without a hitch."

William grunts. "Okay, do it."

The Funeral Director waves the hoist team to come forward with their crane. Workers in the grave hook up the vault. One of the workers shouts, "We're ready."

The cranking starts at low speed. The straps become taut. The operator stops. "We're ready to remove the vault, sir," he says to Hargrove, who turns to William.

He nods.

"Be careful, crane operator," McGraw says.

Inch-by-inch the vault containing the casket of John Dell Sunday rises out of its resting place and is set to one side of the open grave. Workers unscrew the locks and it takes several men to slid the heavy top to the ground. The noonday sun reflects off the top of the copper box that's still in beautiful condition.

William Sunday says. "Good. They can replace the top now."

"We're through until Detective McGraw finishes," Hargrove says.

The Sundays step back.

McGraw nods to Nora "How much of her will be left?" he asks.

"Probably much since the body hasn't been in the ground too long. Some bacteria will have done some damage since the body has not been preserved. Also, the water table can encourage bacterial growth."

She and Larry move to the grave with flashlights. They slip into the hole and step to the sides so as not to step on the body. McGraw lowers their black case. The M.E.'s personnel above shine more lights into the hole.

"She shouldn't be too deep," Larry says. "I guess the vault didn't crush the body."

"I don't think so. They had these concrete barriers poured around the sides to hold the weight of the vault. The body is low enough that the vault wouldn't touch it."

"Yeah, I see that now, doc."

"Let's trowel and brush first to see how deep she is." They smooth away the dirt inch-by-inch. A head begins to appear. Minutes later hands are uncovered and the body is exposed wrapped in the remnants of a thin dress.

"We have a body, McGraw," Nora shouts from the hole.

"What's the condition of the body," McGraw asks, looking down into the hole.

"Not too bad. Some decomp but pretty dirty right now."

She opens the mouth. "We have a tongue, McGraw."

McGraw knew that would be the case; otherwise, why would Carter go to the grave and scream that he should have taken her tongue when he had the chance.

"What do you need to get her out?" he says.

"Tell my lab guys to get the body basket and a couple of sterile sheets from the van."

"We'll get it," one of them says. When they return, he says, "We're lowering the basket now, doc."

The covered body was hauled up to the top.

"Doc? What about these tools?" Larry says.

"McGraw will have the state police techs take pictures and treat them as evidence."

"Haul us up!" Nora shouts.

"Will IDing the body be difficult?" Holly asks.

"Don't know yet," Nora says, brushing the dirt from her clothes. "Some disfiguration of the face, but we'll get her in and let you know."

Chapter 49

How many times has Noah McGraw been to the morgue? More times than he can count on his fingers and toes. Each time he enters this cold, sterile room filled with steel tables and covered bodies lined up for autopsy, he thinks about the victims and their families.

Their pain.

Their loss.

Losing a loved-one is bad enough, but having a member of the family brutally murdered devastates the family even more. This also has an effect on detectives working the scenes. Some citizens may forget that detectives are human, too. Over time they learn to cope with the family's pain by not dwelling on the case, but visions do resurface.

Noah McGraw and Holly Roark enter. Nora Philips is standing over the body taken from Congressman Sunday's grave. A couple of technicians are working on a body across the way. Nora has pulled the overhead light down close to the partially decayed face. She regards the two detectives carefully, who move to the opposite side of the table. The blonde M.E. tries to move autopsies on McGraw's victims in front of others whenever she can.

"We've washed the body and x-rayed her. No broken bones and no blunt-force trauma. No defensive wounds but there's bruising around the neck to indicate she had been strangled. As you can see, the poor thing has some decay on the face and no teeth," she says. "The victim is a woman in her early sixties." Nora lifts up one arm to show them the hand. "No fingers."

Holly stares at the face. She turns to McGraw. "This has to be Laura Evans."

McGraw also has been staring at the body.

Nora says, "Normally we'd I.D. the vic through fingerprints and dental records, but, again, the poor thing has no teeth. So, that's out. We'll have to rely on her DNA."

"Do whatever it takes. We have to be positive that this is Laura Evans," he says. "You know how attorneys can rip us one in court without definitive proof."

She nods. "How well I know it."

Holly has a cagy look.

Nora squints at her. "What are you not telling me?"

"We believe this is Jack Carter's mother."

"What?! The guy in the Crime Lab?"

"Yep, afraid so," McGraw says.

"Jack is your Tongue Collector? You can't be serious."

He nods. "No proof yet. But yes. DNA could tie Laura Evans to him. We may be able to get his DNA."

Nora looks at McGraw. "That would only mean she's his mother. Wouldn't prove he killed her and put her in the grave."

"Wait a minute," Holly says. "We have a witness that saw Jack at the grave screaming and taking off in a black SUV that's been at all the crime scenes."

"Unfortunately, the witness didn't see Jack dump his mother's body into an opened grave," McGraw says.

"Well, there you have it. All circumstantial," Nora says.

"I don't care," Holly says. "No jury would fall for Jack beating and screaming at the congressman's grave because he hated the congressman. How did he know there was a body under him? Because he put it there! That's my case."

McGraw and Nora look at each other and smile. McGraw turns to his partner. "What passion. I like it. Now that we think we have Laura's body; I'll get a warrant from Judge Virtue to search the Evan's home and grounds."

She nods. "I'm confident there's proof there that Jack is the Tongue Collector. I just know it. The black SUV and God knows what else we'd find out from Megan Turner, Jack's live-in. Remember, she's one of his forensic criminalists."

"Excuse my cliché, McGraw, but aren't you treading on thin ice?" Nora says. "I don't think her DNA will prove anything."

"Hell no! Jack is not going to get away with this!" Holly says.

"Well, it wouldn't hurt to have some of Ms. Evan's things when you go into the home," doc says.

"Can do," Roark says as she inhales a deep breath.

Chapter 50

Noah McGraw walks through the dimly lighted dark wood halls of the courthouse to Judge Virtue's chambers. A gold plate with the judge's name is on the door. McGraw knocks.

A muffled, "Enter," is called from inside.

McGraw opens the heavy door and steps in, closing it behind him. The judge is wiping his mouth with a white napkin and takes a sip of coffee before looking up. Apparently, a catered lunch still on a tray.

Judge Virtue is in his mid-sixties, medium built with a full head of gray hair and a handsome narrow face with a neatly trimmed gray goatee. McGraw has heard that Virtue is a swimmer and goes daily to lap swim. His pleasant face has a smile when he sees Noah. McGraw likes the judge. Thinks he's one of the best.

"The famous Cowboy Detective, Noah McGraw," he says, still smiling.

McGraw tips his Stetson and says, "Judge."

"To what do I owe this honor, lieutenant?" The judge is quite the joker, and Noah feels at ease. "Don't tell me. I know. That's a warrant in your hand."

The room is spacious, filled with mahogany furniture and the judge's desk makes two of normal size desks. Virtue has a stack of files in front of him that are probably cases that will be appearing before his court.

McGraw moves in to the only leather chair that faces Virtue but doesn't sit. "Yes sir," he says, handing the paperwork to him.

The judge begins flipping through the pages. A warrant must contain several items: must show probable cause; a crime has occurred or is about to occur—adding witnesses statements help—an affirmation to the truth of the matter supporting probable cause; specifically describes the places to be searched; and persons or things to be searched.

The judge looks up. "This is for the home and everything on the property of Laura Evans. Who might she be?"

"The mother of our perp, sir."

"He's the serial killer I've been reading about?"

"Yes, your honor. He killed his mother and buried her in the open grave of John Dell Sunday. Not much left of her, sir."

"Oh, yes," he says, pushing back into his high back leather chair. "I remember approving the exhumation of the Congressman's casket."

Noah nods. "Thank you, judge, for that."

Virtue looks down at the page in front of him. "And this Megan Turner?"

"She's the perp's live-in at the Evan's home."

"And Jack Carter?"

McGraw looks into the eyes of Judge Virtue. "He's our serial, judge."

Judge Virtue signs the warrant and hands it to McGraw. He's about to say something, but hesitates.

"Yes, your honor."

"Catch the bastard."

McGraw tips his hat. "Will do, sir."

When McGraw gets to his car, he calls the detectives watching the Evan's home. Anything unusual?"

"Nothing, lieutenant."

"Have the night shift stay put, we're going in tomorrow morning early."

Chapter 51

This cold morning a swarm of patrol cars and unmarked black detective units surround the Evan's home. McGraw and Roark bail out of the Silverado.

"When I pulled our surveillance guys, they said Jack wasn't in the house."

"He's probably in the wind," Holly says. "What about aunt Bea?"

"She'll remain under covered until we get Jack."

⎯⎯⎯●❦●⎯⎯⎯

Scared out of her wits, Megan runs from the kitchen to the den for her purse, grabs her cell and calls Jack. Seconds later he answers.

"Where in the hell are you?" she asks.

"Where else. At work. Where did you think I was?"

"Cops have surrounded the place as I speak. Detectives McGraw and Roark have just pulled up and are walking this way. What have you done? You need to get your ass over here now! I don't know what to do and don't want to be alone."

"Get the hell out of there. Now!"

"Why? I've done nothing. They're almost at the door. I see a paper in McGraw's hands. They must have a warrant to search this place."

He shouts in the phone. "Keep your damn mouth shut."

Click.

Megan grabs her things and darts to the back door, but an officer is waiting for her.

"You'll have to step back inside, Miss," the female officer says.

———◦◦———

McGraw bangs on the front door. "Police!" he shouts. "We have a warrant."

The female officer opens it. "I caught the young lady trying to sneak out the back," she says, guiding Megan to the couch in the living room.

"Good work," McGraw says as six officers and McGraw's team of detectives enter. "Get her cell phone, officer."

"I have it, sir," the female office says, and hands it to him.

"Work Megan's cell," McGraw says, handing it to Roark.

She nods.

"Check out the garage and everything in the back. Look for that SUV," he says to the uniforms. "Clean sweep the grounds."

They dart out.

McGraw hands Megan the warrant. "This is a warrant to search the home, phones, and everything on this property." She reaches for it.

"Where did you think you were going when the officer caught you flying out the back?"

She shrugs. "I got scared and just wanted to get the hell away."

Georgia State Police forensic personnel enter dressed in white garb and masks. They know the drill and get after it. They scramble throughout the place, going through all the rooms, closets, drawers, cabinets, night stands, desks, behind every hanging picture and every vase. Fingerprint dusting and flashes of photos are seen throughout the house.

"Where's Jack?" McGraw asks Megan. He knows Jack has taken off somewhere.

"At work."

McGraw hands her his cell. Call him."

She squirms. Several seconds later, she looks up. "He's not answering."

Roark finishes scanning Megan's cell and frowns at her. "You just called him four minutes ago."

"You alerted him that we were here, didn't you?"

"I called him to see where he was and to tell him you cops were surrounding the place and that he should get his ass over here right away. I wanted him here with me to face you guys, 'because I don't know what's going on and I'm scared as hell.'"

McGraw gets a call. He says, "Really? I knew we should have moved faster." He pauses. "Okay. You guys get over here." He turns to Roark. "Capt. told Kramer Internal Affairs swarmed the City Crime Lab to remove Jack to put him on administrative leave."

"Don't tell me. Jack is in the wind," Holly says.

"Yep. You're right. Let's send out a BOLO on him."

"When is the Capt. ever going to learn to listen to you?" Holly says. "They could have gone earlier."

He shrugs. "He's in charge."

She turns and walks into the bedroom.

McGraw heads back to Megan. "That phone number for Laura Evans you promised us. We never got it. Is she still in Charlotte?"

"Detective, I have no idea where she is. I never could get it out of Jack. When I confronted him, he promised he was going the next day to your office and straighten things out so you could talk to her."

"That never happened. And now Laura Evan's has disappeared," he says.

Megan jolts backwards. "What do you mean disappeared?"

He doesn't tell her Laura is dead.

"Do you think Jack had anything to do with his mother's disappearance?" He wondered if she would incriminate him.

"All I know is they never got along and they fought a lot. I believe he hated her."

"You didn't answer my question."

"How should I know? You're the detective."

"You okay, Megan?" Roark asks, returning from the bedroom with a box, and sits it on a chair.

"No! I'm not! Would you be?!" She lowers her head.

"Where do you think Jack would go? Careful now. You could be an accessory," Roark says.

Her head pops up. "An accessory? Accessory to what?" she says. "I know nothing more about what Jack does or what he's done."

McGraw believes her. She didn't move in with Jack until after he buried his mother. "Anything unusual about Jack lately?" McGraw asks.

She wipes tears from her eyes with a tissue the officer hands her and inhales a deep breath. "Jack started going out a lot at night. When I confronted him, he said he worked with a guy who paid him under the table and he couldn't tell me who he was. It was all confidential."

"You have any idea what they did?"

"Jack said he helped the guy with some kind of forensics. I thought it all odd, but he was adamant that he couldn't go against his confidentiality agreement with this person."

"Did you believe him,"

Megan eyes widened. "At first. But now I don't know."

"Oh, why is that?" McGraw asks.

"He's been acting strange. He's become quiet and distant. His eyes have this wolf-like look, like he's stalking, ready to tear you apart. He's been sneaking out in the middle of the night to that shed in the back. He doesn't have a clue that I know. Once when he was at work, I tried to break into his hideaway That's what I call it. Because he hid in there so often. At first, I thought it was to get away from me. But now I don't think that."

"What do you think?" Roark says.

"That place's secure as Fort Knox. I couldn't get in. I was able to widen a crack near the door in the back with a crowbar. All I could see was a laptop on a desk. Paper sheets on the wall. Couldn't make anything out too well."

McGraw tells Kramer and Gomez to tear into that shed attached to the garage. "Let me know what you find"

He turns back to Megan.

"What do you think Jack did in his hideaway?" McGraw asks. He had an idea but wanted to hear it from her.

She shakes her head. "I'm afraid to say."

"Afraid of what? Jack can't hurt you now."

She pauses. "No, no. Not that he's going to hurt me. What I meant was, I don't want to tell something I don't know. I can only guess what he does in there."

"What's your guess."

"Porn. He must be addicted to porn and goes out there to find sexy women on his computer.'

"What about those sheets of paper on the wall?" McGraw says. "Any theory?"

"Probably blown ups of naked women he likes," she says.

"You seem fairly certain it's porn," Roark says.

"Jack hasn't been very good in bed lately. He wasn't all that good before. He never seemed like he enjoyed it. He's worse now. He must like getting it off out there looking at all that stuff. I hear many men are addicted to porn."

Most serials aren't turned on in the bedroom, McGraw thinks.

"How often in the middle of the night did he slip out there?" McGraw asks.

"At least three time a week."

"Does Jack own a black SUV."

"Yes, and a white caddy."

Gomez comes in and whispers something in McGraw's ear and leaves. McGraw nods.

Megan frowns at him. She must be wondering what Gomez whispered to him.

"Jack's caddy's in the garage. Do you know where he might have gone in his SUV?"

She shrugs. "I just talked to him. He was at work."

McGraw believes Jack was lying to her. "Doesn't he normally take his caddy to work?"

She nods. "He does. He never takes the SUV."

"Where do you think he'd go if he were on the run?"

She shrugs. "I don't know. What has he done? You haven't told me what he's done."

"Does Jack have a certain place he goes to for relaxation?" he asks, probing for a possible secret place that Jack might like.

"Now you're not answering my question."

"First, tell me where Jack might go to hide from us."

"He likes to fish." Her brow lowers. "Wait a minute. I remember something. He took me to a cabin once to fish but I don't fish. He loves that cabin. He could have gone there."

"Where is it?"

"Somewhere past Sweetwater Creek. I don't know how many miles."

"I know the general area," McGraw says.

"Jack told me his dad taught him how to fish when he was young. Said his mother never went there. She and his dad had divorced."

"Do you think you could tell our dispatcher the direction to get to the cabin?" McGraw asks.

She hesitates. "I think so. It's been a while."

"Try to be as specific as you can," Roark says.

McGraw calls dispatch on the landline phone. "Sergeant Striker, this is McGraw. Our perp is in the wind and may be heading west to Sweetwater Creek area in a black SUV. I'm turning the phone over to Megan Turner. She'll give you some directions to the place, then alert the highway patrol and get me the number for their super."

"Will do. I saw the BOLO," dispatch says.

McGraw hands the landline phone over to Megan.

Gomez rushes in. "Boss you gotta see this."

McGraw turns to the female officer and tells her to stay with Ms. Turner and write down the phone number that dispatch calls in.

"Yes, sir."

"Noah, wait up," Roark says. "I gave some of Laura's clothing to one of the uniforms to take to Nora."

"Good let's go."

Outside, Gomez leads McGraw and Roark to Jack's lair.

"Whatta you got?" McGraw asks, as he and Roark slip into blue latex gloves.

Gomez shakes his head. "You gotta see this, boss. We had to bust the place wide open." They walk through what could be the front door and step into a small office. A desk one-fourth the size of Judge Virtue's and not as wide, with a photo album, a laptop with a reader attached, and a paperweight on top of newspaper clippings. Pictures of mutilated young women, many of whom are vics of notorious serials like Ted Bundy, hang on the wall in front of the desk.

McGraw studies the area, slipping into a dream-like state. Jack Carter is sitting at his laptop, scrolling, looking up at times at the pics on the wall of naked, mutilated women. With his personality disorder, Jack sees women as objects to use for his own gratification. He becomes calmer when he sees blood and violence in these pictures. Working his computer and looking at the wall pictures satisfies his impulse to kill, and probably has kept Jack from killing more women.

Kramer moves in next to McGraw, bringing him out of his reverie. "Boss, I went through Carter's laptop and camera earlier. He still had the card in the camera and hasn't erased the images. Many are of the ones in the photo album, but with different poses. Guess he selected the ones he wanted to print from his computer. Carter contacted women on senior matching sites. Many of his emails contained sexual innuendos and about meeting the ladies at certain sites. Apparently, he didn't meet them all."

"Check his emails. Hopefully some will be the vics we've identified."

"That's next." Kramer sits at the laptop and fingers the keyboard.

"Is this the photo album?" McGraw asks, turning to Gomez.

"That's it, boss," he says. Wearing blue gloves, he picks it off the desk and hands it to a gloved McGraw. "This will surprise you."

McGraw opens it and stares at the first woman with her mouth closed and the others with their mouths open, and no tongues. Roark comes in and looks over his shoulders. "That must be Jack's trophy book," Roark says. She looks up at Gomez. "Did you find his trophies?"

"In here, Sarge," Gomez says, moving to a hole in the wall next to a book case that has been pulled aside to reveal the hidden space. Roark reaches in to view the jars. She takes one to McGraw.

"Look at this. There are three more. Four in all."

"Get Nora over here. We need her," McGraw says.

McGraw scrutinizes the album. He points to the other four vics with their mouths open. "We went to the home crime scenes of these three: Gail Murdock; Elizabeth Fox; and Alice King. Don't know who the last one is."

Nora enters. "Whatta you have, Noah?" she asks.

"Over there in the hole," he says.

Looking up from the album, Holly waves her to the opening.

"Hey, Holly. What are you hiding in there? "Oh," she says, looking at the tongues in the jars. "Looks like your serial has followed the path of his compadres, keeping his trophies hidden."

"There are four photographs of Carter's vic's without tongues in this photo album," Holly says.

"And there are four jars with tongues. Don't have to be a rocket scientist to figure this one out," Nora says. They laugh.

"This last person in the album hasn't been IDed," Roark says

Nora says, "We now have proof of the grave lady is Laura Evans. I haven't had a chance to tell you guys that I have pictures of her. The forensic anthropologist working with the forensic scientists reconstructed her head and face."

"That's great," Holly says. "Does the model look anything like this first picture in the album?"

Nora holds the album close to the light, and nods. "Yes, I'd say this one," she says pointing to Laura Evans."

"Wonderful. We gotta tell Noah."

Gomez walks over to McGraw. "Boss, forensics has taken the place apart. All his crap is bagged. There are dozens of prints."

"Prints are Carter's. This was his secret hideout. Those in the house will be Laura Evans, Megan Turner and Jack Carter. Take everything to the station."

"Good news for you, cowboy," Nora says.

"How's that, meat lady."

She frowns. He's never called her that before and he's pleased it surprised her. She can be a smart ass at times.

"Well, where did that come from?" Nora says. They laugh. "Anyway, we've IDed your serial's mother."

"Who's we?"

"Your brilliant partner and I."

"And how is that possible?"

"The forensic anthropologist working with forensics made a model of Laura's head and face. I have pics to show you back at the pit, but in looking at the woman on the left is the person that matches the face model back at my lab."

"Great. With the ID of Jack's mother, we can now connect him to her as well as the others in the photo album," McGraw says. "The mystery of Carter's mother solved. Thanks. You can be very helpful at times."

"At times? What the hell do you mean? I'm always helpful. Aren't I, Holly? Tell this crazy boss of yours that I'm the best."

"Well...." She looks over at Noah. "Well, you do know he's just pushing your buttons, don't you?"

"Gotcha, meat lady."

"One for you, cowboy, but look out."

They laughed it off.

Roark asks McGraw. "Whatta we gonna do with Megan Turner?"

He turns to Gomez. "Have patrol take her to the station."

Chapter 52

Jack Carter races off to the east end of Atlanta, while watching in his rearview mirror for patrol cars. He pulls into Eastside Storage. Stops at the keypad pole. Enters the 6-digit access code. Gate rises. He stomps on the accelerator, causing the tires to squeal as he steers the SUV to his left between a series of parallel storage units, stopping at 1020. Shuts off the motor, bails out, fumbling for the key on the ring to open the lock to his unit. Once the lock flips open, he raises the aluminum door, looks around the other units before entering. There's only one car down at the end of the row. He quickly begins loading the SUV with boxes of ammo, his two hand guns, and AR-15s.

He yanks the door down to his unit, doesn't take the time to lock it. Hops into his vehicle. Takes off, ending up at the exit keypad pole. Enters the numbers again and shoots out onto the street, traveling west. He glances around every few seconds, expecting the police.

McGraw has probably issued a BOLO on me.

He reaches into the glove compartment for a sophisticated police scanner and places it on the dashboard. The cops are smart. They now use secure channels to communicate in the field so reporters and bad guys can't pick up on a crime scene. Carter knows their secrets. Leaving Atlanta city limits, he stays five miles under the speed limit. Out here, the highway patrol has jurisdiction and Jack doesn't know the security channel their super uses for communicating to his officers out on the roads. McGraw would know to call in to APD supervisor for a special line to get to the highway patrol super.

About five miles from his turnoff, the four-lane interstate divides around a wide median covered in a thicket of evergreens. Coming to his dad's cabin since he was very young, Carter knows Highway Patrol officers like to hide in there. As he approaches the divide, there's one car partly camouflaged in the grove. If you weren't looking, you'd never see him. Seconds later, the black and white races out from under its hiding place. Jack floors the SUV, hitting ninety in seconds. Flashing strobes are a half-mile behind him, coming at a high rate of speed. Carter slows enough to make his turn off the highway to his right, speeds down the dusty dirt road. Fortunately, it hasn't rained in weeks, and while the road isn't as dusty as in the summer, Carter can still blind the copper. He's flying along at a high rate of speed, bouncing up and down, head hitting the roof, as he tries avoiding most of the bumps and holes the best he can. High-pitched laughter overtakes him when he sees the cloud of dust he's making behind him.

Eat my dust, asshole. No one knows this place like I do. Good luck in finding me.

Jack Carter is racing over a winding route through the area. No sign of the highway patrol. He makes a couple of turns, pulls up his driveway and stops in the back to shield his vehicle from the road. He hops out.

He edges to the side of the building. No sign of the highway patrol car.

Carter's cabin has the advantage of being at the top of an incline and at the edge of a cliff with plenty of tree coverage and a lake below. There's no other access to his dwelling except from the front. Opposite the driveway, lakeside, there's a steep drop-off twenty yards away, and thirty yards behind the cabin is another drop-off with dense foliage, making it difficult to maneuver through.

He unloads the SUV, setting the boxes on the back patio. He knows what he has to do. McGraw and his detectives, the sheriff, highway patrol and maybe even a SWAT Team will be coming after him.

Gotta get ready.

———————◆◆◆———————

"Sarge. This is corporal James. I spotted the suspect in the BOLO driving the black SUV heading west on highway I-20. I took off after him. He turned off on Water Valley road.

"No, sir. I lost him in here somewhere," officer James says, sighing from frustration. "For forty minutes, I've traveled over these roads down to the lake. Haven't found the SUV. No activity in the cabins. It has to be here somewhere. This time of year, most of the cabins are empty, except for one that is occupied with a couple here on vacation, renting, driving a blue Mazda. They hadn't seen nor heard anything. I'm at the end of the only road that ends up high above the lake. A cabin sits up on a hill. It could be where the suspect is hold up..." He pauses. "Sarge, it will be hell getting up there. If our suspect's there, he could have a bead on us trying to get at him. I'm parked behind a couple of trees across the road, facing the cabin. Earlier, I thought I saw movement. I believe he's holded up in there."

He pauses, listening to his supervisor. "Yes, sir. I'll keep watch."

Chapter 53

Back at the station, evidence taken from Evans' home and Carter's hideaway along with his laptop are placed on the extended table against the wall. Megan Turner is advised of her Miranda Rights and placed in Interview Room Two. She tells them she has nothing to hide, they can ask her anything.

He turns to Kramer. "You and Gomez go through the evidence. Work through Carter's computer again. See what turns up."

"Will do, boss," Kramer says.

"Let's see what else we can get out of Megan Turner. You take the lead, sergeant."

"Sure thing, boss," Holly says, smiling. She reaches in her desk drawer for the recorder.

McGraw carries a yellow pad with him, which he doesn't need but feels is a psychological tool that has an effect on the witnesses. Over the years, he's noticed how suspects eye him every time he writes something, just anything, on the pad, wondering what he has written about them. Some fear they've convicted themselves in some way without knowing it. A few even change their stories.

Roark enters Room Two first. Megan looks ruffled.

"How long are you going to keep me here? I haven't done anything wrong. Haven't broken any laws."

"We're here to finish up. To tie up loose ends," Roark says.

"But I've told you all that I know," she says.

"This won't take long," Roark says.

The detectives take the chairs facing Megan. McGraw drops the legal pad on the table to draw attention to it and begins writing a few sentences.

Megan glances at him. And frowns.

Roark flips on the recorder. "We're recording this interview to make sure it's on record."

She frowns. Still eyeing McGraw, who is writing on the yellow pad.

Roark speaks the time and day and who's in the room into the recorder.

"How long have you been living with Jack?" Roark asks.

Megan watches McGraw. "You already know that I work for Jack and have known him for over five years. He moved in with me at my apartment before we moved to his mother's house." She looks up at the ceiling. "We've been living together about four weeks."

"Did you ever meet his mother, Laura Evans?"

She shakes her head. "No. She's supposed to be in Charlotte taking care of a relative, so Jack told me. But I just learned from him that she's there for alcohol rehab."

"Is that what he told you?" Roark asks.

"Yes."

Without looking up from his legal pad, McGraw says. "He killed her."

The shock in Megan's eyes is real. No fake. "Jack would never—"

"He did."

"During your time together, did you ever notice anything strange about Jack other than slipping out to his hideaway?" Roark asks.

"What do you mean strange?"

"Did he ever do anything or say anything to you that you considered eccentric?"

"I've already told you that."

"Please repeat it for the record," Roark says.

"Well, he's good about putting on a pleasant facade. Goes out of his way to be nice, wants people to like him." She pauses as she looks away for a few seconds. "Come to think of it, he's never wrong. Doesn't take the blame for anything. It's always the other guy's fault—"

"Narcissistic," McGraw says interrupting, writing on his pad.

Megan watches McGraw writing. "I'd say so."

"Doesn't like criticism," McGraw says not looking up.

"Why, yes."

"Has a sense of superiority and patronizes you," McGraw says, still writing.

"You seem to know Jack better than I do."

"Psychopath." McGraw says.

There's fear in Megan's eyes. "What are you saying."

"Lieutenant McGraw is saying that Jack Carter is a serial killer. He's killed elderly women, and cut out their tongues."

Megan's skin turns pale. "Jack? A serial killer? I don't believe it."

"Yes," Roark says.

"You mean I've been living with a serial killer?"

"Yes, again," Roark says.

------◦•◦------

McGraw stands and leaves the room for a few moments. He returns with a female officer. "Officer Allison will sit with you for a little while. We won't be long."

He and Roark return to the pit. He throws the legal pad on his desk.

"Anything more on Carter's computer?" he asks his detectives.

"Nothing, boss." Kramer says.

"Really did his homework on the ladies before he killed 'em," Gomez says.

McGraw's desk phone rings. *Maybe it's the highway super*, he thinks as he reaches for the receiver.

"Lieutenant McGraw, homicide."

It's the Highway Patrol Supervisor, Sergeant McCoy. He informs the lieutenant that one of his officers spotted the black SUV described in the BOLO, on I-20, and sped after it, turning in on Water Valley Road ten miles past the Sweetwater Creek area. "He believes your perp is holded up in one of the cabins, but isn't sure which one. He's at the end of the road that goes to the lake. Anyone you know can ID his cabin?

McGraw thinks about Megan. "We'll get back with you, Sergeant," he says and hangs up. McGraw calls out, "Listen up, everyone."

They gather at his desk.

"Highway Patrol spotted Jack's black SUV on I-20 and took off after him, ending up at a cabin past the Sweetwater Creek area in which the officer believes Jack Carter is holded up. But there's no sign of him and the officer isn't positive he's even in there. The supervisor wants us to help locate the cabin. Ask officer Allison to bring Megan Turner in here," he says to Gomez.

"Sure thing, boss."

Megan appears disheveled and scared out of her mind as she walks into the squad room with the officer. Megan's never been in trouble, yet she must feel like a criminal living with a serial killer.

"Am I being released?" she asks, looking down at the floor.

"Not yet, dear," Roark says.

She looks away. "But I've done nothing. How long can you keep me?"

"You said you've been to Jack's cabin," McGraw says.

She turns to face him. "Once."

"Do you think you could find it again?"

She eyes the cowboy with suspicion. "If I help you, does it mean you'll release me?"

"It does."

She perks up. "Well, then, what are we waiting for?"

"Good. We'll be ready in a short while." He motions for her to have a seat by Roark's desk.

McGraw tells his team the Capt. will have to coordinate the capture of Jack Carter with all law enforcement agencies before they head out. He walks over to the chief's office.

The Capt.'s door is closed. He knocks.

"Enter."

McGraw closes the door behind him. "Jack Carter's in the wind," he says. "Got a call from the Highway Patrol supervisor. One of his officers believes Carter's holed up in his cabin in Clearwater Creek but isn't sure which one. He needs us to ID Carter's cabin."

"Howya gonna do that?"

"His girlfriend, Megan Turner. She's been there and can take us directly to his cabin."

"Is she being held?"

He nods. "She's in the squad room with Roark. Megan's been living with Carter for weeks and has told us all about him. We've taken her statement and she's been very cooperative."

The Capt. rises and walks with McGaw out into the squad room. He tells his detectives that he'll work them in with the Highway Patrol Supervisor and the Sheriff and will let them know where to meet them.

Roark stands when the Capt. walks over to her desk. "Is this Ms. Turner?"

"Yes, sir," Roark says. "Megan, this is Captain Dipple, Chief of Detectives."

She stands. "Please sit," he says. "I'm told you know where Jack Carter's cabin is, is that correct?"

"Yes, sir. I've been there once but can find it with no problem."

"What can you tell us about the area?" he asks.

She pauses for a few moments. "I remember there's a wide median filled with lots of trees, where the highway divides around it several miles before Jack turned off. The name of the road is Water Valley."

"That area in the median across from the turn off, is it flat or hilly?" the Capt. asks.

"It's flat and very pretty."

"Thank you." He turns to McGraw. "That could be the command center. I'll check with the sheriff and see what he thinks."

"Chief, I want Drew in on this."

"I'll call upline and tell them the FBI will be working with you on this."

"Thanks, Capt."

McGraw puts a call in to Drew at the FBI.

Chapter 54

Captain Dipple has called a meeting of his detectives for two p.m. While waiting, McGraw and Drew with the FBI are at the evidence boards.

Roark notices the Capt. heading their way. "Here comes the Chief."

Capt. nods to Drew. "Glad to see the FBI is with us. How you've been, Drew?"

"Good. Always ready to help in any way I can."

The Chief nods, again. "I've spent all morning coordinating the capture of Jack Carter with the law enforcement agencies. The jurisdiction of this operation essentially belongs to Sheriff Millhouse of Douglas County and he's taking the lead for the time being." He pauses as Gomez hands him a cup of his favorite coffee. The detectives smile as their attention switches to Gomez, the proverbial brown-nose cop. Gomez shrugs and smiles—his usual response when the others catch him in the act of currying favor. They know he's harmless.

The Capt. continues after several gulps of coffee. "Carter's no dummy. He's sharp. Nick, his father, a cop, was a member of our SWAT Team. He told me once that he taught his son, Jack, games using military tactics and how to shoot weapons from the time he was just a kid. And Jack took to them like a kid to candy."

SWAT (Special Weapons and Tactics) officers are members of highly trained paramilitary units that tackle situations beyond the capability of conventional police forces. These officers usually serve as SWAT Team members as an additional duty to their regular jobs so that SWAT is not a full-time career. The Team is called in to handle situations that present significant risk to law enforcement or the public, that regular patrol officers and detectives aren't equipped or trained to handle.

McGraw says, "Megan described Jack's cabin being at the top of an incline that would be hard to get to except from the front or south side. Cliffs on one side and the back drops off to the lake below. Did you call in our SWAT, Capt.?"

Chief shakes his head. "Sheriff said he doesn't need them."

Drew speaks up. "Chief, FBI can override the sheriff. Our SWAT Commander would be in charge. I'm sure the sheriff would be glad to turn over the mission to them if you let him know the FBI is on the case with you."

"He'd be a damn fool," McGraw says, "if he doesn't."

And get us all killed, McGraw thought.

Most sheriffs in charge of operations occurring in their jurisdiction would be happy to give authority to a SWAT field commander.

The Capt. says, "The Sheriff's set up a Command Center a couple miles from Water Valley road. I'll talk him into having us and FBI SWAT involved." He looks at McGraw. "Remember, Cowboy, don't go off half-cocked and try to take Jack all by yourself. Let SWAT do their job. Patrol super and three of his cars are waiting for you outside," he says heading back to his office.

Drew informs McGraw that a couple of FBI cars are also waiting in the parking lot, and their SWAT commander will have the Mobile Command Center bus there by the time everyone reaches the site.

Holly whisper to Drew so Megan couldn't hear her. "Glad you talked the chief into SWAT. Now we won't get our heads blown off."

Drew smiles, knowing she's right.

McGraw reaches for his Stetson.

Chapter 55

Outside the station, McGraw, Drew, Holly, and Megan wait in the cold for Kramer and Gomez. McGraw finds the patrol supervisor and tells him their mission. "Your officers have their AR-15s in the trunk?"

"Always."

"You're the man. Let's go," McGraw says heading to his black Silverado.

Drew takes the lead of the caravan in his black SUV with Megan in the back seat with a female agent followed by two of his SUV backups. McGraw and Holly follow in the Silverado, and Kramer and Gomez and three other black unmarked APD cars, each with two uniform officers, are at the tail end of the caravan.

After passing Sweetwater Creek, Drew tells Megan to be on the lookout for the median. "The divide is a few miles up ahead," she says.

"We should see the Command Center bus with SWAT vehicles," Drew says. "The other law enforcement vehicles should be parked close by, too."

Several minutes later, Megan shouts, "There it is! Take that road to your left."

Drew spots the FBI SWAT Command Center bus and SWAT vehicles as he drives up the dirt road leading into the median. The Sheriff and Highway Patrol Officers are standing by their vehicles talking. Drew pulls up next to the Sheriff's car and the FBI cars move in alongside, forming a line perpendicular to the Interstate followed by McGraw and the APD cars. The APD officers bail out and hurry over to McGraw and Holly. They walk up to the Sheriff and the Highway Patrol Sergeant and huddle around the SWAT Commander as they greet one another. First thing out of the Sheriff's mouth is, "This is Agent Pascal, FBI SWAT Commander. The Commander will be in charge of this mission."

"Our men are ready," the Commander says.

Next to the Mobile Center are a couple dozen SWAT Team operators and two sniper teams, receiving instructions from their tactical commander. They are dressed in black military BDU's (Battle Dress Uniforms), tactical vests, radios with headsets, black Kevlar helmets, and an assortment of special gear attached to their vests, including diversionary devices that emit a loud percussion sound and one-million-candle-power light in a fraction of a second upon detonation. These hand-thrown devices will be used to temporarily stun and blind the fugitive, Jack Carter, giving the team crucial seconds to move in and control him before he can react.

The briefing ends and the team does a walk-through and entry rehearsal in the wooded area. When completed, the team leaders give the orders to load up and perform communication checks, testing their radios on a private encoded tactical channel.

"Beautiful site," McGraw says.

"I'll second that, "Drew says.

"Who is Jack Carter's girlfriend?" the commander asks.

"Megan," Drew says. "This is she."

The commander looks her over. "You can identify which cabin he's in?"

"Yes, sir," she says. I've been there with Jack."

"Good," he says. "I want Sheriff Millhouse, Highway Patrol Sergeant Miller, Drew, Megan, McGraw and Roark in the Command Center. The others can wait out here. I'm going to meet with the tactical commander for a few minutes before we go in."

On the roof of the vehicle is a Satellite dome with five satellite receiver channels, a multi high-tech camera surveillance system, and a digital HDTV antenna. Six 500-watt bulbs that swivel three-sixty are around the edge of the roof. A waterproof exterior workstation with 43" 4K LED TV, computer network, power outlets, shelf for cellphone/laptop charging station, modulated audio and video system are on the exterior. LED lighting throughout, enormous exterior storage compartments with slide out trays, and a weather display console on the sides of the vehicle.

The bus has a 30' all-aluminum walk style van body. A unique layout with a forward conference room and two workstations, two centrally located café seats or checkpoints and an additional rear conference area with storage, whiteboard and large bench seats, gallery with coffee maker, refrigerator and microwave, and a stainless-steel electric toilet system.

After talking with the tactical commanders, the SWAT Commander opens the door behind the driver's compartment and ushers the group up the step and through the forward work station to their left, with seven monitors on each side operated by officers sitting in front of each one. Walking past them, through a doorway with a sliding door, the group enters a conference room with table and six chairs. On each side of the aisle, against the wall, are cushioned benches. A large TV screen is affixed to the wall and there are several dry-erase white boards on stands. Looking beyond is another conference area, followed by a gallery, and a curved seating area with cushioned benches and a toilet chamber. They move into the second conference room with table and eight chairs with custom-made cushions on each side of the aisle.

After everyone is seated Commander Pascal says, "To bring everyone up to date, a highway patrol officer pursued Jack Carter west on Interstate I-20 and onto Water Valley road but lost sight of him. He eventually ended up at the end of a road with a drop-off to a lake below. He reported only one cabin in the area, which was up on a hill with a steep slant." He pauses while he moves over into the workstation. Minutes later, he returns and a picture of the cabin area flashes on the large TV screen. He turns to Megan and asks her if she recognizes the area.

"That's Jack's road. I remember it well. I didn't let on that I was scared he was going to go over the cliff, but he pulled up into his driveway.'

Pointing to the cabin in the picture on the screen, the commanders asks, "Is this Jack's cabin?"

She nods. "Yes."

"I'll want you in a vehicle with officers to identify the place so you and I can be positively sure. No messups," he says, looking at the Sheriff and the Highway Patrol Sergeant.

Sheriff Millhouse says, "Wise move, Commander."

"Where is the officer that chased our suspect?" Drew asks.

The commander looks at the Patrol Sergeant Miller, who says, "Trooper James is posted at the end of the road, down the hill from the suspect's cabin. He still has eyes on the place until the tactical team is in place."

Commander Pascal tells the patrol Sergeant that he can have Trooper James fall back once the perimeter is set.

"Will do," Sergeant Miller says.

The Commander walks to the front of the bus and exits. Minutes later he returns. "Here's the plan. My scout team is on its way to the cabin. We can watch them on the TV. Once we get their recon, SWAT will move out and setup a perimeter one hundred yards from the cabin and analyze the area on foot. The FBI helicopter unit is almost here. They have been briefed while in route and have the coordinates of the cabin. They will be needed if our suspect escapes and gets past our perimeter."

All nod in agreement.

"Sheriff Millhouse and Sergeant Miller will stay with me in the Command Center. Agent Drew and Detective McGraw will be in the FBI lead car, waiting orders at the perimeter. Detective Roark and Ms. Turner will be in a second FBI suburban that will move through the perimeter to within view of the cabin area. Once Megan IDs the cabin, I want her out of there immediately and back at the Command Center."

They turn their attention to the movements of the scout team on the TV. "There's a porch across the front without any furniture, a door and two large windows next to the door that are visible from the road," scout leader reports. "There's movement inside, sir," he says, looking through his scope. "A man. He stops every few minutes and looks our way, sir."

"Any weapons?" commander asks.

"Subject has a rifle in hand, possibly an assault weapon. He could have an arsenal in there, sir."

"It's obvious that Jack Carter has the advantage," McGraw says. "He's up on that hill with a cliff on the other side of the cabin. We've learned from Megan there's a drop-off about thirty yards behind the building to the east, too. The only way to approach the cabin is from the front—west side—and the south side."

"Sit tight," Commander says to the scouts. "A perimeter is being established one hundred yards from the cabin."

A mile down the highway, McGraw turns off at the sign, *Water Valley Road*. Drew is in the passenger seat. Megan Turner and Holly are in the second car radioing directions to Drew. They pass through the SWAT perimeter.

"Follow this road until you cross a small bridge and then take the road to the right. No direct way to Jack's place," Megan says.

"After crossing the bridge, the road divides thirty yards up ahead. Take the road to your right." Seconds later she instructs them to make a left at the next turn. "Okay," Megan says, "there's one more turn to the right up ahead. It ends at the cliff with a lake below. Jack's cabin will be on the hill on the right. Be careful," Megan says, "there's no barricade. You could go off the cliff."

"I see it up ahead," Drew says to McGraw.

"Positive ID on the cabin, Commander," McGraw radios, "we're turning around and heading back to the perimeter. Megan and Detective Roark are returning to the Center."

As instructed, McGraw and Drew head back and wait in the Silverado for the SWAT Commander to give them the go ahead to enter the cabin.

Back at the Center, Detective Roark steps in with Megan. They view the maneuvers of the SWAT Team as they move in sync and precision from the perimeter, one hundred yards away, toward Carter's cabin, like an army of cockroaches.

⋅•⋅

Jack Carter laughs to himself, looking around the edge of the window. He has a series of AR-15s resting on the window sills. He moves over to the window on the south side, looking over the driveway. He spots the tactical team in the distance.

They think they've got me cornered. Well, I have a surprise for them.

He returns to the window over the porch.

He knows what they're going to say.

We have you surrounded. There's no escape. Surrender now and save yourself.

"Bullshit!"

Suddenly, a barrage of shots from AR-15s rip up the ground, forming a wall of dust in front of the team. Blue team returns fire. Officers blast the west front of the cabin with intense firepower, the windows blow out, the front door shatters into splinters, the wood pillars split in half, causing the canopy over the porch to collapse. Tactical commander raises a hand and the firing stops.

Blue Team leader gives command to hold, while Red Team Leader takes over and gives the command to deploy tear-gas through the side windows. With precision, the tear-gas cannisters are launched through the air, using a military-style hand-held-grenade launcher. Three cannisters enter the cabin after smashing through the windows from the force of the launching weapon. The cannisters explode inside on impact and immediately fill the cabin with white smoke, a chemical agent that will immediately causes burning sensations and pain to the skin and eyes of any occupant. SWAT units move out in horizontal lines 20 yards in front of the other units, as they move up the incline to the house with weapons ready. No barrage of shots comes from the house. All tactical officers are ordered to hold position to allow for the tear-gas to have maximum effect. The SWAT Team Officers are expecting the suspect to come rolling out of the house in excruciating pain, choking and coughing, but instead, the house explodes minutes later with such force that the windows. doors, walls and glass hurl out in all directions. All SWAT operators instinctively fall to the ground, avoiding the blast. All that remains is a structure leveled to its foundation.

McGraw and Drew hear the blast from the distance and Drew immediately throws the SUV into drive and races toward the cabin, sliding to a stop below it. They jump out as the tactical officers are with team leaders conducting a status check on all members of the assault team. McGraw is in disbelief as he surveys what's left of the cabin as he approaches the Red Team leader.

"What the hell happened here!"

"We deployed tear-gas after he fired on us and soon realized we were compromised. The cannisters used were combustible, but wouldn't have done this damage. He must have had setup a bomb in there for the place to have erupted that quickly."

"Knowing Jack, he deliberately set up an explosive device," McGraw says.

"Definitely a possibility," the team leader says. "Guess it doesn't matter. No one could have escaped that explosion. He must have planned on going out in a blaze of glory."

"Don't count on it, team leader," McGraw says. "This guy is no ordinary suspect."

Something's not right. Carter would not have given up this easily.

"We're looking at a recovery operation," Drew says to McGraw with the team leader standing close by.

"There won't be much to recover, sir."

"Probably right," Drew says.

"If there's nothing more you need, sir, we're out of here."

"Can you take some of your guys and hold the perimeter for a while?" McGraw asks.

"Sure thing, lieutenant. No problem. We'll stay as long as you need us."

"I'd appreciate it," McGraw says as he walks across the lawn toward the cabin. With a puzzled look on his face, Drew slowly follows him, probably wondering what the hell McGraw is thinking.

The team leader motions to his members and they depart as smoothly as they entered. At the edge of Carter's property, the teams gather their gear, load into their assault vehicles and pull away, as well-organized as they came.

"What's troubling you, cowboy?" Drew says.

"Carter didn't vanish in this explosion," McGraw says. "He's too damn smart." McGraw walks around the cabin and begins removing some of the rubble. "He planned it. I'd bet my life on it."

"Noah. C'mon. He couldn't have survived. Just look at this place" Drew says. "You're giving him too much credit."

"That's the point. He wants us to think that. Did you see that sewer pipe extending out over the lake on the north side?"

"Yeah. So what?"

"Don't you think it strange that there'd be another sewer line running in the opposite direction."

"Probably pipelines from other cabins feeding into this line."

"There aren't any cabins withing miles of this place," McGraw says. "Anyway, where would the sewage go? No, this pipeline was used for something else."

Jack could have slipped out through this system in some way after the explosion. But how?

Little by little they removed what boards they could.

McGraw grabs his cell and makes a quick call. "Anyone at the Command Post have a K9 (canine)?"

"Yes, we do."

"Good. Get them up here right away." Before Drew can say a word, McGraw says, "They're on their way."

"What's going on, Noah? Why do you need a police dog?"

"I'm convinced that explosion was a deliberate diversion for Jack to escape."

Within minutes, a Sheriff's Department SUV K-9 vehicle pulls up. A young uniform deputy jumps out. "Watcha need, lieutenant? I'm deputy Clark." The K-9 is jumping from the front seat to the back barking.

"Is your dog good at tracking?" McGraw asks.

"The best in three counties, with commendations to prove it."

Deputy Clark opens the car door and grabs the lead, yanking his K-9, Hoyt, from the SUV. The dog is a three-year-old, 75-pound, Belgian Malinois with beautiful black and tan markings. Hoyt is jumping around as he pulls at Deputy Clark's lead. Belgian Malinois are a very popular K-9 choice among police departments due to their extremely high drive, stamina and work ethic, and are extremely fast afoot with a very powerful bite and apprehension capability.

Deputy Clark orders Hoyt to *platz* and immediately he lays down in a crawl position, waiting for his next command.

"Impressive," McGraw says, convinced that Hoyt is well trained by his young handler.

Drew nods in agreement.

McGraw instructs Clark to conduct a search around the cabin for any fresh human odor. He explains that the tactical team has contaminated the front (west) and south sides of the property, and directs him to the rear (east) side.

Clark quickly places Hoyt on a thirty-foot lead and gives the command to *suuk*—seek and track. Hoyt instantly places his nose a few inches off the ground and begins a crisscross pattern across the back and southeast corner of the property, heading to the cabin. McGraw and Drew watch the K-9 work energetically, purposeful, and with determination. Several minutes later, Hoyt shows excitement in a pile of wood covering an area close to the southside.

"He senses a strong human odor, sir," Deputy Clark says, as he pulls back some of the boards.

McGraw and Drew rush over to remove more boards.

"There's steps here, sir," Deputy Clark says.

McGraw reaches into his pocket for his flashlight and heads down the steps with Drew in tow. Not much is disturbed, just plenty of dust. Drew shines his light around but says nothing.

"Footsteps over here in the dust," McGraw says.

Drew shines his light in the direction. "Yeah, they don't lead anywhere."

"Don't be too sure."

The K-9 rushes over to them guiding his nose a few inches from the floor. Hoyt circles and barks.

"We have something," Clark says.

McGraw begins hitting the wall with his fist.

"Fake wall," he shouts. Clark and McGraw begin removing the paneling. They come upon an opening that leads into a pipeline large enough for a six-foot man to stand erect in it. The smell is atrocious.

Chapter 56

McGraw turns to Drew and says, "Can you get a chopper up here to pick you up? I'm sure Jack used this pipeline as his escape route and he's got a head start on us. We have no time to lose."

The deputy and Hoyt wait at the opening for instructions while McGraw runs down the front of the property to his Silverado and retrieves his M-4 rifle and portable radio. When he returns, he says to Drew, "I don't know how far this pipeline goes, but radio Roark and tell her to get our APD guys to help cover the area around the perimeter. I'm not sure where it comes out but we'll need air support."

"Can do," Drew says. "I'll have some of our men with them."

Several inches of slimy water seeped in from the ground splashed over their feet. Clark begins working the dog. He grabs the end of the lead and gives the command to *suuk*, and Hoyt picks up a scent and barrels through the slippery water, pulling his handler along, running as fast as the slime will allow. Finally, they come out into a woody area about twenty-five yards beyond the perimeter. McGraw and Clark glance around. The late afternoon sun barely penetrates the trees and branches.

Jack could be anywhere by now, McGraw thinks.

Hoyt circles the area near a tree, which has a camouflaged six by six mesh tarp lying on the ground. The canine is circling the tarp at a frantic pace.

McGraw turns to Clark. "Shit! Jack's in an ATV."

Clark nods in agreement. Tire marks and the disturbed ground lead through the woods in a northwest direction. McGraw radios to the air unit.

"Have you lifted off yet, Drew?"

"We're just off from the Command Post," Drew says.

McGraw gives his location and tells Drew to use thermal imaging to try and pick up a heat signature in the area northwest of his location. McGraw adds that they will continue to track on foot through the woods. The Command Center is joining in by tracking McGraw's radio GPS along with the air unit search location. Command Center notifies SWAT team to redeploy and set up a containment area surrounding approximate one-hundred acres of woods.

McGraw and Clark and Hoyt approach a steep incline leading down into the woods. As Clark descends, being pulled by an overactive Hoyt, he loses his footing and rolls head-over-heels for nearly twenty yards down the ravine, coming to rest on his back next to a large hickory tree. Clark cries out in pain, grabbing his ankle. "I heard something snap," he says. McGraw rushes to his side. It's obvious Clark is in excruciating pain.

"I think my ankle is broken," Clark says.

McGraw kneels down by his side and examines the ankle. "I'll radio for help."

"You just keep going, sir."

"I just can't leave you here alone."

"I'm not alone, Hoyt can protect me from anything. Wish I could send him with you, but he's a meathead and will only listen to me. Sorry."

"No problem. You and Hoyt did a great job putting us on Jack's trail."

"Well, get out of here and catch the bastard, sir." McGraw rises and takes off.

What a great cop. Tough, too. He should work for me, McGraw thinks as he heads off into the woods.

After navigating through one hundred yards, McGraw realizes he is at a loss without Hoyt. A few minutes later, he notices a clearing fifty yards up ahead.

Perfect place to land a chopper, he thinks.

McGraw radios Drew to request a pickup by the chopper in the clearing. He then calls Command Center to update them on Deputy Clark's location and his condition.

Hopefully Jack hasn't made it too far, ditching the ATV and taking off in another vehicle, he thinks.

Jack emerges from the tunnel, works his way to the ATV he camouflaged earlier, throws off the tarp, hops in, and drives west through the woods, making sure he doesn't make too much noise to draw attention. He doesn't know where the officers have set up their perimeter. In the ATV, Jack has his M-4 rifle, multiple extended magazines of rifle ammo, binoculars and a Glock 40-caliber handgun with extra magazines. He's prepared to take them on. Jack figures he has about thirty minutes to make it about four miles west before the cops locate the sewer system. He knows that if he can make it to the State highway, he will have no problem flagging down some idiot wanting to help an injured hiker. Jack laughs as he thinks how stupid the cops are. *They have no idea who they are dealing with. They'll soon find out.*

Chapter 57

As the chopper lands, McGraw jumps into the rear passenger side, and after getting situated he shakes his head, seeing Holly sitting in the other seat, holding her M-4 and wearing flight earphones.

"What the hell are you doing here?" he says, knowing it would have taken the SWAT team to stop her from getting on the chopper.

"I figured you needed me to cover your ass. Remember the last time?"

McGraw nods.

Drew turns around and holds his hands up in defeat. "I couldn't keep her away." McGraw gives a thumbs up and instructs the pilot that the suspect is traveling west, based on the tracks from the ATV. He banks the chopper and maneuvers about two hundred feet above the tree-line. McGraw knows the FBI pilots are competent, being recruited from the special forces of the military. This bird is a Bell 407 that files at 162 mph, carries five passengers and costs 3.1 million. Not as big as the Sikorsky Blackhawk, also owned by the FBI, which costs 5.3 million.

Within minutes, the pilot alerts Drew about movement in the woods directly ahead.

"Roger that." Drew, busy managing the thermal imaging unit, detects the heat signature of the vehicle from roughly 1/5th of a mile. Holly grips her binoculars and shouts, "I have him in sight. A red ATV travelling west."

McGraw asks the pilot to take them down closer, but not close enough to give the suspect a clear shot at the chopper. "I'm sure Drew won't want to explain how he lost a three-million-dollar chopper."

"Me?" Drew says. "I'm not the pilot."

The pilot laughs.

"Experiencing a crash landing has never been on my bucket list," McGraw says.

As they descend, the ATV slows and Jack turns to release a barrage of automatic rifle fire. A couple of rounds glance off the chopper. Holly returns fire with her M-4 from the open door. Jack's ATV flips. Jack is thrown out.

"Nice shot," Drew says. "The vehicle has flipped."

McGraw sees Jack jump to his feet and take cover behind a large tree. He tells the pilot, "Pull up now, I don't want him drawing a bead on us."

McGraw scans the area and sees a clearing about seventy-five yards in front of them. "Put it down in that clearing up ahead."

The pilot says, "I can get you close but can't set her down. Can't risk shutting her down. You'll have to drop down a few feet."

"Copy that," McGraw says.

When the pilot descends to about 6 feet, he gives the command, "Go!"

McGraw is the first to push out and hit the ground, tucking his head as he rolls. He jumps up to see Holly perform the same maneuver. She bounces to her feet as the aircraft quickly ascends over the trees.

Holly turns to an open-mouthed McGraw. "Amazing," he says.

"I'm a quick learner. Let's go!"

McGraw follows her, amazed at how focused and driven she can be during stressful operations. Heading west in the woods, she turns to her partner and asks as they move forward, "How do you want to play this?"

McGraw explains that when they get close to Jack's location they will split up and flank him. "We can use the chopper to draw his attention. Hopefully, he hasn't seen us and we can get the drop on him."

"And…if that doesn't work?" she says.

"Then we'll go to plan B."

"What is plan B?"

"I'll let you know when I figure it out."

"Oh, fine," she says trying to be cute with him, but knows that all tactical operations are based on plans. They don't always go as anticipated and when they fail, good cops rely on instinct, the ability to improvise and to adapt.

Silence.

McGraw knows his partner has confidence that they can pull this off.

Chapter 58

McGraw calls up to Drew with his plan to use the chopper to re-locate Jack and draw him out.

"Roger that."

He instructs Drew to update Command Post with Jack's location. Drew explains that the SWAT Team is already heading toward their location to set up a containment perimeter.

I love working with a guy who thinks ahead and knows his job, McGraw thinks.

Moving forward, McGraw and Holly get a message from Drew that Jack is dead ahead about fifty yards. McGraw motions to Holly to break away to the south. As they move in unison separated by forty yards, McGraw spots Jack near the base of an oak tree. Jack is concentrating on the chopper as it approaches. McGraw hand-signals Holly indicating he has eyes on Jack. She responds with a thumbs up.

As they get within thirty yards of Jack, McGraw sees him preparing for a shot at the chopper.

McGraw shouts, "Drop your weapon, Jack!"

Jack freezes for a few moments, lowers his weapon, slowly turns around with his assault weapon held in both hands pointing down at the ground. He cries out, "Well-played, lieutenant!"

He pauses. McGraw has his rifle aimed at Jack's chest with his finger on the trigger.

"Cowboy, you know I can't let you take me."

"I figured you'd say that."

Jack waits a few seconds, probably thinking about his fate.

McGraw is ready.

"Well, cowboy, at least those bitches got what they deserved, and best of all, I won't have to listen any more to the voice of that bitch of a mother I had."

Jack slowly raises his weapon to take aim at McGraw.

The lieutenant squeezes the trigger of his weapon and gets off two rounds. Simultaneously, another shot in the distance goes off and hits Jack in the head. He hits the ground. McGraw motions to Roark. They walk over to Carter's body. Roark's shot blew off the right side of Jack's skull and McGraw put two holes in his chest. While looking at the remnants of pure evil lying in a pool of blood, McGraw says to Holly, "It's over."

McGraw continues to stare at Jack's body. and after a brief silence, Holly asks, "You alright, boss?"

"It's just that I don't feel anything for this guy. Not sure that's normal."

"I understand," she says, as they slowly turn and walk away from Jack's corpse.

McGraw radios the chopper that the suspect is down and the scene is secure.

"Copy that," pilot says.

"Meet you at the Command Post," Drew says.

As the two detectives are walking to the perimeter, Holly grabs Noah's hand and says, "Boss, how about a few days off at the Circle M? We could use a break."

McGraw gazes into Holly's big brown eyes. Feeling this strong commitment filled with pure love, he says, "That's the best idea I've heard in a long time."

Chapter 59

Walking the grounds of the Circle M in the early hours before dawn, wearing his Atlanta Falcons jacket, Stetson, and carrying a steaming cup of coffee, Noah McGraw is contemplating the day. He forgoes his usual talks with his equine friends because of what is weighing heavy on his mind.

This day is unlike any other he has ever faced.

Capt. Dipple has been working with Sylvia Sunday, the wife of the powerful congressman who is buried in Pinelawn Cemetery, to make sure that Laura Evans, the mother of dead serial killer Jack Carter, is interred in Pinelawn with a proper burial service.

McGraw has been struggling to justify in his mind how such a woman, who abused her son to no end and who is responsible for driving him into becoming a psychopathic killer, can receive the same honor as most loving mothers.

He walks around the barn drinking the last of his coffee and sits on his favorite bench close to the wooden fence. Whitey comes out of the barn and eyes Noah, comes over and sits next to him.

"You haven't come in to visit your pals, boss," he says.

"Can I ask you something," Noah says.

"Sure, boss."

"How long have we been friends?'

"Oh, since grade school. Why?"

"And we've ridden a lot of miles together, right?"

"Sure have."

"Then how is it you, too, are now calling me boss?"

"I heard your detectives calling you that. I thought out of respect, I should, too."

"No way, man. I want you to go back to calling me Noah, or I'll have to take you down an inch or two like I used to do."

"In your dreams."

They laugh.

"Okay, boss. He clears his throat. "I mean, okay, Noah."

"Good. That sounds better from a true friend."

"What's up with you, Noah? It's not like you to not come into the barn to see us."

Noah shakes his head. "Something's been bothering me." He begins by telling him about Laura Evans's life, her treatment of her son, Jack, and her burial to take place today.

"So, you're thinking she doesn't deserve the respect paid to other mothers?" Whitey asks, then pauses for a few seconds. "Don't say, 'it's the principle of the thing.' That's a cop-out."

"To be honest, I don't believe she does. She's getting a lot attention she doesn't deserve. I blame her as much as Jack Carter for the death of all those poor women victims. If she were like Anna Marie and her son turned out bad, I'd say she deserves the best, but she was a bitch."

"Did you stop to think that maybe this Sylvia lady is doing this because she might have had a mother like Jack that she didn't bury?" Whitey says.

Noah stares at his buddy for a few moments, then grabs his head in a bear hug and rubs a knuckled-fist through his hair. "Whitey, you're a damn genius. Did I ever tell you that?"

"Not enough, b-o-s-s," he says in a playful way.

They laugh.

———————

On his way to the station in his Silverado, Noah reaches over on the seat for his cell. Calls Holly. "Run Sylvia Sunday for me. Find out all you can on her."

"What's up? I'm about to close up for our little vacation."

"I'm headed in to get you. Will explain when I get there." He flips off and throws his phone on the passenger seat.

Thirty minutes later, McGraw enters the bureau and stops at Roark's desk. "Anything yet?"

"You'd be amazed."

"Let's have it."

"Sylvia was a prostitute before she married Congressman Sunday. He must have brought her out of the gutter. A religious thing, I think."

"Whatta you got on her parents?" McGraw asks.

She gestures. "It's interesting that you ask. They both were arrested multiple times, dealing drugs. But the mother was a holy terror. She was hauled in for domestic abuse and beating her only child on several occasions."

"Sylvia?"

"Oh my. You're a genius." She laughs. "What? You're not laughing at my humor anymore?"

"Whitey and I talked this morning. I was upset because Sylvia Sunday is going all out for Laura Evans, an evil person in my mind. I wondered why. He suggested that Sylvia's mother may be more like Jack's mother, and that's why Sylvia might have a reason for wanting all this fanfare for Laura Evans."

She frowns. "Well, Whitey's right. Sylvia's mother not only beat her daughter, but drove Sylvia into prostitution when she was only sixteen. Mama was more like her pimp. Sylvia got arrested and so did mama. Don't know what happened to the mother. After that last arrest, nothing more in the system. That reminds me. Most girls know about Cinderella. She had an abusive and cruel stepmother and mean stepsisters. She was the most unlikely girl to appear at the ball. Guess Congressman Sunday was her prince who searched for her and rescued her like Cinderella."

"Wow! What a beautiful analogy. But still, I don't know why Sylvia's doing it. It's difficult to comprehend how she still has feelings for an abusive mother, after all the bad things she did to her," McGraw says.

"Maybe she learned from the congressman what the Good Book says, "'Love Your Enemies,'" Holly says, "and through the years she came to forgive her mother."

McGraw nods. "Apparently he taught her that when he rescued her from the Devil's grasp." He sighs. "Guess I need help in that area, too."

He looks at his wrist watch. "Grab your coat. We gotta meet Nora in five minutes."

⎯⎯⎯◆◆⎯⎯⎯

When Noah and Holly arrive in the morgue, Nora Philips is standing in her overcoat by one of her polished metal dissecting tables. On the table is a wooden box.

"It's about time you guys showed up," she says.

"Is that Laura Evans in there?" McGraw asks.

She nods. "It contains her remains, which is going to be placed in an area in Pinelawn. We're running behind and I'm sure the funeral director is chewing on his lip."

"We saw the hearse outside," Holly says.

"Yes, provided by Sylvia Sunday," Nora says. "We better hurry. You guys can ride with me. We can follow the hearse once it is loaded."

The Environmental Health Officer, Funeral Director, and Minister from Sylvia Sunday's church, and Mr. Cotton Hargrove, the manager of the Pinelawn Cemetery, are waiting for the Coroner and funeral hearse, the Detectives, and Sunday family to arrive. Moments later, they all pull up behind the hearse in single file and roll out of their cars. Nora moves out ahead of everyone, rushing over to the Funeral Director, while McGraw and Roark wait for Sylvia and her brother-in-law, William Sunday. Sylvia smiles as they begin walking up the small incline together but William doesn't look at them. He guides Sylvia by her arm. Noah and Holly follow.

The officials are standing close to a plot that has been chosen and paid for by Sylvia Sunday. The opened grave is ready to receive the remains of Laura Evans, and the Funeral Director and his assistant lower the box into the hole. The minister moves to what could be considered

251

the head of the coffin area to begin his funeral homily, while the others stand around the plot.

As the minister delivers the eulogy, McGraw, sandwiched between Holly on his right and Nora on his left, tries to concentrate on the service but he's in a cloud. The minister's words are inaudible to him. Surprisingly, however, he's finding it in his heart to forgive Laura Evans as he stares at the box.

Anna Marie would be very happy with me, he thinks. *She taught me to forgive my enemies, and now I really know it's more than words.*

The End

A Note to Readers

It's always a pleasure when authors finish their novels. But the pleasure doesn't stop there. Readers interested in their genre must be reached. Some gurus say people read less these days because of all the electronic gadgets, but we believe there are still many readers out there looking for an interesting story, whether in print or as an ebook. We hope you've found it in *The Tongue Collector*—interesting and enjoyable, as much as we did in writing it.

Thank you for reading *The Tongue Collector*.

We would greatly appreciate reviews. If you would write one where you purchased the book, we'd be grateful. Reviews help readers to find new stories. You can find more of Magarian's titles in ebook and paperback at your favorite online retailer.

Every quarter I (Magarian) have a drawing for a free autographed copy of one of my novels. Please go to my website and sign up. Directions are given on how to register.

Detectives Noah McGraw and Holly Roark have become enduring fictional characters. They will definitely appear again, but they are thinking about marriage at the moment and don't want to be bothered. I've told them, I would give them some time, but they should not take too long.

Website: www.robertamgarian.com
Facebook: www.facebook.com/authorRam
Twitter: www.twitter.com/authorRam
LinkedIn: www.linkelin.com/in/robertmagarian
Email: author@robertmagarian.com

Acknowledgments

Having a team brings life to a novel and makes the many lonely hours spent by the author worthwhile.

The author (Magarian) wishes to thank those who have contributed to this novel in many ways.

My co-author, Colonel Scott Waldrup.

Detective Mike Isaac (ret) of the Norman, OK PD. Enjoyed our meetings together reviewing the novel, and working through your many suggestions.

Editing: Nancy Hancock, the consummate language scholar, eagle-eyed corrector, and best advisor a writer can have.

Cover design: Peter O'Connor, www.bespokebookcovers.com

Print formatting: Amy Atwell, Author E.M.S.

My brother, Dr. Edward O. Magarian, for reading and making suggestions and treating me like an author.

Use of name: Thanks to my friend Bea Kunz from middle TN, chemical free herb farmer and educator for healthier foods. I've always called her aunt Bea and that's the name used in this novel. Hope you like your fictional character with the purple hat.

To my family: Love you all.

ROBERT MAGARIAN, B.A., BSPH, Ph.D., is emeritus professor of pharmacy and medicinal chemistry. Since his retirement he has been writing fiction and has created several fictional characters in medical thrillers and detective mysteries. The two most popular characters are: Detectives Noah McGraw and Holly Roark of the Atlanta PD. Magarian is introducing Colonel Scott Waldrup as his investigative collaborator in *The Tongue Collector*.

Magarian is the author of four thriller novels: *The Watchman, 72 Hours, You'll Never See Me Again: A Crime to Remember,* and *The Tongue Collector*. In addition to his fiction, Robert is the author of two nonfiction essays: *Follow Your Dream* and *A Journey into Faith*. He lives with his wife Charmaine in Norman, Oklahoma.

SCOTT WALDRUP, B.A. in Criminal Justice and graduate of Session 228 of the FBI National Academy, spent 34 years working general crimes and narcotic investigations and was a member of a Major Case Squad, and SWAT Team, becoming its Team Commander. After 30 years with the Alton police department in the Illinois Metro East, Captain Waldrup, now Colonel, moved on to become Chief of Police in an Illinois metro east community. He lives with his wife Lupe and family in Mascoutah, Illinois.